THE REDEMPTION OF HATTIE McBRIDE

I hope you enjoy reading my book as much as I enjoyed writing it!
Dawnelle

DAWNELLE GUENTHER

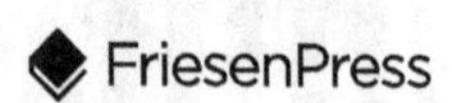

Suite 300 - 990 Fort St
Victoria, BC, V8V 3K2
Canada

www.friesenpress.com

First Edition — 2021

ISBN
978-1-03-910127-2 (Hardcover)
978-1-03-910126-5 (Paperback)
978-1-03-910128-9 (eBook)

1. FICTION, MYSTERY & DETECTIVE, HISTORICAL

Distributed to the trade by The Ingram Book Company

DEDICATION

This book is dedicated to my husband
Tony *Edward* Guenther.
Of all the adventures we've been through,
writing this book with you has
meant the most to me.
Thank you with all my heart.

ACKNOWLEDGEMENTS

Writing a novel has been a life-long dream, one I would have never achieved without the help and support of so many.

Thanks to the volunteers at the Princeton Museum (BC) and the Mennonite Historical Society of BC for helping me with my research.

I am blessed with an astonishing group of friends and family who have encouraged me throughout this five-year process. I wish I could list you all by name, but you know who you are.

Special thanks to my parents, John & Esther and my friends Laurie Anne, Joan and Sue. I think I would have quit a long time ago if not for your constant encouragement, honest critiques and the many *how's the book coming?* messages.

To my daughters: Eleah, Jenna & Tessa. You've heard your mother talk about *the book* for so long… and while I'm thrilled that my dream has been realized, you three are my greatest achievement.

A NOTE FROM THE AUTHOR:

Hattie McBride was a real person. It's believed that she lived in Greenwood and later moved to Coalmont where she opened a brothel. She was murdered in 1920 but the murderer was never found. Hattie was buried in the Granite Creek Cemetery but history records little else about Hattie McBride, not even a photograph. Sadly, that's where her story ends.

From the moment we were 'introduced' to Hattie McBride, my husband and I were intrigued by her tragic tale. When I decided to write my first novel, he suggested a story loosely based on her life.

It is important to note that this is a work of fiction. While based on a real woman, the rest of this story is purely from my imagination.

I hope you enjoy this tale of Hattie McBride. Thank you for reading!
Dawnelle Guenther

PROLOGUE

COALMONT, BRITISH COLUMBIA—NOVEMBER 21, 1920

HATTIE MCBRIDE JUMPED OUT of the wagon and into the familiar yard. Dolly, a beautiful Appaloosa mare, nickered as she passed by and Hattie took a moment to give the horse an affectionate scratch. She cast a glance over her shoulder and looked down the street once again, making sure that no one had noticed her arrival. It was a cold November afternoon and, fortunately for her, most of the townsfolk were inside, keeping warm. A few sounds drifted down from the east end of Main Street: the spin of a blackjack wheel, a woman's laugh. For the moment it was still and quiet, but soon Coalmont's saloons and red-light district would come to life.

In 1885, a hapless cowboy named Johnny Chance discovered gold in Granite Creek and word spread like wildfire. The town of Granite Creek seemed to spring up overnight, like a mushroom after the rain. But by the turn of the century, prospects of Granite Creek were dwindling, and the mining companies began to shift their interests to the staggering amount of coal found in what would be known as the Tulameen Coal Basin. In 1910, the Columbia Coal and Coke Office was opened in the newly formed settlement of Cardiff, just west of Granite Creek. A year later, Coalmont was born and Cardiff became known as Upper Town.

Prospective miners, fortune seekers, and businessmen all followed the irresistible lure of riches. Many tried their luck panning for gold along the countless streams and rivers but few made their fortunes. The real gold was not found in the mountains and streams, it was found in the businesses, opened by the men and women who arrived after the miners, catering to their every whim and need.

There were times that men in the boomtowns outnumbered women fifty to one. Some men became so lonely that they would think nothing of spending all they had for just a short visit with a woman who smelled of lavender, making him feel like he was loved.

Hattie McBride was not a fool and there had been a time when she had not been averse to using that knowledge to her advantage. But she was no longer that woman.

Her business, affectionately called Hattie's Place by her clientele, had been a lucrative one, but, much to her relief, it was finally time to move on.

Hattie shivered and drew her cape more tightly around her. She shuddered again and wondered if her growing unease was from being back at this place or from the chilly autumn air. Trying to shake her apprehension, she stepped into the barn and looked carefully into each of the stalls. She was alone. Letting out a pent-up breath, she began to relax when she heard a small chuckle behind her.

She whirled to face her intruder. She tried to keep her voice even, but it trembled with fear. "What are you doing here?" she demanded.

"I believe you owe me something."

Hattie stood slowly, ready to run, but it was too late. Before she knew it, she was dragged into the old cabin that stood in the shadows of the barn. There was no time for regret. No time for redemption. It was over before it even began.

Later, the townsfolk would say that it was the smell of smoke that first caught their attention, alerting them to something that was dreadfully wrong. By the time they had rushed down the street to the old cabin, it was fully engulfed in flames and beyond saving. It wasn't until that next morning, after the ashes had cooled, that they found what remained of Hattie's body.

Surprisingly, despite the nature of her profession, many had mourned the loss of Hattie McBride. Somehow, she had managed to work her way into this small community, earning the townsfolk's trust and proving that first impressions aren't always correct. Some even called her "friend."

CHAPTER ONE

FRASER VALLEY, BRITISH COLUMBIA—PRESENT DAY

Ed pulled a crumpled hanky from his jeans pocket and swiped at the beads of perspiration collecting on his forehead. Sweat had begun to gather on the back of his neck and he could feel it inching its way down his spine. He stared longingly at the window, wishing for the thousandth time that he could open it and let some fresh air into the tiny room.

"Ed." His wife shot him a disapproving glance. "You made me spill my tea." She transferred the china cup to her other hand, the side furthest from her fidgeting husband, and picked up a napkin from the small coffee table. Dabbing at the spots on her skirt, she whispered. "Could you please attempt to sit still?"

"Sorry Hannah," he said grimacing, "but this couch is so uncomfortable and…" he tugged on his collar, "…does it have to be so hot in here?" He squirmed again, trying to find a spot where the ancient couch springs didn't jab his backside.

Hannah smiled in sympathy. Just a few days before, Ed had been in Tulameen, at King Valley Ranch, helping their friend Sam with the fence lines that surrounded the enormous property. He had come home last night, bone tired and saddle sore, and this was the last place he wanted to be. Still, she brought her finger to her lips. "Shhhhh. She might hear you," she said quietly.

As if on cue, the other woman in the room spoke up. "What's the matter, dear? Did you need some more tea?"

Ed smiled but shook his head. "No, Aunt Elsie," he said loudly. "I'm just fine." *The last thing I need is more hot tea*, he thought.

Elsie smiled at her great nephew. Despite the heat in the retirement home, Aunt Elsie had a crocheted blanket draped across her legs and a shawl over her shoulders. Just looking at her made Ed sweat. He twisted around to lay his cup back on the side table and nearly knocked over a framed photograph that they had given Aunt Elsie of their three grown daughters—Emma, Justine and Lydia—for Christmas. He caught it just in time, preventing it from hitting the floor and the inevitable knick-knack disaster. The room was so overwhelmingly full that every time they came to visit, he truly felt like a bull in a china shop. But Aunt Elsie could not for the life of her throw anything away. Every family photo, every birthday card, every memento was sitting out, displayed with pride.

Even as a small child, Ed had always known that his great aunt Elsie was special. She had a naivety and innocence that had made everyone want to protect her. She was, what they would have said in her day, "not quite hundred percent." She had never married; instead, she was content to dote on her sister Helen's family, showering them with love and gifts like they were her own children. She was loyal and honest to a fault. Unfortunately, she believed that everyone else in the world was as trustworthy and truthful as she was. The family had worked hard to protect Elsie, shielding her from those who would take advantage.

Ed had never known a time when Aunt Elsie hadn't lived with someone in the family. For most of her life she lived with Helen, who was Ed's grandmother. When Helen passed away, Elsie moved in with Ed's parents' and had stayed with them until they discovered that Ed's mother, Elizabeth, had cancer.

It was a difficult decision to move Aunt Elsie into a nursing home, but with her usual good humour she agreed, trusting that her family knew best. When Elizabeth was in her final days, she implored Ed to watch over the old woman and, of course, he promised he would.

"Ed, do you remember this trip we took to Banff?" Elsie thrust the black photo album at her nephew, bringing him out of his contemplation. She pointed a knobby finger at the old black-and-white photograph.

"Yes, Aunt Elsie, I remember," Ed said and smiled. *How could I possibly forget?* he thought. *We bring that album along every time we visit.*

"And this picture was taken on my parents' wedding day," Elsie continued. "Wasn't my mother pretty?"

Hannah smiled and nodded, turning the page. "Oh yes," she said, "she is so pretty and you can tell that she is very happy too." Pointing to the faded sepia photo on the next page Hannah asked, "And that's your family, isn't it?" The photo was cracked and worn from years of wear, but it clearly showed five children standing in a row, each one a little shorter than the next, their backs ramrod straight. The last two in the row were obviously sisters, they looked so much alike. They had long braids and were holding hands.

Elsie smiled wistfully at the photo and ran her gnarled fingers over the faces. "Yes, that's Henry, Frieda, Nettie, Helen, and me." Elsie's finger lingered over the face of her sister. "Helen was Ed's grandma, you know," Elsie said absently. "Papa was so proud of us that day."

The picture of the Thiessen children had been taken shortly after their family settled in British Columbia, after moving from Saskatchewan. Elsie loved to tell the story of how proud their father had been that day. The photo had been taken during their first harvest and it had been a bumper crop. They made more money than they had ever dreamed of, enough that their father could afford to hire a photographer. He talked of their family who remained in Russia. They wouldn't even have considered spending money on such extravagances in their small village of Gnadenheim. Elsie's father had loved their new home country of Canada and the opportunities it afforded.

Hannah, of course, remembered Ed's grandmother very well, but Elsie had forgotten that they had any connection and Hannah didn't remind her. Elsie had good days, when she remembered everything, and she had her bad days. Hannah just nodded and smiled. It was the same every Sunday; the same pictures, the same tea, the same stories, but every visit was precious to their great aunt.

Elsie ran a weathered hand over the photo and got a faraway look in her eyes. Ed knew what was coming next. "She's gone," Elsie said. "She died and left me all alone." Her eyes filled with tears as she continued. "She was always so good to me." Hannah took a box of tissues from amongst the paraphernalia on the side table and held it out in front of Elsie. The old woman smiled and took one, dabbing it under each eye and her nose. Hannah knew she needed to come up with a distraction quickly or Aunt Elsie would begin her descent into the past and start weeping in earnest.

"This place looks familiar," she said, turning the page and pointing to the photos of their cabin in Tulameen. The cabin had been in Ed's family since he had been a boy and, when her health had been good, Elsie had loved spending time there with the rest of the family.

"Hey Elsie!" The door to Elsie's room opened and Ruth, one of the nurses, poked her head in the door. "How are you doing today?" She spoke the way that most of the nurses spoke at the Menno Home, loud, clear, and with great exaggeration.

Elsie beamed at Ruth, wiping her glittering eyes with the tissue. "I'm just fine." All thoughts of her dead sister were instantly forgotten and she motioned for Ruth to come over. "Have you met my nephew, Ed? He comes to see me every Sunday you know." Elsie patted Ed's knee as she spoke.

Nodding, Ruth smiled and winked at Hannah and Ed. "Yes, I know Elsie." She knelt in front of the old woman's wheelchair and tucked the crocheted blanket tighter around Elsie's small legs. "Aren't you lucky? To have a family that loves you so much?"

Elsie nodded and glowed at Ruth's praise. Ruth stood and said, "It's almost time for dinner. I hope you're hungry because it sure smells good down in the dining room!" She gathered their empty teacups and was about to go back into the hallway when she paused and turned back to face them. "Oh, that's right. Elsie, did you tell Ed and Hannah about your special visitor yesterday?"

Ed and Hannah exchanged looks. Special visitor? The few friends of Elsie's who were still living, lived in retirement homes like she did. No one ever came to visit her except their family and her pastor.

"You had a visitor, Aunt Elsie?" asked Hannah.

Elsie turned to look at Hannah. Confusion crossed her lined face as she groped for the answer that she knew she was supposed to give. Instead, she repeated Hannah's question. "I had a visitor?"

Ruth put the teacups down, crossed the room, and crouched again in front of Elsie. She patted Elsie's frail knees and gave them a small rub, meant to reassure her. "It's okay, dear. You just forgot with all the excitement. Remember? A policeman came to see you yesterday."

Ed sat up. A policeman? What on earth would a policeman want with his ninety-seven-year-old great aunt? He leaned forward and touched her on the hand. "A policeman came to see you Aunt Elsie? What did he want?"

Turning, Elsie looked at him with a blank expression on her face. He was certain that she had completely forgotten the visit. Elsie could remember events from her past with astonishing clarity but had trouble remembering what she had for breakfast. Suddenly her eyes brightened and said. "Oh, that's right, I remember now." But as quickly as she brightened her face fell. When she looked back at Ed, he was shocked to see that she was about to cry again. What was going on? Aunt Elsie's gaze dropped to the blanket on her lap and she started picking at the multicoloured strands of yarn that had pilled in the crochet work. When she spoke, her voice was small, and she didn't look up. "He came to give me some news about my brother…" Her voice faltered. She made a small sound at the back of her throat and tried again. "My brother, Henry," she finished.

Ed frowned. Her brother Henry? "Didn't he pass away a long time ago?" Ed asked.

Elsie's brow furrowed and she nodded, still not looking up. "Yes, he did. In 1967."

Looking at Ruth, Ed hoped for some clarification but the nurse just shrugged, "I wasn't here when he came yesterday," Ruth said. "Karen was working that shift. When we did our shift change, she told me about his visit. Apparently, he brought something with him but decided not to leave it, but Karen said he left a card."

Ruth walked over to Elsie's small bedside table and opened the top drawer. "Yes. Here it is." She handed the card to Ed. "Constable Mark Harrison. There's a note on the back of the card saying he's back on duty tomorrow at 7 a.m."

Ed was lying in bed, staring at the ceiling. The alarm clock on his nightstand ticked loudly and made each passing hour feel interminable. Suppressing a groan of frustration, he rolled over onto his side and tried to turn his brain off. It was only 3:10 a.m.

Why was it that the night seemed to drag on forever when you couldn't sleep?

Reaching out, Ed turned the alarm clock around so that the glowing numbers no longer mocked him. *Maybe that will help*, he thought. But it was futile. Every time he closed his eyes he saw his great aunt and the pained look on her face.

He couldn't make sense of it. His Aunt Elsie had always been an open book when it came to her family. They meant everything to her, and during the past few years, her devotion had not diminished. If anything, it had grown. She talked about every one of her siblings, reiterated their virtues, and reminded everyone of their accomplishments. She was so proud of who they had been except for one, her brother Henry. She never mentioned him. Ever.

Sighing, Ed rolled over, trying to shake the growing feeling of unease that was building in the pit of his stomach. His thoughts strayed back to his great uncle and he tried to recall what he knew about the man. Precious little, he realized. Once, when Ed was about eight, they had a family dinner at his oma's farm and he had been delegated to the kiddie table. He was so mad at being left to look after his infantile siblings, that he had stomped off to where the adults were. Carrying his plate and his protestations to the dining room, he stopped short when he realized that someone in the room was crying. Tiptoeing closer, he overheard low murmurings and he realized, to his horror, that the person who was crying was his oma. *Tante* Frieda's shrill German caught Ed's attention, and for the first time he wished he had paid more attention to *Frau* Giesbrecht during those dreaded German School classes on Saturday mornings.

Someone (it sounded like his *Tante* Nettie) said, "It's not our fault he went his own way. And now, with this, he's trying to make amends. He was always a black sheep." Her voice sounded brittle. Ed knew, instinctively, that they were talking about their brother, Henry.

That evening, when they had driven home from the family farm, his parents were uncharacteristically quiet. He saw his mother's red-rimmed eyes and his father's grim expression, but he didn't have the courage to ask why they were upset. He never told his parents what he had overheard and wondered for days afterward what his great uncle had done to make him a "black sheep." It couldn't have been good for it made everyone sad. His great uncle was never mentioned again. It was like he never *was*.

Ed sighed again and swung his legs over the edge of the mattress. Turning, he glanced at Hannah who was sound asleep, her dark hair in disarray over the pillow. He quietly slipped out of bed, so he wouldn't wake her. Walking to the kitchen, he put the kettle on, hoping a cup of tea would calm his stomach, and then settled himself in his favourite armchair to watch the sunrise.

CHAPTER TWO

ABBOTSFORD, BRITISH COLUMBIA—PRESENT DAY

Constable Mark Harrison was pouring himself another cup of coffee when the lunchroom door opened. A petite blonde poked her head inside.

"Oh, there you are, Mark. I rang your desk, but you didn't answer."

Mark smiled. "Sorry, Tracy. I was in desperate need of more caffeine. What's up?"

"There's a man downstairs asking for you. Says you're expecting him?" she said.

"Is his last name Janzen?"

She glanced at the yellow sticky note stuck to her palm. "Yes, that's right. Ed Janzen. Is it okay if I send him up?"

Mark nodded. "Sure," he said. "Just give me five minutes."

She ducked out as quickly as she had arrived, and Mark was again alone in the lunchroom. He added some sugar to his coffee and liberally laced it with some questionable cream from the staff fridge. Stirring his coffee, he recalled the conversation with the old woman who lived at the Menno Home. He shook his head and chuckled to himself. It had been an interesting exchange, and after about five minutes it was clear that she was an old soul who was living in the past. She was determined that they have tea together and he must have told her at least five times that they were not related, but there was no convincing her. Finally, in exasperation, he had left his card with the floor nurse on duty, hoping that someone from her family would contact him.

He had been quite surprised when a man, claiming to be her great-nephew, had phoned him early this morning, at 7:10 a.m. *Well, that didn't take long*, he thought, and was glad to know that Elsie Thiessen had someone looking out for her.

Mark walked into his office and had barely settled himself behind his desk when a man appeared at the door. Mark guessed he was in his mid-fifties, judging by the greying beard, but he was caught off guard by the man's hair. It was curly and long, hanging almost to his shoulders. Mark stood, holding out his hand. "Mr. Janzen?" The man stepped forward and shook Mark's hand with a surprisingly strong grip. His skin was burnished by the sun, testament to countless days spent in the outdoors. Laugh lines creased the corners of his eyes when he smiled and said, "Yes. But please, call me Ed. Mr. Janzen is my father."

Laughing, Mark gestured to the empty chair across the desk. "Well, Ed," he said, "thanks for contacting me so quickly. Can I get you a cup of coffee?" Ed sat in the chair and shook his head, "No thanks. I already had a few cups at home."

Nodding, Mark sat down and grabbed a yellow pad and a pencil. "Before we go any further, I just need to confirm your relationship to Elsie Thiessen. Did you bring identification like we talked about?" Ed nodded and pulled out his wallet. He placed his birth certificate and driver's licence on the desk so Mark could see it. The constable made a few notes on the pad. "And Elsie Thiessen is your great aunt?"

Ed nodded again. "Yes, she is my grandmother's youngest sister."

"And what are the names of her siblings?"

Ed listed his grandmother's siblings starting with the oldest: "Henry, Elfrieda, Aganetha, Helena, and Elsie. My Aunt Elsie, who you met at the Menno Home, is the youngest. Helena was my oma." When Mark looked up at the last word, Ed explained. "That's a German word for grandmother." Ed took a deep breath, hoping to calm his nerves while Mark's pencil made quick scratching noises, the only sounds in the otherwise silent office.

Putting the pencil down, Mark took another sip of his coffee. "You sure that I can't get you a cup?" he asked.

Ed shook his head. "To be honest I've been up since 4 a.m. Couldn't sleep." He shifted a bit in his chair and Mark watched him twisting his wedding ring around. Recognizing the nervous gesture, Mark smiled and reassured him. "There's nothing to be worried about."

Ed said, "We visit my Aunt Elsie every Sunday and she's never had a police officer come to visit. Guess I am a little on edge."

Mark smiled, "It's nothing serious, but it does concern your family."

Ed frowned at the mention of his family. "That's the one thing my Aunt Elsie did remember. She said your visit had something to do with her brother Henry?"

Mark reached down to the floor beside his chair. Ed watched, intrigued, as the police officer lifted an old suitcase up onto the desk. "Yes," Mark said, "We're pretty sure that this belonged to him."

Ed stared at the case. It was dark brown leather, with two brass clasps. Years of dust had filled the cracks in the leather, like grout between tiles, and the brass fittings were dull and badly tarnished. It was like something straight out of a cheesy detective novel. The moment Mark placed it on the desk, Ed was overwhelmed with curiosity.

"Where on earth did you find this?" he said, reaching out to touch it.

Mark wiped some dust from his palms and said, "I guess it was about two weeks ago that we got a call from the RCMP in Quesnel. Apparently, a young couple were working on remodelling their house in Wells." He looked questioningly at Ed. "You know where Wells is?"

Ed nodded, "Yes, just before Barkerville."

Mark was impressed. He had no idea where Wells was until he googled it. "Well, they were ripping out the floorboards in the attic and they found this case hidden between the floor joists. The officer I talked to said they had looked through the case and felt they might have found something important. So, they brought the case to the detachment in Quesnel. Once the officers there determined that the original owner had a living relative in Abbotsford, they contacted our detachment.

Ed blew out a low whistle. "Wow," he said as he ran his hand over the dusty grain of the leather. "I don't know what I was expecting, but certainly not something that actually belonged to my great uncle."

Mark looked at Ed and tried to read his expression. "I take it that you didn't know him that well?"

Ed shook his head. "No. To tell you the truth, I never met the man and, as far as I know, no one knew where he lived." He fingered the clasps and then asked, "Do you know what's inside?"

Mark nodded and smiled. "Yes, I do. That's how they found your Aunt Elsie." Mark turned the case to face him and snapped each clasp open with his thumbs, the sounds like rifle reports in the small office. He lifted the lid and instantly the musty smell of a forgotten past filled the room. "It's mostly old postcards and a couple of old photos," Mark said. "Not much to go on and then one of the officers found this card in the old Bible."

He handed a small ivory coloured index card to Ed. It read, "Immigration Identification Card." Under the title, written in beautiful script, was his great uncle's full name, Heinrich Johann Thiessen. Ed recognized the next line. He read it out loud, "The Mercator." He paused for a moment. When he looked up, Mark was waiting for him to continue. "That was the name of the ship that brought my great grandparents and their family to Canada. They were emigrating from Russia."

Mark nodded. "That was the clue that we needed. After that, it was simple, really. It's amazing what you can find on the internet. Apparently one of our police officers went on one of those ancestry sites, typed in a few particulars, and there it was: a list of your whole family and your family tree."

Ed grimaced. "That's pretty frightening."

Mark grinned. "I know what you mean. I'm afraid nothing much is private these days." He reached inside the case and drew out an envelope, which he handed to Ed. Tapping the side of the suitcase, he grinned. "This suitcase is quite unique you know. These items were hidden under a false bottom."

Ed raised an eyebrow, feeling his pulse quicken.

Mark continued, "I put them inside the envelope to keep them safe. They're pretty old and official."

Ed took the envelope from Mark's hand and carefully withdrew two pieces of paper. The first one was a document with an illegible signature in one corner and a red seal in the other. It wasn't until he read the title of the document that he recognized its significance.

He leaned back in his chair and took a deep breath. A million questions were swirling in his mind, but before he could voice them, Mark put up his hand to stop him.

"Wait," he said. "It gets even better." He picked up the last document and handed it to Ed. Ed could make out a few words... mineral, British Columbia... and his uncle's name. He saw the date written in script under the signature: December 6, 1920.

Ed looked at Mark with confusion. "Is this what I think it is?"

"Yes," Mark nodded and smiled with satisfaction. "Not only did your uncle own a fair chunk of land, he also owned a mine."

CHAPTER THREE

GREENWOOD, BRITISH COLUMBIA—MARCH 1914

William McBride sat at the large dining table in his home, slumped in a hard-back oak chair, a sullen expression on his face. He toyed with the glass tumbler that was on the table in front of him, rolling it back and forth on its edge. The amber liquid inside the glass sloshed from side to side. Every so often, he took another large swallow. "Fortification," he would tell Sarah. She used to laugh when he said that, but that charade was long over. Now, when she looked at him, she saw only a pathetic drunk and a sorry excuse for a man.

He brought the glass to his lips again and threw his head back, downing the contents in one gulp. The fiery liquid burned as it ran down his throat, but he didn't care. He stared at the empty glass for a long moment. Leaning forward, his emotions warring, he set the glass down and put his face in his hands. Disgusted with himself, he vowed to put the bottle away. He should go outside and get some fresh air, he told himself. God knows it would do him good.

But before he could take his own advice, the crushing disappointments of the past few years came back, the memories as fresh as a new wound. It was too hard to relive, and having no desire to, he grabbed the bottle and refilled the tumbler instead.

William stared at the floor, watching the shadows growing longer. The pendulum of the Seth Thomas wall clock ticked loudly, the only sound in the vast empty house, and grated on his nerves. He leered at the clock and for a moment thought about knocking the thing over, if only to stop its constant reminder of a past he could never erase.

Sarah McBride picked up her skirts as she hurried down the street to the house that she shared with her husband, William. She had coiled her long black hair in a bun that morning, but some tendrils had worked their way free and they streamed behind her like a kite tail. She was flustered and worried and she knew that she had no one to blame but herself.

Sarah had met her friends for lunch and afterwards they had persuaded her to join them at Wilson's Millenary to see the new arrival of hats. They had a lovely time trying on every new creation, but she had lost track of time and by now William would be waiting for her to start supper. If he had already dipped into the whisky today, then there was no telling what his mood would be. She dreaded walking through their front door, but there was no putting it off.

Sarah had married William McBride, an affluent businessman, in Greenwood nine years before. When she had first met him, he was handsome, polite, and obviously enamoured with her. He had charmed her with his manners and his sense of humour. She loved to laugh, and William told the most amusing stories. It seemed like she was in giggles whenever she was in his company. He took her to see a play and to dinners out. They walked along Copper Street at night and looked in all the bright shop windows. It was a storybook romance and after a five-month courtship, William asked Sarah to marry him. She said yes without hesitation.

Sarah and William built a lovely home on Skylark Street that overlooked the town. It was a two-storey Victorian painted butter yellow with white trim. A large wraparound porch encircled the entire house and white gingerbread enhanced every corner. Two enormous willow chairs sat on the porch by the front door. They had belonged to Sarah's grandmother, Beth. Sarah's parents had both died when she was a child, so her grandmother had raised her. She had so many wonderful memories of long talks with Grandma Beth in those very chairs, but what Sarah loved most were her lilac bushes. When Sarah married William, Grandma Beth had given the newlyweds some cuttings from the lilacs that grew in her farmyard. William had planted them in a row in front of the porch and Sarah had pampered them until they grew and then flourished. The first year that the bushes blossomed, Sarah was ecstatic. The light purple flowers were so delicate and their scent perfumed the warm summer nights, reminding her of her childhood and her grandmother.

For the first two years, their marriage was idyllic. It wasn't until they decided they were ready to start a family that their troubles began. At first, they weren't too worried. Many couples they knew took some months to conceive. But when Sarah's period arrived every month like clockwork, they were devastated. When a few months turned into a year and then turned into two, the tension between them grew. Soon, it became unbearable. William and Sarah tried not to blame each other, but sometimes in the heat of an argument they would throw careless accusations at the other. Each word inflicted a new wound and before too long there were just too many to heal. Once upon a time they made love because it was just that; now it was a chore. Instead of facing the reality that loomed in front of them, they both found other things to occupy their time and their thoughts. They avoided spending time together. Sarah devoted most of her time to friends, took care of her and William's investments, and the rest of her days she filled with shopping. The only thing that William found that he really cared about was whisky, drowning his guilt, his regret and his insecurities in the bottom of a glass.

Sarah stepped through the front door of their home. The house was dark and silent and, for a tenuous moment, Sarah hoped that William was out. But as she walked by the formal dining room, she saw him sitting there in the dark.

"William! You scared me." She pressed a hand to her heart. "I thought that maybe you were out."

"Out?" he sneered. "Why would I be out?" Some people, when they drank too much, became the life of the party. But some, like William, became belligerent and downright mean. "Where have you been?" he said, looking at her with watery, bleary eyes.

"I was out with Lillian and Evelyn," she said, her voice trembling. "You knew that. I told you before I left this morning."

"You told me you'd be out with them for lunch, but I didn't think you'd be gone all day." He stood up, swaying slightly, and placed his palms flat on the table, leaning towards her. "What did you expect me to do here all day alone? Huh?"

His breath was fetid in her face and she lost her temper. "Well, I guess I thought that maybe you'd do some work around here!" She threw her handbag on the table and yanked off her gloves. "The porch needs repainting and the roses could be pruned. What exactly did you do all day?" She stared pointedly at the empty whisky bottle on the table.

He stared at her for a long while. "So that's all I am to you now?" he reiterated. "Your handyman?" He stared into her eyes, willing her to deny it.

She shook her head, immediately contrite for losing her temper. "Of course I don't think that William. I just want you to do something productive with your time like you used to. The city council even asked you to be an alderman and you turned them down. Why would you do that?" But she knew why, even before she asked the question. Because he was heartbroken, just like she was. She lifted her pleading eyes to his face. "Please, William. If I can get over this, then surely you can."

"This?" He repeated the word like it was distasteful. "What is it that you want me to get over? That I'm unproductive and useless or that I will never be a father? Take your pick." He looked at her for a long while and when she didn't answer he walked over to the front door and grabbed the doorknob.

"Where are you going?" she said, taking hold of his arm.

He yanked it out of her grasp. "I'm going out to do something productive." His words were so filled with bitterness and acrimony that her eyes instantly filled with tears. Walking out the door, he slammed it so hard she was sure the neighbours had heard.

Sarah stared at the closed door for a long time and then slowly walked over to one of the chairs at the table. Her heart heavy with regret, she sat down and gazed out the large windows until the sun sank behind the mountain and the sky was dark. Then she laid her head on the table and wept.

They entered a silent truce after that. She never mentioned William's drinking again and he ignored the fact that she was never home. Sarah spent more and more time in town, shopping, and filling her days and their home with useless bric-a-brac and her closet with dresses that she would never wear. When they happened to be in the same room they barely spoke, just saying enough to take them from day to day. Occasionally they would talk about the weather, both pretending that everything was back to normal. Never again did they talk about what was weighing so heavily on them both, the harsh reality that they would never, ever, have a child of their own.

CHAPTER FOUR

FRASER VALLEY, BRITISH COLUMBIA—PRESENT DAY

Ed drove straight home from the police station and carried the case into the house. Placing it on the kitchen island, he pulled up a bar stool and popped the lid open. The musty aroma once again overpowered his senses and Ed wondered at how long the case had been hidden in that house.

He carefully lifted each item out and placed it on the counter. It was an odd assortment of ephemera. There were the usual keepsakes: cards, a couple of photos, and postcards. But there were other things, too. A Bible, a brittle brown flower, and a silver baby rattle. Picking up the toy, he shook it a little and heard the beads rattling within. Why did Uncle Henry have a baby rattle? He couldn't believe he knew so little about this man who was his relative.

Ed picked up the Bible. Surprisingly, it was well used. The cover was cracked and worn, the corners were dog-eared, bent from years of handling. A brown frayed ribbon, used as a bookmark, was sewn into the binding. When Ed opened the book, he was surprised to see that it was a German translation. It fell open to where the ribbon had been placed, at 2 Timothy and Ed saw that someone had underlined a verse on the page. His German was pretty rusty, but it didn't matter, he knew the verse off by heart. He read it out loud in English. "I have fought the good fight, I have finished the race, I have kept the faith." Ed couldn't help but smile when he read the verse. It had been his mother's favourite.

Looking at the things his uncle had collected, Ed wondered why they were hidden. They all seemed benign enough. But it was the land title and mineral claim that he kept coming back to. His uncle had hidden them under the false bottom. Uncle Henry never intended for anyone to know that he owned land, or a mine, and Ed was dying to know why.

Glancing at the clock, he was surprised to see that it was nearly 4 p.m. Hannah would be heading home in about half an hour and he hadn't given a thought to what their dinner would be. Although he had been retired for a few years, Hannah still enjoyed her job as an office administrator, so by tacit agreement, Ed had taken charge of supper on her work days.

He rummaged through the freezer and found a frozen lasagna, which he popped into the oven. Then, heading down to the ancient basement, he made his way to their modest collection of wine. After selecting a bottle, from their favourite local winery, he went up to finish making their dinner. By the time he heard tires crunching on the gravel drive, the lasagna was brown and bubbling, he had thrown together a green salad, the wine was open on the counter, and he had nearly run out of patience.

Hannah walked into the foyer, depositing her keys and jacket on the deacon's bench by the front door. She was surprised when he met her there. She gave him a quick kiss. "Mmmmm," she said, rubbing her nose on his rough cheek. "Smells good in here. You started supper?" She was famished.

He kissed her back. "Yup, I've been waiting all day for you." He handed her a glass of the wine.

She took a sip and gave a small sound of appreciation. "Old Settler?" she asked, recognizing her favourite. Curious, she raised one eyebrow and asked, "What's up?"

He chuckled. "I went to the police station this morning and it was pretty interesting," he said. He grabbed her other hand, pulling her towards the kitchen. "Let's eat. I can't wait to show you what the constable gave me."

Hannah marvelled at the assortment of things that were spread out over her counter. "Wow," she breathed. "Look at all this stuff."

"I know," said Ed. "I've been looking at it all afternoon. It's quite a collection, but there doesn't seem to be any rhyme or reason to it. It's like he just threw a bunch of things in a case."

Hannah gave her husband a dubious look. "Well, obviously, they meant something to him. Otherwise, why would he have gone to such great lengths to save them? And hide them away."

Ed shrugged, then handed her the mining certificate. "I can understand why he kept this, though."

Hannah scanned the fragile document. "What is this?" she said. "It looks very official."

Ed nodded. "Yes, it is. It's for a mineral claim called *The Linnea*. Apparently long-lost Uncle Henry was a miner of some sort."

Hannah's eyes grew wide. "Really? Who's Linnea?"

Ed shook his head. "Beats me," he said, chuckling. "And look at this!" He put a hand inside the case, lifting the bottom. "He had hidden that paper and another one under this."

Hannah stood to look inside the case, her mouth open in amazement when she saw the false bottom. She ran her fingers along the inside, noting the grooves around the edge holding the extra piece perfectly in place. If Ed hadn't pointed it out, she doubted she would have noticed. She looked at Ed questioning, "You said there were two documents under this?"

Ed nodded, took the certificate from Hannah, and picked up the other paper. This was with it." He handed her the land title deed. "Seems he owned some land as well."

Hannah stared at the deed, trying to read the faded script. "This is almost impossible to make out," she said, looking at the elegant longhand.

Ed took the deed back from Hannah and examined it. "I know. I was thinking I'll have to do some digging to find out where the land is, but I don't even know where to start." He shook his head and then took another sip of his wine. When he set the glass down, he rubbed a palm across his forehead. Making a steeple of his hands, he pressed his fingertips deep into his bottom lip. Hannah saw the troubled looked on his face and knew the frustration he must be feeling. "I hate the fact that this man was a stranger to me," he said finally. "And that I'm finding out things, important things, about him after he's gone." They both sat in silence, sipping on their wine, their lasagna growing cold, until Ed spoke again. "What's bothering me most is why? What did he do that was so terrible that our entire family wanted nothing to do with him?"

Hannah walked around the kitchen island and wrapped her arms around her husband, placing her chin on his shoulder. Gazing at the paltry collection of what had belonged to Henry Thiessen, she said quietly, "I don't know. But I think it's about time we find out."

CHAPTER FIVE

GREENWOOD, BRITISH COLUMBIA—AUGUST 1914

It was early in the morning, but Copper Street was already coming to life. Store owners greeted each other as they rushed to open their shops, delectable smells of baking wafted on the morning breeze, and the great smoke stack of the copper smelter heaved and belched white smoke as it came to life, melting down the ore that was the lifeblood of the little city.

Sarah trudged down the street and tugged her shawl back over her shoulder with irritation. On most days Sarah loved the vibrant energy of downtown Greenwood, but today she was in a bad mood. No, she decided, she was in an *exceptionally* bad mood. Not only was her marriage deteriorating by the minute, but last night William hadn't come home until the wee hours of the morning. More often than not, she was left to manage all their business dealings. When there were problems she muddled through, doing her best, while William just got drunker than usual. "Perfect," she muttered under her breath. "Just perfect."

Sarah sighed and looked at the sky. The clouds were thickening and getting blacker. *Great*, she thought, *not only am I in a foul mood, but I'm about to get soaked too.* Well, at least the weather matched her disposition.

It had started out as a beautiful day, so she hadn't even thought to bring an umbrella. But shortly after leaving the house, the weather had turned and the wind started in earnest. She was hurrying between the druggist and the mercantile, hoping to avoid the worst of it, when the first drops began to fall. If she didn't find shelter sometime soon, she would certainly be soaked to the skin. Sarah yanked her shawl over her head and bent into the wind. She had her head down, trying to get ahead of the rain when she ran right into another pedestrian doing the very same thing. Landing on her backside with a thump, her packages spilled out in every direction.

"Oh! I'm terribly sorry," he said. "I was so intent on getting out of this weather that I wasn't even watching where I was going." He instantly reached for her hand, helping her to stand.

"Well, I can't admit to having any better manners," she grimaced, pulling her filthy wet gloves off her hands. "I think we're both guilty of wanting to stay dry!"

Sarah used her gloves to wipe at the grime from the front of her skirt but soon realized it was an exercise in futility. Her hands were covered in grit and she looked at them, at a loss at what to do next, when he produced a linen handkerchief. Taking it, she smiled at the courtesy. She wiped her hands as best as she could. When she handed the cloth back to him, she looked at his face. It was the most handsome face she had ever seen. He had large brown eyes with lashes most women would kill for. Perfect, white straight teeth. Black curly hair and a beautiful thick moustache. He returned her smile and then quickly bent to pick up her dropped packages.

"Please, allow me to get these for you," he said with a dazzling smile. Sarah couldn't help but notice the dimple that appeared in his cheek when he smiled and she realized, to her horror, that she was staring. The handsome stranger didn't even seem to notice how flustered she was as he picked up one package after the next. "My goodness! It is positively horrendous out here!" He tucked her packages inside his coat and then asked. "Are you all right? I didn't hurt you, did I?"

Sarah was still a little dumbstruck. "Oh no!" she said when she found her voice. "I'm just fine. A little wet but fine."

Taking her elbow, he quickly drew her into a small alcove between two buildings, providing them with a little shelter from the coming deluge. He smiled at her again and looked her over for a long while, long enough that Sarah found a blush creeping up her cheeks. Finally, he extended his hand and said, "Where are my manners? Simon LaMont."

Sarah looked at his outstretched hand and finally managed, "Sarah. Sarah McBride."

"Well, Sarah McBride. How about I buy you a cup of tea and let's see if we can't wait out this storm?"

Sarah's first reaction was to say no. It wouldn't be proper for her, a married woman, to be seen having tea with man who wasn't her husband. She was about to decline when the first small inklings of resentment began to work their way into her heart. It had been so long since she had done something just for her. She was too busy managing their affairs to take the time anymore. And really, what could it hurt? They'd be in a very public place and it was about to rain. And, she reasoned, she really would love a cup of tea. Sarah looked into Simon's beautiful brown eyes and decided to throw caution to the wind. She smiled and said, "That would be lovely."

CHAPTER SIX

TULAMEEN, BRITISH COLUMBIA—PRESENT DAY

It had been a frustrating week for Ed. Since leaving the police station that first day in Abbotsford, he had spent every spare moment talking on the phone. No, that wasn't quite accurate. He spent every spare moment listening on the phone—to the most annoying recordings. "Press one" for this person, "Press two" for that person, "We're sorry, that is not a valid number." Only Hannah's cooler head had kept him from throwing the blasted phone out the window. All he wanted to know was if Uncle Henry still owned the land on the deed and where it was. They weren't hard questions. The difficult part was finding a live human being to ask!

Finally, after talking to a real person—wonders of wonders—Ed found himself in a tiny cubicle, in a windowless office, with a paper cup of tepid vending machine coffee in his hand. Sitting across from him was a man who was, apparently, an expert on tracking down old land titles and deeds.

"Hmm"... the man said for the tenth time, peering at the computer screen and then back to the deed in front of his face. He tapped on the keyboard a few more times, pinching his bottom lip, and staring at his screen in concentration. Ed was about to leave for another cup of coffee when the man spoke up. "I've found it!" he said. Ed felt his heart rate increase in anticipation. The man followed the words with his finger. "Yes, here it is." He said finally tapping the computer screen in front of him. "The property is near Tulameen. Do you know where that is?"

Ed had made it as far as the parking lot, his mind whirling. He thought that he would get some answers today, but instead the story of his great uncle just got more bizarre. He sat in his truck staring at the land title deed. Uncle Henry owned land on Otter Mountain, if that expert had been correct. Otter Mountain was so close to their cabin, they could practically walk out and touch it. It seemed like a pretty big coincidence and Ed didn't believe in coincidences.

Hannah was in her garden when she heard Ed's truck come down the road and turn onto their gravel drive. She stood to wave, smoothing her chestnut hair from her face and then continued to tackle the weeds that threatened to overtake her tomato plants. She was sure that the weeds had grown overnight, but everything on this piece of land seemed to flourish without any help from her.

Ed and Hannah lived on five acres of rolling hills on Mount Lehman Road in Abbotsford. They had purchased the land from Hannah's grandfather shortly after he retired from farming. The two-storey, red-and-white farmhouse had been built by her Grandpa John. Together with his wife, Tina, they had raised five children on this land, including Hannah's mother. The house was old and dated, but the view overlooking the Fraser River was spectacular and more than made up for the tiny bathroom and squeaky wood floors. Every morning when Hannah looked out her kitchen window, she saw the beautiful Golden Ears mountains and was filled with gratitude. She couldn't imagine living anywhere else.

"Hey," Ed said as he walked through the garden gate.

Hannah smiled and tugged at another tenacious dandelion. "How did it go at the land title office?" she asked, turning back to the weed. When he didn't answer, she looked at him and then saw his face. "What?" She could see that something had happened. "What did you find out?"

"You're not going to believe it." He walked over to an old bench in the corner of the garden and sat down. "The land is on Otter Mountain."

"What?" Hannah was confused. "Otter Mountain? You mean *our* Otter Mountain? By the cabin?" Ed nodded, still not sure he believed it, either.

Tossing her gardening gloves on the ground, Hannah stood and walked over to her husband. She sat on a nearby willow chair, her weeding forgotten. "How can that be?" she asked, incredulous. "How could he have owned land in the same area as the family cabin and yet have nothing to do with the family?" It seemed so implausible.

"I don't know." Leaning forward, Ed put his elbows on his knees and stared at the ground. They were silent for a while, both trying to assimilate this new information. "The guy at the office said he'd do some more investigating for me." He tugged absently at a small seedling that was coming up in the dirt between his boots. "I can't imagine that the land still belongs to him."

"Remind me," Hannah said. "When did your family buy the land for the cabin?"

Ed did the math in his head. "I was about nine I think… so around 1968?"

"And what do you remember about that time?"

Ed's forehead puckered as he tried to dredge up those days from so long ago. "I honestly don't remember exactly when we bought it. I just remember how excited I was when my parents told us we were going to build a cabin in Tulameen." He bent to pick a sprig of sage growing in a nearby oak barrel and toyed with it absently. "I had no clue where Tulameen was, but it sounded so exotic," he laughed. "We cleared the land ourselves you know; boy, did our dad ever put us to work. And we poured the foundation with cement we mixed in this old mixer. Took us forever!"

Hannah watched her husband's face transform, the way it always did when he talked about his childhood." He smiled, then shook his head, "It took us two summers to frame it up but when it was done, it was better than Christmas."

Turning to Hannah he said, "You know, Oma Helen cried that day. I assumed that she had bought the land for our family. She always talked about how important it was for us to be together." He threw the piece of sage on the ground. "Now I'm starting to wonder." He stood and walked over to the fence that bordered the vegetable garden and looked at the view.

When he didn't continue talking, Hannah walked over to stand beside him. "So, when your oma died, the land went to your mom and Aunt Elsie?" she asked.

Ed nodded. "They were the only two left. We had no idea where Uncle Henry was, Tante Nettie died in China, and even if Tante Frieda had been alive, she wouldn't have wanted it. She never seemed to care for the cabin much." Ed chuckled remembering the grouchy spinster.

Hannah smiled and laced her fingers through his. "And now it's ours," she said.

He turned to her and smiled. "Yup. Finally."

When Ed and his siblings were young, the family went up to the cabin as often as they could; every long weekend and most of their summer months were spent in Tulameen. But then things started to change. The children became teenagers, they got jobs, and couldn't get away as often. His sister, Marlene, married a great guy named Peter whose family owned a cabin on Sheridan Lake. After they were married, they went there every summer. Ed's younger brother, David, was married to a girl who loved travelling to Mexico and Hawaii and her idea of a great holiday did not include hiking or fishing. Consequently, neither of his siblings had used the family cabin in years.

After a lot of thought and discussion, Ed proposed to each of his siblings that he buy their shares of the property, along with Aunt Elsie's. His brother and sister both readily agreed.

Ed leaned forward, resting his elbows on the fence and Hannah rested her head on his shoulder. "Do you think that the mine is still there?" she asked, giving voice to what they were both thinking.

"He shook his head. "It could be, I suppose." He picked at a piece of white paint that had flaked free from the fence. "Maybe even a cabin? He might have lived there." He turned to her and smiled. "But there's only one way we're going to find out."

Turning, Hannah started toward the house.

"Where are you going?" Ed asked. Was their conversation over?

She smiled at him over her shoulder and shrugged. "I better throw some food together if we're going to the cabin tonight."

CHAPTER SEVEN

TULAMEEN—PRESENT DAY

DEPENDING ON THE TRAFFIC and Ed's mood, it usually took them about three and a half hours to drive to Tulameen. They had made the same trip over a thousand times, but Hannah never tired of it. There was always so much to see, so much beauty. There were countless dairy farms, fields filled with wild swans, and stunning views of the Cascade Mountains. The flood plain of the Fraser Valley extended for more than 50 kilometres and after driving through the fertile Sumas Prairie, they turned and began their foray into the forest. The flat farmland ended so abruptly it always made her smile. It was as if a giant hand had flattened the land and then, changing its mind, made the mountains instead.

Once they passed Bridal Falls and the quaint town of Hope, they left the Trans-Canada Highway, and continued east on the Hope-Princeton Highway. This small section of the Crowsnest, as it was also called, had been built in 1949, and for the most part it followed the original Dewdney Trail. It was here that Hannah would begin to feel that delicious pull into the past.

They passed the Hope Slide, where in 1965 more than 47 million cubic metres of rock and debris came crashing down, leaving a jagged scar on the mountain, still plainly visible today. About ten minutes later they drove by Engineers' Road, a small remnant of the original road built to replace the Dewdney Trail in the 1860s. Ed always marvelled that the original stones were still intact, having withstood nearly a hundred and fifty years of mud and snow, countless mule trains during the gold rush, and thousands of tourists.

Ed guided the truck effortlessly, following the road as it shadowed the snaking curve of the Skagit River. Just past the summit of Allison Pass, they stopped for coffees and muffins at Manning Park Lodge, taking a few minutes to feed peanuts to the whisky jacks.

After they arrived in Princeton, they turned north and crossed the one-lane bridge at the edge of town, again turning west towards Coalmont and Tulameen.

Anyone driving into Coalmont for the first time can be caught off guard. Two large signs at the entrance of the tiny village declare, among other things, that the chief sports of the town are sleeping and daydreaming and that there is a predominance of bachelors living in town. All women are given fair warning.

As they drove through the small village, Ed waved at a couple of familiar faces gathered on the front steps of the Coalmont Hotel. The three-storey establishment, with its bright peach edifice, was one of the few original buildings still standing from the town's glory days. It was built at a time when everyone believed that Coalmont was certain to become the "City of Destiny." Today, it stood as a testament of the tenacity of the town's residents; just like their beloved hotel, they refused to go down without a fight.

Hannah sighed. They were about ten minutes from Tulameen and usually around this leg of their journey, she would start to feel the anticipation of arriving at their second home. But this time she felt an unfamiliar ache in her stomach, like she had eaten a sour apple.

Hearing her sigh, Ed turned to her with concern on his face.

"What?" she said, looking back at him.

"You just sighed. You okay?"

Hannah wrinkled her nose. "I'm fine. I just feel out of sorts, I guess." She turned her gaze to the hotel, like she always did. "I guess I don't like this uncertainty. Not knowing what Uncle Henry was about."

Ed smiled, reaching across the truck's bench seat to squeeze her hand. "I feel the same way. I have since that policeman came to see Aunt Elsie." They drove for the next ten minutes in silence until Ed parked the truck in front of their cabin. He turned the engine off and then spoke into the silence. "Tomorrow," he said with certainty, "we'll start to get some answers."

The next morning could not come soon enough for Ed. He waited, not very patiently, as Hannah drank her morning coffee and then put together a lunch for them to take along. Hannah was not a morning person and during their 35 years of marriage Ed had learned that there was no rushing her. But it took everything he had to keep his mouth shut.

Finally, they were on Otter Mountain. Ed had found a Forestry Service Road that brought them as close as he could get to the edge of his uncle's property line. When he got out of the truck, he surveyed the mountain in front of him. "I always assumed that this was Crown land. I can't believe that at one time it belonged to someone in our family." He shook his head still trying to assimilate this new turn in their lives.

They grabbed their packs from the truck and began to climb the hillside. After about 30 minutes, Hannah stopped to catch her breath. Although she considered herself an active person, she had never been a great climber. It didn't take long before Ed was far ahead, as usual, but she didn't bother saying anything. He would notice soon enough.

When he finally did, seeing her far below, he shot her an incredulous look. "Seriously? He threw his hands up in the air. "You're stopping already?"

Ignoring her husband, Hannah sat on a nearby boulder and pulled a water bottle from her pack. "I'm sorry, but I'm not part mountain goat like some people I know." She gave him a dirty look but there was teasing in her voice.

As if to reiterate her opinion of him, Ed came back down the hill to her, jumping from boulder to boulder, belying his fifty some years. Hannah could not get over how spry and lean he was; especially when he was in the mountains and, despite being married for almost thirty-five years, the sight of him in his element still did something to her insides. The man couldn't send an email or text to save his life, but plunk him in the wilderness and he exuded confidence. Today he was wearing a mismatched ensemble of camouflage, denim, and khaki with an old faded backpack and a rifle in its scabbard on his back. Everything about him testified that he was entirely comfortable in his own skin.

Ed pulled a protein bar out of his pack and handed it to her. "What?" he asked.

She took the bar from him and shook her head. "Nothing. I was just thinking how content you look right now."

"Yes, I guess I am. I feel like today we are finally doing something."

They ate their bars in companionable silence, soaking in the silent beauty of the mountain until Ed broke the stillness. "Okay," he said, "that's enough resting. Let's keep moving or it'll be dark before we get there."

Hannah shot him a withering look. "It's nine o'clock in the morning."

Grinning, he took her hand to help her stand. "That's right. No time to waste!"

They continued up the hill, walking through the tall bunch grass and jack pines, which gave off a familiar, pungent aroma. Ed closed his eyes for a moment. He loved that smell, like spicy tea.

Following an old game trail, they came to a break in the trees. Hannah stopped to appreciate the view. "Look at that!" she said. "The lake looks incredible from up here."

Ed looked at the valley and at the tiny town below. "You can see our cabin from here," he said, pointing at the cluster of cabins hugging the lakeshore. "I still can't believe that he lived here somewhere." He kept his eyes on their small cabin. "All this time and we never knew."

They walked on, the stillness broken only by the wind and crunch of the countless pinecones beneath their hiking boots. Suddenly, Ed stopped. Turning to her he said, "Do you hear that?" Hannah stopped and listened. Yes, she knew that sound. Ravens, lots of them, making a racket in the pines just over the ridge. Without a doubt, Ed knew. They had found something dead.

Ed pressed a finger to Hannah's lips. Motioning to follow his lead, he pressed low to the ground and silently crept on hands and knees to the ridge. When they reached the top, he peered over and scanned a small clearing below. It didn't take long to spot. A dead mule deer buck was lying under the nearby trees. The surrounding foliage was flattened and the area around the deer was dark with blood and littered with hair and bone.

Ed scanned the forest and debated whether he should take a closer look. It was a big buck with an impressive set of antlers, but he knew that the only predator capable of bringing down a buck like this would have been a mountain lion.

Hannah's stomach lurched as she watched her husband pull his rifle out of its scabbard on his back and check the chamber, making sure the gun was loaded. When he stood up, she grabbed his wrist. "What are you doing?" she hissed.

He handed her his pack. "I just want to take a look. I'll be right back."

Stepping over an old log and making sure the gun safety was off, Ed pointed the muzzle of the gun to the ground as he walked. It was not a big gun, just his dad's old .243, but it was good enough to deter a mountain lion. Ed was not afraid of the big cats, but he had spent enough time in the forest to know that you could never be too careful. As much as he loved being in the wilderness, he knew this was their territory, not his.

As he neared the deer, the ravens scattered, their black wings beating the air with great whooshing sounds. They cawed loudly to show their annoyance at having their dinner interrupted but that's as far as their courage took them. They flew to the tree branches just overhead and continued to complain at their uninvited guest.

Ed laid his rifle down, ignoring the birds, and knelt beside the head of the magnificent animal. He ran a hand over the smooth antlers and counted the points. It was a remarkable buck in the prime of its life. He sighed and stood and that's when he took a good look at the deer and the area around it. He saw three fresh piles of bear scat and the buck was half buried. Dirt and debris were piled on top of the deer in a random, haphazard way. Ed felt his pulse quicken. Only one animal he knew buried its food like this. He knelt to examine the ground more carefully. Bear tracks. Ed stood slowly, every muscle in his body taut with apprehension, adrenalin coursing through his veins. A cougar may have brought this deer down, but it had definitely been absconded by a bear. And, by the size of the tracks, Ed was sure it was a grizzly.

He picked up his rifle and cautiously took a few steps backwards. Ed had experienced a grizzly encounter only once in his life and that was one time too many. A grizzly would not hesitate to protect its newly acquired food source and if it was feeding on a kill it never left it for long. Ed's rifle was starting to feel like a little toy. He knew it was no match for a big grizzly. A shot from this gun would just piss off a massive bear. They needed to get out of there and now.

It happened so fast after that. For a moment Ed felt like he was suspended in midair and then he slammed into the ground. He writhed in agony, struggling for breath as a sharp searing pain shot up his leg. Then everything went black.

CHAPTER EIGHT

GREENWOOD, BRITISH COLUMBIA—DECEMBER 1914

SARAH WAS CLEANING HER house. She moved from room to room, scrubbing and tidying, with a frenetic pace that matched her mood. She had no idea what to do with the jumble of emotions coursing through her. Whenever she felt like this, she cleaned. For some reason Sarah could sort out her thoughts best when she was scrubbing a floor.

Throwing a dirty, sopping rag into her bucket, she stopped for a moment to collect herself. She knew full well what was eating at her. Well, it wasn't a "what," it was a "who." His name was Simon Lamont.

"Simon." Just saying his name out loud sent a thrill through her. He consumed her thoughts and that, of course, was the problem. How had this happened? She was completely infatuated with a man who she barely knew. And, despite all evidence to the contrary, she was still a married woman.

It had been a few months since they first met on that stormy day. They had had a very enjoyable time getting acquainted over fresh scones and two cups of Darjeeling. Sarah had to admit that it had been so refreshing to once again spend time with a man who was interested in her. There was no hidden agenda, no guilt to avoid. He seemed to truly care about every word she said and before they knew it, they had sat and chatted for over an hour. The rain had stopped long before either of them had noticed. When they finally left the shop, Simon had bowed over her hand and said, "It was a pleasure bumping into you Sarah McBride. Hopefully we will 'bump' into each other again." He gave her a wink and she had blushed at his brazen attitude.

Sarah hadn't rushed home that day. William no longer waited for dinner and was usually fast asleep or in a drunken stupor by the time she got home. No, she was in no rush. She had strolled home, unwilling to have the pleasant afternoon come to an end. She found herself smiling at passersby and even humming a tuneless tune. But illusions are fleeting. When she walked into their parlour that afternoon, William was there snoring loudly and sprawled on the chaise, an empty bottle on the floor beside him.

Sarah sighed heavily as she returned to the present and her cleaning, pulling the rag from the bucket and wringing it out. *I should have ended it right then and there*, she thought, as she tackled the floor again. That would have been the sensible thing to do. What was it about the man? Whenever she was in his presence, she completely took leave of her senses!

Instead of refusing his invitations, she welcomed them. They had met for tea again. They had gone for a stroll in town. Simon had taken her dismal, empty days and given her something to look forward to. He was attentive and listened to every word she said, and he made her feel desirable. It had been so long since she felt like that and she had to admit that it was a heady sensation, one that she was becoming addicted to.

Sarah sat back and stared at her shiny floor, contemplating her newest dilemma. Simon had asked her to meet him for dinner that evening. Up until now their meetings had been rather random and benign, but this was different. This time she would be making a deliberate decision to spend time with a man who was not her husband. Sarah closed her eyes as she waged war within herself.

It's just dinner. What can happen? she thought.

Plenty can happen and you know it.

Simon makes me happy.

William made you happy.

William doesn't even care anymore.

Is that why you've been "carrying on" behind his back?

I haven't been carrying on!

Then why are you feeling so guilty?

Just leave me alone!

Groaning in frustration, Sarah stood abruptly. Hefting the bucket, she carried it to the sink and dumped the filthy water down the drain. As she stood watching it, her thoughts swirled too; around and around until they disappeared. She had made her decision.

Two hours later, Sarah walked through the doors of one of the best restaurants in Greenwood. She spotted Simon immediately, sitting at a small table near the back. When he looked up and saw her, his face lit up like a rainbow. Her heart leaped and she realized then how much she had been anticipating seeing him again. She let out a long, shaky breath, smoothed her hands over the front of her skirt and walked towards him, leaving reason and her conscience at the door.

The evening had been exquisite down to every detail. Simon had ordered for them both. They dined on fresh trout and sipped on a very expensive bottle of Merlot. The candles on the table cast a warm glow and they lingered in the intimate atmosphere. When Simon reached for her hand over the table, she didn't pull it away. When he laced his fingers through hers, she felt reborn. They talked and talked until most of the patrons had gone home.

Simon took another sip from his wine and gazed at her over the rim of his glass. He set the glass down and then he squeezed her hand. "Sarah," he said, "this has been the most wonderful night. I never imagined that I would meet a woman like you."

Sarah blushed and he continued. "You're beautiful and funny and smart. Do have any idea how desirable you are?"

Sarah watched him, mesmerized as he lifted her hand and kissed the inside of her wrist where her pulse was pounding. His warm lips sent shivers through her and she had the overwhelming sensation that she was losing herself. She opened her mouth to protest, but he spoke before she could. "Sarah, I know that you're a married woman, but I can't help how I feel."

She struggled to be the voice of reason; she couldn't possibly allow this to continue, but when he produced a posy of lilacs from under the table, she forgot what she was going to say.

His eyes never left hers as he kissed her hand again. In a throaty whisper he said, "Sarah. I'm falling in love with you."

And with that, she was lost.

CHAPTER NINE

GREENWOOD, BRITISH COLUMBIA—DECEMBER 1914

SIMON LAY IN BED with his hands behind his head, staring at the ceiling. Sighing in utter contentment, he could not believe his good fortune and how this night had ended. He rolled over and slid a hand along the mattress until he touched her bare thigh. She sighed and rolled towards him, throwing an arm over his chest. "Mmmm…" she said snuggling under his chin. "I must have fallen asleep. I forgot where I was."

Chuckling, he asked, "Occupational hazard?"

She groaned and said, "What time is it?"

He took his pocket watch from the pine table beside the bed and held it up to the lantern. "It's nearly midnight." He said. "I still own you for at least another half hour."

She snuggled deeper under his chin and said, "So tell me about your evening. How did it go with your lady love?"

Simon ran his fingers up her bare arm and when she shivered, he laughed. "It could not have gone better," he said with pride. "Sarah McBride is absolutely putty in my hands."

Kate Alexander leaned up on one elbow. Even when she wasn't trying, she was bewitching. Her long blonde hair cascaded over one shoulder and pooled on the mattress between them. She rested her chin on her shoulder and looked down at him quizzically. "So, she's actually falling for this? She's falling in love with you?" She was incredulous that a woman could be so naïve.

Simon laughed again. "She is. It's sad, really." He shook his head. "And, in a way, I'm disappointed. I was hoping for a bit more of a challenge."

Kate sat up, wrapping the sheet around her body. "You are a despicable man Simon LaMont; you know that, right?" He laughed and grabbed her wrist, pulling her back into the quilts. He leaned over her. "If I'm so despicable why are you here with me?"

Kate rolled her eyes. "I'm here because you paid for me." She traced a finger lightly down his bare chest. "And I can't seem to say no to you."

"That's right," Simon said, nibbling at her collar bone. "And, thanks to you, I know how Sarah McBride is going to make me rich."

Simon was quite proud of himself, for the entire idea had been a stroke of genius, he was sure.

A month before, he had been feeling particularly frustrated and so he stole away to the red-light district and had indulged in a night with Kate and bought her "off the floor." As the owner and madam of Alexander House, one of the high-class brothels in Greenwood, buying her off the floor took a significant amount of cash. But it proved to be a wise investment for Simon. Later that night, as they lay in bed together, in a momentary lapse of indiscretion, Kate had told Simon how much money she made in one night. Simon was astonished! That's when he realized that, while there may be gold lying in wait all over the mountains, the real gold was in establishments like hers. Simon knew that this was where he would find the mother lode. *Let the miners pan for gold,* he thought, *let the saloon owners pour whisky and ale all night long.* He knew where the real money was lying. It was lying between the sheets in the red-light districts.

Kate pushed at him in a half-hearted attempt to get free. "Please don't give me credit for your deviousness." She knew her moral compass didn't always point true, but still, a small part of her niggled with guilt when she considered Simon and his newest mark.

She felt his smile against her skin. "Devious?" he asked. "I wouldn't go so far as to say I'm devious." He rolled back to look at her and grinned. "Determined would be more precise. I just know I was meant for a life of luxury and I came so close, I could taste it." Kate watched his face grow dark for a moment. "If it hadn't been for that damned Archibald Wilton," he said, "I would be married right now."

Six months previous, Simon had set his sights on a beautiful young heiress from Leavenworth, Washington, named Lillian Wilton. Lillian had easily fallen for Simon's charms and good looks and soon Simon was picturing himself living a life of leisure, safely ensconced within the Wilton family and their fortune. But what Simon hadn't bargained for was Lillian's father.

Kate had heard this lament a thousand times before and it was always the same. Simon had misjudged Lillian's father, but he was loathe to admit it. Archibald Wilton had spent the better part of a decade confined to a wheelchair and Simon assumed that the decrepit old fool could be hoodwinked as easily as his daughter had been. Wilton may have been imprisoned in a body that no longer obeyed his commands, but his mind was as sharp as it ever was.

"Your ship will come in soon." Kate said, trying to soothe him. She had no love for Simon, but his dark moods frightened her. She brushed a fingertip over his beautiful mouth.

Simon kissed her fingers but scowled at the ceiling. "Wilton seemed so happy to have me for a son-in-law. I never dreamed that everything he said was an act and that I was being followed."

Simon rarely spoke of what happened after he was found out, but Kate had heard from a reliable source that Simon, while courting the demure Lillian, was also having an affair with the wife of one of Leavenworth's more notorious citizens. When Wilton learned of Simon's peccadilloes, he summoned him to his palatial home and informed Simon that, if he ever came near his daughter again, evidence of the affair would reach the husband's ears. He suggested that if Simon would like the protruding parts of his body to remain intact, he would leave Leavenworth immediately.

Simon raked his fingers through his dark hair as he relived the humiliation of those days. Glancing at the pocket watch, Kate sat up. "Your time is up," she said, a little too brightly. She was getting out of there before his mood got blacker. Simon nodded and managed a small smile for her benefit but continued to stare at the ceiling.

After she dressed, Kate stopped at the door and turned to see that he was still brooding. "Will I see you again?" She didn't really care but she thought it polite to ask.

"Not if things go according to plan." I'll be leaving Greenwood soon and taking Sarah with me."

Kate nodded and touched her fingers to her lips. "Good luck, Simon," she said, though she didn't mean it. "I hope you get everything you deserve." She blew a kiss in his direction and then walked out the door.

"Everything I deserve." Simon repeated Kate's parting words to himself.

He rolled over and reached under the bed to retrieve a half empty bottle of whisky. Not bothering with a glass, he pulled out the stopper and drank straight from the bottle, replaying the last few months in his mind.

It had been sheer terror that had driven him north to Canada and, at first, he had no intentions of staying in this little mining town. But Greenwood was different. Greenwood had a charm and permanence about it. Gorgeous wood buildings lined the street and some were made of brick! It was a far cry from the many crude mining camps that had sprung up all over the province. There was money here. He could just smell it. And so he decided to stay; he was glad that he did, for it was here that he laid eyes on Sarah McBride.

Simon took another swallow from the bottle and smirked. Sarah suited his needs perfectly. She was beautiful and elegant but, more importantly, she was a woman of means. When Simon learned that she had an alcoholic husband, he knew he had found an easy mark.

After he "accidentally" bumped into Sarah during that summer storm, he put his plan into motion. He played to the emptiness that he knew she must be feeling. It had been so simple to sweep her off her feet. Simon made sure that he portrayed himself as the perfect gentleman, never doing anything that she would consider crass or unseemly. He prided himself in his ability to read women and his inherent talent to say just the right words at just the right time. Actually, it wasn't all that difficult. Women were so gullible.

Simon took another long pull of whisky and thought back to the days when he had "courted" Lillian. She had been so trusting, but her father had derailed Simon's future. *You thought everything was going according to plan*, he reminded himself. How it had gone so sideways was still a fresh humiliation. The memory made Simon groan.

Swinging his bare legs over the side of the bed, he scrubbed his face with both hands. "Not this time, by God," he said under his breath. He tossed the empty bottle on the mattress and laughed. "This time I will get what is coming to me."

CHAPTER TEN

TULAMEEN, BRITISH COLUMBIA—PRESENT DAY

ED WOKE IN SLOW degrees of consciousness. Screaming. He heard screaming. Someone was shouting his name. He rolled slowly onto his side and cried out when he moved his leg. The pain was so intense that a wave of nausea hit him and he forced himself not to throw up.

"Ed!" There was that screaming again. Like coming through a fog, Ed pushed his way past the haze and finally realized that the person who was hysterical was his wife. Hannah was somewhere above him. He lifted his head and looked around and was instantly filled with a stab of panic—all he saw was darkness—nothing but blackness. Dirt was in his mouth and he felt the grit between his teeth. The smell of stale air and moist earth filled his nostrils.

He pushed himself up to sit and tried to answer her. He couldn't seem to form the words. Spitting out some dirt, he tried again. "Hannah?" he managed in a croak.

Her voice came back to him in the dark, filled with relief and fear. "Ed? Are you there? I can't see you!"

He moaned. "Yes, I'm here… what happened?"

She said, "You were coming back after looking at that dead deer, when you just disappeared. Right in front of my eyes!" Her voice sounded calmer, now that she knew he was not lost to her. "It looks like you fell into a hole." Ed closed his eyes to let them adjust to the darkness and to take in Hannah's words. He willed himself to not panic. When he opened his eyes again, he could make out some murky images. Looking up, he saw a bright spot of sky above. He realized that Hannah's face was framed by the blue above her. She was looking down through the opening, trying to see him.

"I can see you," he said with relief. She was about fifteen feet above him. Ed got on his hands and knees, sucking in his breath as the pain shot up his leg again.

Hannah heard his quick intake of breath. "Are you hurt?"

Ed considered lying, just to keep her calm, but he was never good at hiding things from her. "I think my ankle might be broken."

"What are we going to do?" Ed could hear the rising hysteria in her voice.

He needed to stay calm for both their sakes. "Find my pack. I took it off somewhere up there," he said. "I need a flashlight. And then check your cellphone. See if you can get a signal." Ed knew the chances that their phones would work at the top of this mountain were slim, but it was worth a try.

"Okay. I'll be right back," she said. He waited for what seemed an interminable amount of time when her head appeared at the opening again. "I found your pack. And I checked for a signal. There's no service here."

Ed nodded in the dark, trying to think of a plan. "Okay. Can you drop my pack down to me? Nice and easy." She dropped the pack and he managed to grab it with one hand before it hit the ground.

Quickly he dug into the pack and found his flashlight. The beam flooded the dark space and he breathed a huge sigh of relief. Ed shone the light around in great arcs, taking in all that was around him. It wasn't just a hole; it was a mine shaft. He saw timbers above him and some old tools leaning against one wall. Some grey, weathered wooden crates were stacked to his left. "It's a mine," he yelled to Hannah. "I must have fallen through an old ventilation shaft." He swept the flashlight over the ground. "There are old steel tracks in here! That means there must be a way out. Hannah, look around for an entrance to this tunnel. It will probably be somewhere on this side hill. If you can find it then maybe I can find my way out of this mess."

She didn't answer right away and Ed knew that she was skeptical. "Trust me, honey. It's gotta be here. It will be close by."

"Okay," she said but didn't leave. "Are you going to be all right?"

Ed laughed ruefully. "Don't have much of a choice, do I?" When she didn't respond, Ed reassured her. "I'm okay. It's nothing that's going to kill me. I just need to get out of here."

Hannah forced down the panic that was rising within her. Never, in all their years together, had she been the one to rescue them. Whenever they had got themselves into a jam, she always knew that Ed would come up with a solution. She was always telling people that "he could 'McGyver' his way out of anything." But this time it was all on her. She took a deep breath. "I'll be back as soon as I can."

When Hannah disappeared, Ed prayed that his hunch was right. Another stabbing pain shot through his leg and he closed his eyes, breathing through it. Crawling over to the crates, he set the pack down. He propped the flashlight on top of a crate marked "Sundries" and took everything out of the pack: three sandwiches, two granola bars, a bottle of water, an emergency space blanket, matches, his flashlight, and a small first aid kit.

Ed spread the space blanket on the cold dirt floor of the mine and moaned as he slowly lowered himself onto it, trying his best to keep his weight off his left foot. Leaning back against the crate, he rubbed his sleeve over his forehead, swiping at the sweat that had started to collect. He let out a long shaky breath and then opened the first aid kit. Thank God he always kept pain killers in the kit. Ed took two of the pills with one swallow of water and a couple of bites of a granola bar. He closed his eyes, leaned his head back on the crate, and collected his thoughts. He knew that he needed to look at his leg, but he was afraid of what he might see.

Reaching down as far as he was able, he pulled up his pant leg. Just above his boot, he could see that his leg was bruised and swollen. The skin felt hot to the touch but, thankfully, there was no blood. Somewhere in the recesses of his mind, Ed remembered that he should keep his boot on. It would keep the swelling down and if he took his boot off, he'd likely never get it back on again. Twisting around, Ed grabbed one of the smaller, empty crates that littered the mine floor. He lifted it and then slammed it as hard as he could on the ground. The crate fell apart enough that Ed could wrench two of the smaller boards free. He pulled his pant leg back over the top of his boot and then placed a board on either side of the swelling. He grabbed the tensor bandage from the first aid kit and then slowly wrapped the bandage around his leg and the two boards, winding it up and down. The immobilization gave him some relief and he leaned back and sighed. Wiping again at the sweat on his forehead, he took a deep, shuddering breath. He had done all he could do; the rest was up to Hannah.

CHAPTER ELEVEN

GREENWOOD, BRITISH COLUMBIA—FEBRUARY 1915

Sarah went to great lengths to keep her affair from William. But Greenwood was a small town and even though William had been spending less and less time in town and more time in the saloons, word finally reached his ears about his wife devoting most of her free time to a man named Simon LaMont.

William had been living the past months in a drunken fog, but he wasn't dead, not yet anyway, so when he heard about Sarah and Simon Lamont he was not surprised. Oh, he was angry all right, but he was not surprised. He knew that someone else was occupying her time. He saw it on her face every time he looked at her. She avoided his eyes whenever he was around. Her guilt was as plain as day! When he couldn't take the humiliation any longer, he finally confronted Sarah. She thought about denying it but then she decided to lay it all out on the table.

"Yes," she said defiantly, "I've spent some time with Simon, but it has been completely innocent. Some walks along the river and a few cups of tea. I've done nothing wrong."

William looked at her for a long time. "Nothing wrong? You can honestly stand there and tell me your carrying on is innocent?"

Sarah tried to keep her chin level, but her last dinner with Simon and his declaration of love gnawed at her and she dropped her gaze, unable to meet William's eyes. He saw the guilt and his voice rose in anger; without warning, he threw his glass across the room where it hit the wall and shattered into a thousand pieces. Sarah's heart seized with fright and for a moment she thought he might strike her. He walked closer to her until they were just inches apart. "My wife"—he said the word "wife" like it was something nauseating—"is parading about town with a dandy and I should be all right with that? Tell me, wife, how would you feel if our roles were reversed?"

She knew instantly that she would be mortified, but she couldn't bring herself to apologize. For years she had been making excuses for him. She had run their affairs and taken care of their home while he squandered his life, and all the talents that he had been born with. She had finally found a little happiness with Simon and she had to admit that she was reluctant to let it go. When Sarah didn't answer, William knew that their marriage was no longer her priority. He grabbed his whisky bottle and walked out of their home without a backward glance.

It had been a stressful time for Simon. Feigning love took a lot of concentration and a lot of work. He had no idea how people did it every day. Whenever Sarah was in his presence, he had to make sure that he was smiling. He had to make sure that he said the right things. He had to make sure that he was forever attentive. Heavens… it was downright exhausting! And unfortunately his time was running out. Simon had very little money left and if he wanted to continue in the lifestyle that he was accustomed, he soon needed to put the final pieces of his plan in place. At least one thing had worked in his favour: William McBride was out of her life.

Sarah had told Simon that William had walked out on her and she hadn't seen him in weeks. He had returned once, presumably for some of his clothes and personal possessions, but she hadn't been home at the time. She had arrived later that evening to find that most of his clothing was gone. Simon had watched her face carefully when she told him William was no longer a part of her life. She seemed resigned to the fact, but still Simon was careful to proceed with caution. The next step in his plan was crucial. If she balked at his idea, all his hard work and the investments he had made into this "relationship" would be for nothing.

Simon used every last cent he had to prepare a special evening for Sarah. He was sure that this new business venture could make him a very rich man, but he knew that Sarah would never agree to it. Not if she knew what he had in mind. So, his plan was to bend the truth a little and to give her as few facts as possible. Then, when she had committed to it and when he had her money in his hand, there would be no way she could back out. He would see to that, one way or another.

Simon took Sarah to the Leland Hotel, the most prestigious establishment in Greenwood, where he had reserved their best table. When Simon ordered lamb, roasted potatoes, and wild greens Sarah was impressed if not a bit surprised. When Simon ordered coffees and lemon ice for dessert, she looked at him quizzically. "Are we celebrating something that I don't know about?" she asked smiling.

Simon was waiting for this and was ready to begin the dramatic story that he'd prepared. He took Sarah's hand, doing his best to act dejected and morose. He had to make this look good. "I'm sorry Sarah," he said, "but I just found out that I have to leave Greenwood and I wanted to make tonight special. I'm sorry to say that this will be our last dinner together."

"What?" Sarah was horrified. "What do you mean, you have to leave?"

He shook his head. "The business plans that I had have fallen through and I have exhausted all other possible avenues," he sighed heavily. "I can't make a living here." He looked at her with sad eyes. "You can't imagine how hard it will be for me to leave you." He gave her hand a squeeze.

Sarah stared at Simon for a long time. She couldn't believe this was happening. When William had left her, she had been devastated but now she honestly thought it had been providence. She was meant to be with Simon. She realized that she had imagined her entire future with this man. She took a shaky breath and managed, "What are you going to do?"

This was the moment he had waited for. He took a deep breath. "Well, I have heard of an opportunity in Coalmont. They say it's going to be a great city one day and the opportunities are endless. I've heard of some prime property for sale and it's perfect for opening a boarding house. There are miners coming from all over the world to British Columbia and they need places to stay." He held his breath at the white lie. *Boarding house* was often used to describe a respectable brothel. If Sarah knew this, then his plans would be for naught. But Sarah only nodded, so he continued. "The trouble is, I have enough money to buy the land but not enough to build the business…" He let his voice trail off and then stared off into the distance. He waited the length of a heartbeat, then two. The wait was excruciating. Then she spoke.

"How much do you need?" Her voice was barely above a whisper.

"What?" he kept his voice calm and even, pretending he didn't understand.

"How much do you need?" she repeated. "To get your business off the ground?"

Simon swallowed and then managed to give her a sum that he hoped sounded fair. She thought for a moment and then said, "I can give you the money."

Simon did his best impression of startled bewilderment, but inside he was ecstatic. This was exactly what he had been hoping for. "Sarah, I can't take your money." He managed to look pained.

"You're not taking it," she said, forcing a smile. "I'm giving it to you as a loan. A business loan. It sounds like an exciting opportunity and you will pay me back, I know." Tears filled her eyes and she brushed them away, embarrassed. "Besides, this will give you an excuse to come back to Greenwood."

Simon wiped at her tears with his thumb, then took her hand, kissing her palm. He shook his head. "I don't need any excuse to see you. I want you with me, always." He gazed lovingly into her sad eyes. "I will take your money, but only on one condition—that you come with me. I want to build this business together with you."

Sarah stood up and walked to the picture window facing the street. Crossing her arms over her chest, she shook her head. "Simon, I can't go with you. I can't leave Greenwood. I have a husband."

Simon walked up behind her and forced himself to stay calm. "Some husband. When's the last time you saw him?"

"Okay," she admitted. "I haven't seen him in weeks, but that doesn't mean I'm not married! How can I just leave?"

"Sarah," he said, grabbing her shoulders and turning her so that they were face to face, "this is your chance to start a new life. No one would know about your past. No more whispers behind your back. You can start all over again with me; you and me in the City of Destiny. Just imagine what we could accomplish together!"

Sarah looked into his beautiful brown eyes and she knew then that she would not argue with him. She swallowed all her misgivings and nodded. "Yes," she whispered simply. "Yes, I will go with you."

He closed his eyes, swallowed hard, and nodded, trying to hide the overwhelming relief he felt inside. He took her in his arms and because his duplicity knew no bounds, he asked, "Can I kiss you, Sarah?" She nodded, closing her eyes as his lips met hers.

CHAPTER TWELVE

COALMONT, BRITISH COLUMBIA—PRESENT DAY

HANNAH WAS TRYING NOT to panic. She had been wandering the mountainside for at least thirty minutes and had seen nothing that looked like access to a mine. She was beginning to doubt Ed's certainty that an entrance was nearby and if he was wrong, she didn't know what they would do. Sighing, she sat down on an old stump to collect and calm herself. She would be no help to either of them if she didn't pull it together.

Hannah took a water bottle from her pack, took a drink, and scanned the hillside once again. The terrain was semi-open, bunch grass covered the slope, and jack pines grew sporadically around her.

Hannah was confident that if there was a mine entrance it should be visible in this open territory. She bit her bottom lip and fought off tears of frustration. Maybe she should go back to where Ed was and tell him they needed to come up with plan B, if there was a plan B. She stood, turning to leave, when she noticed a large pile of boulders up the mountain to her left. Something about them caught her attention and when she went closer, she felt a surge of hope. What she had thought were old logs were hewn timbers. Her heart pounding, she clawed at a small rock that was leaning against a beam. She ignored the pain and broke one nail and then another, when the boulder finally gave way and rolled down the mountainside. Instantly she caught a whiff of cold stale air. Hannah looked at the exposed beam and caught her breath when she saw that someone had carved letters into it. Her fingers traced the rough letters that weren't buried by the mountain: N, E, and A. This had to be it. She had found the mine.

Ed was shivering. He was sure that shock was setting in and, on top of that, it was damn cold in the mine. He had wrapped the space blanket around himself as best as he could, but he still couldn't stop shaking. How long had Hannah been gone? It seemed like hours since she went looking for the mine entrance. The waiting was horrible and he squelched down an uncharacteristic moment of panic. He had no control over his situation, a feeling that he was unaccustomed to.

"Ed? Honey, are you okay?" Hannah's head appeared in the hole above him.

Ed was flooded with relief and he realized how worried he was. "Yes," he grimaced, "I'm okay but I'm freezing. Please tell me you have good news."

There was a moment of hesitation before she answered him. "Yes." But Ed knew that there was something she didn't want to say.

"What is it"? he asked.

"I did find the entrance but, honey, it's covered with rocks. That's why it took me so long. I didn't see it at first."

"Is it caved in?"

"No, I don't think so. I shone my flashlight inside the hole I made and I saw the tracks."

Ed sighed. "Well, at least there's a way out. Which way do I need to go?"

Hannah stood and got her bearings. She had always had a great sense of direction, even when she was a child, and knew instantly which way was north. "It's about 50 metres south of you. Do you think you can make that?"

"I think so. I took a codeine pill, which has definitely kicked in but I'm going to have to crawl or find something to use as a crutch. Just a minute."

Ed struggled to stand, using the crates for balance and wondered how on earth he was going to make it fifty metres. He shone his flashlight behind the crates and there, leaning again the shaft wall, was a pickaxe. He grabbed the pick and flipped it upside down, using the pick like a cane handle. Carefully, he put his weight on it and prayed that the handle hadn't rotted enough to break. It held his weight and he thought, *well this will have to do*.

"Okay, I'm ready," he shouted to the ceiling. "Hannah, you need to go to the entrance and yell and I'll head towards your voice, okay? When I get to you, then we'll figure out how to move the rocks." He waited for a heartbeat. "Hannah? Are you still there?"

She answered back, her voice thin and strained. "Yes," she managed to say with more conviction than she felt. "I'll meet you there."

Hannah left Ed and ran to the mine entrance. Running through the pines, she skirted boulders and jumped over fallen logs. Her mind raced, keeping pace with her body and countless scenarios played out in her head. What if he couldn't make it to her? What if the tunnel was blocked? What if they couldn't move the rocks? With every thought, her anxiety increased and with every breath she said the same prayer over and over again: please let him be okay… please let him be okay.

She reached the entrance, dropping to her knees at the opening that she had made before. She yelled his name into the blackness. "Ed! Can you hear me?" She held her ear to the darkness, straining to hear his voice, any sound that would let her know that he was coming to her. She waited, unconsciously holding her breath. Nothing. "Ed! Can you hear me?" She shouted it again and she heard the fear in her own voice. Closing her eyes, she willed herself to stay calm. Suddenly, she heard a sound coming from deep within the mine. She held her breath and listened. There it was again, unmistakeable this time. He was coming. She held her face to the opening, shielding her eyes from the sun. As her eyes adjusted to the darkness within the mine, she saw it. A flash of light. "Ed?" She waited, willing him to answer.

"I'm coming."

Hannah nearly collapsed with relief at the sound of his voice. It reverberated off the stone walls and she could hear the effort it took for him to walk. The light was drawing closer when suddenly there was a crash, metal against stone. She heard Ed cry out in pain and then it was silent.

"Ed!" she screamed. She heard him moan. "What happened?"

"I don't know. I tripped over something. I dropped the pick and the flashlight, but I can see it. I think it's still working."

Hannah heard him crawling, rocks tumbling as he fished for the flashlight in the dark.

"Got it!" he said.

Hannah breathed a sigh of relief. She waited for him to continue towards her when she heard him yell again but this time it was different. It wasn't a cry of pain, it was fear. "Ed? What is it?"

He was quiet for so long that Hannah thought maybe he had passed out.

Finally, he spoke. "I see what I tripped over." There was another long pause. "There are bones in here."

Hannah imagined a dead raccoon or maybe a bear. "Is it an animal?"

"No," he said. "It's a skeleton." His voice was tight. "A human skeleton. Hannah, someone died in here."

CHAPTER THIRTEEN

TULAMEEN—PRESENT DAY

ED SHONE THE FLASHLIGHT over the bones and then slowly over the skull. Sightless eyes stared back at him and he shuddered. Spending as much time as he did outdoors, Ed had certainly seen dead animals before, but this was different. These bones were human.

"Ed?" Hannah's voice echoed down to him from the end of the mine.

He tore his eyes away from the gruesome sight and called back to her. "I'm coming." He grabbed the pickaxe from where he had dropped it and heaved himself back to an upright position. Once again, he started toward his wife's voice, doing his best to keep the weight off his left foot and paying better attention to the mine floor in front of him.

As he neared the end of the tunnel, he turned a small corner and there he saw a sliver of light. "Hannah?" A shadow moved across the opening and relief washed over him.

"I'm here," she said. Like a moth to a flame, Ed stumbled toward the light, reaching out a hand through the crack to her. Hannah grabbed his hand and was alarmed to feel how cold it was. "How are you doing, honey?"

He laughed a small laugh. "I've been better."

She immediately released his hand and silently berated herself for not moving the stones while she waited. She said, "We need to get you out of there." Hannah climbed up on the boulder in front of her. It was less than a metre tall but thin and flat on top and covered with smaller rocks, branches, and debris. Hannah realized that with some effort she could probably dislodge most of them. "Look out, honey. It might get a little dusty." She climbed a little higher, sat and used her legs to push the stones. Since they were on a sidehill it didn't take much. Once she pushed a rock far enough, gravity did the rest. The stones tumbled down the hill, each in turn throwing up dust and pine needles in its wake. As Hannah worked, Ed lowered himself on the cold ground, watching as the light in the mine grew brighter with each rock she dislodged. He smiled as Hannah made small grunts and groans with the exertion and thought at this moment how he couldn't love her more.

Hannah worked for at least twenty minutes without stopping until she realized that there were no smaller rocks left. She looked to see how much headway she had made and was elated to see Ed's face looking up at her.

"You are a rock star; you know that right?" Despite his pain, he laughed at his terrible joke.

"You're funny," she said as she wiped the sweat from her forehead with her sleeve. "What do you think? Can you fit through this gap?"

Ed eyed the opening dubiously and wobbled his head. I don't think so. But all I need is a just a few more inches." He placed his hand on the flat boulder, the only thing that separated him from her. "Let's try to move this one together, okay? You use the pick and I'll push from inside here." Hannah started to protest but he stopped her. "I'll be okay. We can do this."

Ed turned himself around and placed his back on the boulder. He braced his right leg against the wall of the mine. "On the count of three, okay? One, two, three." Together they strained to move the last boulder. Ed pushed as hard as he could.

Hannah pulled on the pick handle. She groaned with the effort, but when the boulder slid a few inches forward she was elated. "It's moving!"

Finally, when Ed couldn't push anymore, he stopped. "That's all I can do," he said, panting with the effort.

Peering over the boulder, Hannah saw his grimace and knew that he was in a lot of pain. "What do you think?" she asked, praying that it had been enough.

Looking up and squinting against the bright sky, Ed judged the opening. "I think it might be big enough." With a wry smile, he began to stand. "Good thing I'm skinny." Twisting his body to match the space they had made, Ed squirmed and manoeuvred through the narrow opening.

It's like watching a butterfly wriggle out of its cocoon, Hannah thought. She held her breath until Ed raised his hips above the rock. With one last effort, he heaved himself out of the mine and on top of the narrow boulder. When Hannah saw that he was free, her relief was palpable. "Thank you, God," she said to the sky. She stood between his knees, looking up at the face she loved so well and felt the hot sting of tears, her emotions overwhelming her. "I don't know what I would have done if I hadn't been able to get you out of there," she said through her tears, now white rivulets on her filthy cheeks.

Ed touched her dirty nose with his grimier hand. "I'm a lot tougher than I look. And I never doubted you for a second."

She chuckled and rested her forehead on his legs. "You're such a liar." Taking a shaky breath to steady herself, she said, "Let me help you down."

Ed placed one hand on her shoulder and the other on the boulder. Doing his best to land on his right foot, he carefully lowered himself to the ground. When he was down, they slid together to the earth in an exhausted heap.

They sat wrapped together, not moving, and processed all that happened in the last few hours. Ed and Hannah had had their share of adventures, but this one took the cake. The mountain breeze blew around them and Hannah caught a whiff of air from the mine. It was old and stale, reminding her of what lay inside. She stood and reached for Ed's hand to help him stand. "We need to get you to a doctor, and we need to call the police."

But Ed grabbed her wrist. "Wait," he said, pulling her back down next to him. "Maybe we shouldn't call the police just yet."

Hannah looked at him incredulous. "What? Why? Why wouldn't you want to call the police? There's a skeleton in there."

Ed nodded. "That's just it. Don't you get it, Hannah? This mine was probably Uncle Henry's. And there's a body in there! I'm not so sure I want the police involved just yet."

Hannah shook her head, completely unconvinced.

But Ed persevered. "Look," he said, "obviously those bones have been in there a long time. No one has missed him… her… whoever that is." He shifted, grimacing with the pain but continued. "Can you imagine what this would do to Aunt Elsie? You saw how upset she got when that policeman came to visit her. Can you even picture what it would do if they started questioning her about a dead body found in her brother's mine? It would kill her, literally! Our family means everything to her."

Hannah picked up a small pinecone and toyed with it absently as she thought about Aunt Elsie. She knew he was right. Aunt Elsie would be severely traumatized by a police investigation. "OK," she said. "We won't call the police."

He looked relieved.

"Yet," she added. "So, what's your plan?" Hannah looked at Ed's face and instantly knew that she was going to regret agreeing to this. "What?" she asked again, warily.

He pointed to the mine. "You need to go back in there."

CHAPTER FOURTEEN

PRINCETON, BRITISH COLUMBIA—JUNE 1915

THE STAGECOACH RATTLED DOWN the road, leaving a choking cloud of dust in its wake. Despite the dust, Sarah leaned her head out the window and tried to catch a breath of fresh air. Since leaving Greenwood, she had been on various modes of transportation and she felt like a chicken caught in a coop. At first, she had been excited, embarking on this new adventure, but the novelty had quickly worn off. Sarah hoped that she might get this coach to herself, but that had been wishful thinking. There were four others travelling with her; five bodies in such close quarters left very little time for reflection and it left very little time for personal hygiene.

She smelled, to her chagrin, like a miner's boot and her fellow passengers weren't faring much better. She had extracted a fan from her valise, but it did little but move the fetid air around. Gulping at the warm wind at the window, she once again suppressed her misgivings. But it was too late for second thoughts. All she needed was a hot bath, she told herself, and to be alone with her thoughts. Then she'd be right as the mail.

For the most part, she had enjoyed the company. The young man with them, a Mr. John Spencer, was travelling onward to Vancouver to begin a new teaching position at McGill University College. Mr. and Mrs. Langston were joining her husband's family who had started a dairy farm in the Fraser Valley. The last passenger, a young woman, had joined them at Rock Creek. When that one had climbed into the coach, they had all been slightly taken aback, for there was no ignoring her.

She wore a gown of blood red with a matching plumed hat. Her black hair framed a perfect heart-shaped face and her dark eyes were fringed with thick lashes. She drew stares wherever she went, and she knew it.

Holding out her hand to Sarah, she introduced herself. "Hello!" she said to the group in large. "I'm Madeline, Madeline Forrest, but nobody calls me that. Everyone calls me Lena."

"Lena," John Spencer said, sliding so quickly across the seat that Sarah was surprised he didn't slide right out the door. "Please sit here." He patted the now vacant spot on the leather bench beside him.

Madeline smiled a broad, beautiful smile and cooed, "Why, thank you."

Sarah hid a grin behind her fan as Mrs. Langston glowered at her husband, elbowing him in the ribs until he finally closed his mouth.

Madeline Forrest was obviously very aware of the chaos she caused wherever she went, but she had an openness and charm that was infectious. Sarah liked her immediately.

The travellers were beginning to think that they would never arrive at their destination when the driver, a wizened old soul named Turkey Jack, bellowed from the driver's seat above, saying that they would arrive in Princeton in about an hour. Sarah's relief was palpable. Despite the tedious and bone jarring ride, she had appreciated many things about the trip. The landscape during the last two days had changed dramatically. The forest began to thin and became almost desert-like. Sage brush grew everywhere and it scented the air with a delicious aroma.

At one point during the journey, they saw some mountain goats. They were beautiful, shaggy animals, covered with long, snow white fur and they had short black horns. When Turkey Jack slowed the rig so that his passengers could get a better look, the herd spooked. The mountainside next to the road was nearly vertical to the earth, yet they had scrambled up it like they had been on level ground. Sarah had never seen such a thing and she was mesmerized.

"Here we are folks. Princeton, British Columbia!" Turkey Jack pulled the team up as they steered into the stagecoach depot in Princeton. Sarah had never heard sweeter words. The horses had barely stopped before they were clambering out of the coach, nearly falling over themselves to get out. They had arrived.

Sarah took some time to say goodbye to Mr. Spencer and to the Langstons. She wished them well and good luck in their future endeavours. When they walked away, Sarah turned, surprised to find that Lena was waiting for her. Lena took Sarah by the arm and squeezed it, like they had been friends for a lifetime. "Did I hear you say that you're continuing on to Coalmont?"

Sarah nodded and Lena squealed with glee. "Me too." She pulled Sarah towards the hotel. "You know what?" Lena said as she took in the busy street. "It's been a long time since I've gone dancin'. What do you say to joining me?"

At first, Sarah had no intention of going anywhere with this flagrant young woman, but Lena's enthusiasm proved to be irresistible. Before Sarah could object, she and Lena were checked in at the Similkameen Hotel on Vermilion Avenue. The desk clerk assured Lena that the hotel provided the best food and entertainment in

Princeton. Sarah admitted that she was ravenous, so she conceded, agreeing to meet Lena in an hour for dinner.

Sarah wasn't too sure how she felt about this loud and exuberant woman living in the same town as she, but she was sure that once they got there, they wouldn't need to see each other too often. After all, it was predicted that the population of Coalmont would soon reach 10,000. She could easily lose herself there.

Despite her misgivings, Sarah had initially enjoyed her evening with Lena and it seemed that most of Princeton had gathered at the hotel that night. They danced every dance and men bought them drinks all night long. Although there were more women living in the north than there had been fifty years before, the man-to-woman ratio was still in a woman's favour. Sarah and Lena had their pick of the crowd that night and the men did everything to impress them. Unfortunately, the pickings weren't that great.

Sarah had no intentions in spending the night with some random stranger, but Madeline seemed to have other ideas. She fielded propositions, thwarted more than her share of inappropriate gropings, and turned down two very sincere marriage proposals. All the while, she shimmered and shone with a smile that never dimmed. Sarah didn't know how Madeline did it. She herself had been ready to castrate more than a few men by the time the evening was over and she had nowhere near the attention that Lena had received.

At two in the morning, Lena left the saloon on the arm of a young miner named Tom. As they were walking out Lena turned and winked at Sarah. "See you tomorrow," she mouthed. Then she turned and beamed at Tom, apparently hanging on every word he said. As they left, Sarah overheard Lena gush, "Oh Tom, you're just so funny! That's the best story I've ever heard!"

Sarah had endured Tom's stories over the last round of drinks and in her opinion he was as boring as mud. She had no idea what Lena saw in the man. It wasn't until she saw Tom hand over a large wad of bills to Madeline that Sarah's suspicions were aroused. Sarah watched them, mesmerized, as Lena took the bills and stuffed them into her ample cleavage. Then she kissed him. It was a wet open-mouthed kiss, so immodest that Sarah had turned away. When she finally looked back, the couple were walking arm in arm, heading straight for the hotel.

It was at that moment that Sarah recognized Lena for what she was—a prostitute.

The next morning Sarah woke late. She was famished. The night before had been entertaining and rather illuminating, but it had left her with a headache and an empty stomach. After dressing and splashing some cold water on her face, she made her way down to the main floor, only to find the dining room closed.

"I'm so sorry," said the hotel clerk. "Breakfast is no longer being served. But dinner is at noon." He offered her a weak and apologetic smile. *Perfect*, thought Sarah. *I could eat half a cow at this moment and you want me to wait another two hours?* She turned from the front desk in exasperation and walked outside.

Looking up and down Vermilion Avenue, Sarah decided to search for an open restaurant. As she strolled, she took in the names of establishments: King & Gibson Hardware, the Canadian Bank of Commerce and, she chuckled, Undertaker D. M. French, who could apparently supply coffins at short notice.

Sarah basked in the sunshine and the fresh air, feeling her headache begin to ebb. She was about to return to the hotel when she caught the aroma of something delectable. Quickening her pace, her stomach urging her on, she came upon an older woman selling pastries in a vacant lot by the side of the road. Seeing the large array of baked goods spread out before her, Sarah was astonished. She looked all around, but saw no evidence of a restaurant or shelter of any kind.

"Did you make these?" she asked the woman.

"I did, dearie," she said with a smile. "Would you like one?"

Sarah nodded so hard she nearly lost her hat. The woman laughed, handed her a strudel, and took Sarah's coins.

Sarah immediately took a bite and could barely stifle a groan of ecstasy. It was the best thing she had ever tasted. "This is absolutely divine!" she exclaimed. "But I don't understand." She looked all around again. "There's no oven here, not to mention a kitchen! How did you do this?" Sarah then realized her rudeness for not introducing herself and grimaced. "I'm so sorry. I'm Sarah McBride." She held out her hand. "It's a pleasure to meet you and your baking!"

They both chuckled. The woman brushed the flour off her hands and then shook Sarah's hand." My name is Minna. Minna Cooper. And no offence taken. I'm so glad you're enjoying my baking. There is no better compliment."

Minna Cooper was about five foot nothing with blue white hair bound up in a thick braid that hung down to her waist. Under her apron, her dress, was bilge-water grey, the hem badly frayed and stained. She was about as shapely as a barrel and when she walked, it reminded Sarah of an old goose. But it was her face that made Sarah pause. Her cheeks were round and apple red and she had a tiny little button nose. Her eyes were the bluest Sarah had ever seen. When Minna grinned the entire effect just warmed you to your bones. When Minna smiled directly at her, Sarah was struck with a sudden premonition: *This woman is going to change my life.*

Minna wiped her hands on her apron, settling her bulk on a small crate behind her table. "And, as to your question, Mrs. Hardy, who owns the boarding house where I've been staying, has been kind enough to let me use her kitchen. I start as soon as breakfast is over and as long as I'm out of there by dinner, she doesn't mind. I bring my wares out on the street and hope to make enough to pay for my room and board."

Sarah looked down at Minna's work worn hands and dirty apron, sure that she detected a note of sadness in the woman's voice. "I'm sorry if I'm getting too personal," said Sarah, "but why are you selling baking on the street? You should be running a restaurant or a bakery with your talent."

Minna looked up at her and Sarah saw the glint of tears in the older woman's eyes. "Dearie," Minna said, "when you're all alone, you do whatever you can do to survive. And right now, all I can think about is survivin'."

Sarah listened to the cadence of the older woman's voice and asked, "Where are you from? If you don't mind me asking?"

Minna smiled and shook her head. "I'm from Tennessee."

"Tennessee?" Sarah was fascinated. Tennessee seemed a world away. "What brought you here?"

"We came out west so my husband Nathan could work on the railroads." She brushed at a fly that tried to land on an apple pie. "My, but that man loved trains." Minna chuckled softly while staring at her dirty apron. "That's what he was doing the day he died. He was working on the tunnel for the railroad here in Princeton when he had a heart attack. He was gone in seconds, they said. I never even got to say goodbye."

Minna's voice trailed off and she was silent for a long time. When she looked up, Sarah saw a tear rolling down her cheek. Minna quickly wiped it away and continued, "He was the love of my life. I had no idea what I was supposed to do. It never crossed my mind that I might end up on this journey alone. But yet, here I am!" She held her arms out wide in a flourish, making light of her dismal situation. Sarah's heart broke in two.

Sarah stared at the delicious apple strudel that she held in her hand and before she could second guess her decision, she blurted out, "You should come and work for me!"

"What?" Minna looked at her disbelievingly.

"Yes," said Sarah. Now that she had said the words out loud, they made perfect sense. They were going to need a cook and Minna was the best cook Sarah had ever met. "You should come work for me," she repeated. She quickly hurried on before Minna could object. "I'm opening a boarding house in Coalmont and we'll need a cook. God knows I can't do it. No one will ever come back once they taste my cooking!"

Minna laughed but looked at Sarah dubiously. "Are you sure?'

"Absolutely!" Sarah exclaimed. She had never been so certain of anything in her life. "Please say yes."

Minna could not believe what was happening and she wasn't altogether sure she had heard correctly. Not long ago, Minna's wonderful life had crumbled around her. There were times she felt like she was caught in an avalanche; it was all she could do to keep her head above the deluge. She had spent the last eight months trying to keep from drowning in her own sorrow and self-pity; now a stranger was offering her a chance to start over.

Minna took Sarah's hand in hers and, when she looked at Sarah, her eyes were bright and shining. She nodded and simply said, "Thank you."

CHAPTER FIFTEEN

TULAMEEN, BRITISH COLUMBIA—PRESENT DAY

"ARE YOU CRAZY?" HANNAH stood up and took three steps backwards. "I am not going in there!" She shook her head vehemently.

"You have to," Ed said. "I can't go back in. I'm barely going to make it off this mountain, let alone crawl back in there."

"But why do I have to go in?"

She sounded like a five-year-old who had to go to the dentist, but he refrained from saying so. "Because we need a better idea of what we're dealing with," he said. "You need to look for some clues and you need to take pictures." She kept shaking her head, so he took a deep breath. "Hannah. You're one of the bravest women I've ever met. How many adventures have we've been on? It was your idea to climb to the caves in Savona and you're the one who nearly died on those ridiculous cliffs in Proctor looking for rock paintings. You can do this."

She covered her face with both her hands. "I know," she said through her fingers, "but those things were fun and there were no skeletons involved!" She made a sound at the back of her throat;

the sound she always made when she was frustrated. He waited, allowing her to process.

"Fine," she growled once more, knowing that she was beaten. "I'll do it."

Ed smiled. "Ok, in the pack is my little camera and here's the flashlight." He pulled off his sweatshirt. "And wear this," he said, handing it to her. "It's cold in there."

Hannah climbed the boulder and lowered herself into the opening. "I can't believe I'm doing this," she said through gritted teeth. "This has got to be the craziest and stupidest thing I've ever done. She took a deep breath and let her eyes adjust to the darkness of the mine. The musty smell reminded her of the root cellar at her grandma's farm. Her stomach trembling, she stepped deeper into the darkness. Around the corner, Ed had told her, then about ten more metres and the bones would be on her right. It didn't take long and Hannah saw it. It took everything she had not to turn around and bolt, but she forced herself to move forward. She knelt beside the bones and willed herself not to retch.

The bones were not as white as she expected but quite green, probably from being in such a damp place. Surprisingly, the clothing was still reasonably intact although rodents had made quite a mess of it, chewing it here and there. On top of the skeleton was a long-sleeved garment. It looked like a suit jacket, Hannah thought, which surprised her. Long pants were on the bottom and boots still covered the feet. Hannah took the camera and started snapping photos. In the darkness, it was impossible to see what she was taking, but the flashlight, propped on a ledge just above, helped a bit.

Once Hannah had taken about ten photos, she stopped to review them, hoping they would be good enough. She scrolled through each one, happy to see that the flash had gone off like it was supposed to and everything was quite illuminated. They would get a better look at them on their computer screen at home.

Hannah was about to turn the camera off when she noticed a glint in the corner of the last photo. She pressed the zoom button to get a better look. *That's odd*, she thought, *it looks like there's something shiny in the photo*. Hannah put the camera down and grabbed the flashlight to look at the jacket more closely. There was a pocket. She picked up a small piece of wood next to her knee and used it to lift the pocket open. She nearly screamed when a small object fell out and landed on the mine floor with a tiny clink.

Shining the flashlight on the item, Hannah saw what it was. "It's a necklace," she breathed and picked it up. "Oh," she said as she looked at it closely, "it's beautiful." It was a gold heart-shaped pendant on the delicate chain. It was badly tarnished and coated in grime, but Hannah could see that the front of the pendant was covered with intricate engravings. She couldn't wait to get it out in the light.

Tucking the necklace deep into her jeans pocket, Hannah considered the face of the skeleton, her fear beginning to ebb. She shook her head in confusion. "Who were you? And who left you in here?"

Ed was sitting against a pine tree, letting the sun warm his frigid bones and straining to hear sounds from the mine. Finally, he heard Hannah coming.

"You won't believe what I found!" she said the moment she crawled from the tunnel. She jumped off the flat boulder and wiped her grimy hands on the front of her jeans.

"What?" He was already filled with anticipation.

She sat down on the ground beside him and then pulled out the pendant. "Look at this," she said, handing it to him. "It was in the pocket of the jacket."

Ed took the pendant and brought it close to examine it. "Wow," he said. "It looks like gold." He handed it back to her. Ed saw how Hannah's eyes lit up with excitement as she considered the necklace. It was the same look she got whenever they were embarking on a new adventure. He grinned. "How did you do in there? Did you get some pictures?"

She shuddered involuntarily. "It was so gross, but yes." She held up the camera. "At least ten."

Ed smiled again and then grimaced. Hannah put the necklace in her pocket and turned her attention to her husband. She held out her hands to help him stand. "Ok, enough is enough. It's time to get you to a hospital."

CHAPTER SIXTEEN

FRASER VALLEY—PRESENT DAY

Ed was beyond bored. He had always hoped that his death would be quick; nothing drawn out but simple, like falling off a cliff or being mauled by a grizzly. At least those deaths would be interesting. But he was wrong; he was going to die a slow death lying on this couch with daytime television droning in the background. He was just about to roll over to have his third nap of the day when he heard, thank God, Hannah's keys in the front door. When she walked into the kitchen, she dropped her purse and keys on the kitchen island and went to the couch.

"Hey sweetheart," she said, walking over and plunking a kiss on his forehead. She sat on the love seat beside the couch and kicked off her shoes. "How was your day?

"Just amazing," he said. "Did you know that someone famous wore a pink dress last week and then she had the audacity to wear the same dress again yesterday? They even have the photographs to prove it. The world will never be the same again." He rolled his eyes in disgust. She was just about to answer when he blustered further. "And I watched a show today and there was a guy on there named Ransom. Who names their kid Ransom?"

Hannah laughed and kissed him again. "It's called a soap opera and I'm sorry you have to go through this, but you know what the doctor said." She ran her fingers through his grey curls. "Six weeks. You have to stay off that leg for six weeks if you want it to heal and you want to walk properly." Ed smiled at her, but she recognized the look. It was the face he made that said, "I'm smiling so that you will stop talking."

But Ed knew she was right. It was the only thing that kept him from ignoring everything the doctor had said. The thought of never hiking again, never climbing a mountain again, terrified him. "It's only been three weeks," Ed said. "How am I going to last another three weeks lying on this couch?" He picked up a throw pillow from the floor and plopped it over his face.

Hannah chuckled, but didn't answer. She picked a piece of popcorn from a discarded bowl on the coffee table and chewed it absently, then said what had been on her mind all day. "Ed, how much longer are we going to keep this secret? It's been three weeks and we haven't discovered anything that we didn't know already. What if we don't find anything? I feel like we should tell the police."

"I know," said Ed, his voice muffled from underneath the pillow. He looked out at her, squinting with one eye. "Let's wait till my leg is healed. When the doctor gives me the go-ahead, I'll take one more trip up to the mine and then if we haven't found out what Uncle Henry was involved in, I'll go to the police. Sound okay?"

Hannah smiled and immediately felt better now that they had set a deadline; but when she looked at Uncle Henry's suitcase, she shook her head. They hadn't found a thing that resembled a clue and she doubted they would find anything in three months, let alone three weeks.

Since discovering the mine and the skeleton, Hannah and Ed had gone over every item in the suitcase countless times, spending nearly every evening dedicated to the task. It had become their evening ritual; they had supper, had a glass of wine and Hannah brought out the suitcase. They pulled out every item and tried to glean some clue as to what Uncle Henry had been doing when he lived on the mountain. And who was the poor soul that was left in that mine? They talked and surmised but it had been an exercise in futility. There was not much to go on. The only hope they had was that they pendant would provide some clue. Hannah had taken it to an antique dealer in Abbotsford who specialized in jewellery restoration, but they had yet to hear from her.

The fire crackled and Hannah took another sip of her wine. Ed was snoring softly on the couch beside her, having given up playing detective about an hour before. The suitcase was lying open on the floor and most of its contents were strewn about her. She sighed and picked up the old Bible. Running her hand over the worn leather cover, she closed her eyes and tried to conjure some sense of who Uncle Henry was. He was obviously a man of some moral conviction and faith, but beyond that he was an enigma. Hannah opened the Bible and fanned through the pages. So many of the verses were underlined and Hannah wished, once again, that she had met the man who owned this book.

It was when Hannah was sifting through the pages that she noticed something different between the two covers. *That's odd*, she thought. While the front cover was soft and supple, the back cover was rigid. She flipped to the back of the Bible and ran her fingers around the fabric that lined the inside cover. Her heart skipped a beat when she felt a slight ridge around the edges. Examining it closer, she saw that the fabric was worn and frayed and slightly askew, like someone had glued it on but didn't get it quite right. Tossing the fleece blanket off her lap, she rushed to the desk with the Bible in her hand. Rummaging through the top drawer she found the letter opener. With trembling fingers, she made a neat slice about a centimetre from the edge of the binding and then ran her fingernail into the opening. There was something inside. Her heart racing, she grabbed her purse and found a pair of tweezers. She inserted them carefully into the cut and extracted a small photograph that was tucked neatly inside.

Hannah brought the photo back to the couch and held it under the bright reading lamp. It was a gorgeous sepia brown, like coffee with just the right amount of cream, and the words Laurentson Photography was stamped in gold at the bottom. Hannah looked at the strangers looking back at her. In it were four people: two men and two women. The men were standing and the women were seated in front on ornate armchairs, yet the photo had been taken outside. There was an oriental carpet spread out in front of them and a small side table between the chairs. It was so incongruous with the mountains, rocks, and trees in the background that Hannah chuckled.

Their faces were solemn and unsmiling. Hannah wondered why people never smiled in those days. Obviously, they cared enough about each other to take a photograph together; why not show that you were happy? These four looked like someone was holding a gun to their heads, though, Hannah noted, the older man had his hand on the shoulder of the woman in front of him. There was obviously a connection between them.

Both men in the photo were quite handsome and judging by their age, she wondered if the younger might be a son. Although he was much taller than the other man, by a good six inches at least, he still had that gangly appearance of a boy who was hovering on the verge of manhood. He wore a long coat that nearly reached the ground and his dark hair was long and unruly. The older man was quite handsome, Hannah thought, in a rugged, outdoorsy way. He sported a large brimmed hat and a very impressive moustache, and, on closer inspection, it seemed that there was just the slightest smirk on his face. Perhaps these people weren't so angry after all.

The two women in the front couldn't have been more different from each other. The one seated on the right in front of the young man was an older woman; Hannah guessed that she was maybe in her sixties. She was a chubby little thing with a round face that matched her body. Her grey braid was long. It hung over her shoulder and ample bosom all the way to her waist. She was obviously not very tall since her feet dangled from the chair, hanging inches from the ground. She reminded Hannah of a little garden gnome.

The last person that Hannah studied was the young woman. Although she was wearing a simple plain dress, she had a bearing and stature that bordered on regal. She sat ramrod straight, her ankles crossed perfectly in front of her, her hands folded neatly in her lap. Her hair was pulled up into a bun, but many tendrils had worked their way free. They reminded Hannah of the white morning glories that grew over their back shed, all wild and untameable. The woman was gazing intently at the camera. There was just something about her. Hannah's brow furrowed. How could this beautiful woman possibly be connected to their great uncle? It was so mysterious.

Hannah turned the photo over and, to her delight, saw that there was something written on the back. *"Mir mit Jake, Hattie und Minna,"* it read. "Mir?" Hannah knew enough German to know that "mir" meant "me." She turned the photo back over. The two women had to be Minna and Hattie. But who was "me"? Hannah looked more closely at the men's faces, then concentrated on the young man. There was something familiar about that face. "Oh, my goodness!" she exclaimed suddenly and ran to the bookshelf. She pulled out the photo album they took with them whenever they visited Aunt Elsie. She turned the pages quickly and found the family photo of Aunt Elsie and her siblings. She stared at Uncle Henry in the album and then at the photo in her hand. He was older and much more grizzled, but it was him.

Hannah smiled at the young man. "There you are, Uncle Henry," she whispered. She wiped a finger over his face as if to brush the hair from his eyes. "Who are these people in your life and what on earth were you up to?"

CHAPTER SEVENTEEN

COALMONT, BRITISH COLUMBIA—JUNE 1915

Lena Forrest paced the confines of the small bedroom, wincing when another crash reverberated to the second floor. *That sounded like glass*, she thought. It had been like this for over an hour. When the crashing had started, accompanied with a cacophony of verbal assaults, the sound was like two bears let loose in the house. With growing trepidation, she realized that they were now throwing things and that she, in part, had brought this upon them.

She heaved a sigh and stood, pressing hands against her stomach to steady it. She had been in this room since they arrived and had put away the contents of her valise and her dresses were hung in the wardrobe. Her shoes were lined along the north wall and her hairbrush and combs lay on the dresser. She had done all she could do.

Lena absently picked up her hairbrush as she walked over to the second-storey window, hoping that attending to her hair would distract her from the din below. She looked over the town that was to be her new home. The street below was clogged with mules, wagons, and miners, their travels grinding the street beneath them like a millstone. Beyond the town, the mountains rose all around them, encircling Coalmont like a mother hen over her chicks. But instead of feeling safe, Lena was agitated and uncertain. She pressed her forehead against the cool windowpane, hoping to ease the headache she knew was coming. At any other time, she would have thrown herself into her new environs like she always did, with as much bravado as she could muster. But Lena wasn't feeling much bravado now; it was a feeling she was completely unaccustomed to.

Lena had been so excited to move to a new town and start afresh. Simon had been a regular when she worked at Miss Laci's in Leavenworth, Washington. He was always charming and was so handsome. Lena had to admit she had been quite smitten with the man. When she received word from him that he was opening a brothel in Coalmont and that he wanted her to work for him, well, she had jumped at the chance. She had to admit that she had, quite naively, pictured her and Simon in a partnership, running this new business together. Never in her wildest dreams had she expected the events that had unfolded this morning.

They had travelled on the same stage to Coalmont together, she and her new friend Sarah and the cook Sarah had hired in Princeton. Sarah had told Lena that she was meeting her business partner in Coalmont. They were going to open a boarding house together. When Sarah had asked Lena what her plans were in Coalmont, Lena had just laughed and waved a hand in the air. "Oh, you know. I'm sure I'll find something to do." Sarah had silently scoffed at Lena's noncommittal answer. Everyone on the stage knew exactly what profession Lena planned to pursue when she arrived in town.

When the stage had pulled into the depot in Coalmont, Simon had been there, waiting. He looked so dapper in his brown suit and bowler hat. The minute she stepped off the coach, she couldn't resist. She went running into his arms and kissed him right then and there. But he didn't return her kiss as she expected him to. In fact, when she kissed him, he had gone as stiff as an ironing board and immediately tried to disentangle himself from her arms. She had leaned back to search his face and that's when she saw that he wasn't looking at her, he was looking over her shoulder. He was looking at Sarah.

Lena had watched a swirl of emotions cross her new friend's face: happiness, confusion, disbelief, and anger. When Simon took a step towards Sarah, she took a step backwards. Lena had watched them both in bewilderment. Sarah pointed a shaking finger at Lena and said, "What's going on here. Simon? How do you know Madeline?"

Simon had tugged at his collar and cleared his throat. He glanced quickly at Lena and then back at Sarah. "I… umm… well yes… I mean…." His voice faltered. "Well, it seems you've met an old acquaintance of mine. From when I lived in Washington." He had managed to look sincere and contrite when he added, "But, Sarah darling, I had no idea Madeline was coming to Coalmont."

Lena had stared at Simon in disbelief. No idea? She had just spent the better part of ten days to get here. To meet him. To work with him. And he had the audacity to say that he had no idea she was arriving? This was all his idea for heaven's sake! Lena had railed on him then. "What are you talking about?" Her voice had risen to a fevered pitch. "This was all your idea! You're the one who sent for me, Simon Lamont. How dare you act like you don't know me? I know you," she ran her gaze up and down his body, "better than anyone here. Pretty certain of that!" She was shouting now.

Heat crept up Simon's neck and Lena watched as it travelled to his face, colouring it the most unbecoming shade of red. They had drawn an audience and he was losing control. Simon never lost control. He had gestured to the street then and said quietly,

"Why don't we continue this conversation someplace else? Where we have a little more privacy?"

Lena hadn't cared a lick who heard what she had to say but Sarah was obviously uncomfortable, and she liked Sarah enough not to cause her more distress. "Fine!" she had snapped and then added "What about our things?"

"I'll have a boy come and fetch them for you," he said. "Trust me. I have everything under control."

"Trust you?" Lena had snorted at him. "I'm supposed to trust you? Perhaps, Simon, you shouldn't use words that you don't understand." And with that she had stomped down the platform steps and into the street.

It was hard to believe those events had taken place just that morning. This whole day had been so different from what she had imagined. Sighing, she walked over to the bed, throwing the brush on the hand-pieced quilt and then sitting down beside it with a plop. Suddenly she was very tired. She reached up and began to take the pins out of her hair, uncoiling the long tresses that, at one point that day, had been a tidy bun. Her hair was black and as coarse as a horse's mane. She had always felt that her hair was her best feature and she would have liked to thank her parents from whom she had inherited her striking looks. Sadly, for Lena, that was an impossibility, for she had no idea who they were.

Lena knew very little of her past. All she had been told was that someone, presumably her birth mother, had left her on one of the pews inside a Catholic Church in New Westminster. One night, while walking through the church vestibule, Father Murphy had discovered her, hearing her faint mewling inside, near the altar. She was wrapped in a ragged and filthy point blanket with nothing on but a sodden rag as a diaper, the umbilical cord still attached to her tiny pink body. Oddly, Father Murphy found small fir needles stuck to the baby, so he did his best to give her a bath, all the while wondering who the poor creature was who had birthed the child. No one ever came back to claim the infant, so the priest did what he thought best. He gave her to a couple in his congregation, but not before he christened her, Madeline Grace Forrest.

Lena's foster parents, the Connollys, were hardworking and treated her well. They were also very intent on fulfilling God's commandment to be fruitful and multiply; Lena often felt lost amongst their large brood of eleven children. It didn't help that she looked completely different from every one of them. While Lena's hair was jet black, straight as an arrow, and her skin golden, her foster sisters were plain, washed out, and dowdy.

At first, when they were young, it didn't seem to matter much. The Connollys had been very honest about how she had come to be part of their family, so she accepted that she was different. But then, as her foster sisters began to entertain gentlemen callers, their lack of beauty soon became a source of contention. Lena had grown into an exotic beauty and she drew men to her like flies to honey. Her "sisters" began to resent her and they grew tired of living in her shadow. When Lena had been caught in a compromising position with her foster sister's fiancé, they made sure that she was banished from their home and their lives. It didn't matter that the fiancé was attempting to seduce Lena at the time. Some people just saw what they wanted to see.

Her foster parents had suggested that maybe it was time that she went out on her own. She was astonished that they hadn't believed her. Lena left the only home she had ever known, disillusioned and heart sore.

A small knock on the door caused Lena to start and drew her out of her contemplations. She wasn't sure if she wanted to talk to anyone yet, especially if it was Simon, but she said the words anyway. "Come in."

Minna's round face appeared from behind the door and Lena let out a relieved breath. Minna was carrying a tray laden with teacups, a teapot, and a plate of cookies.

"Hello Madeline. I was in desperate need of some tea and I thought maybe you'd like to join me?"

Lena wasn't quite sure what to say to the unexpected kindness but she managed a nod and Minna entered the room, closing the door behind her with her ample backside. Setting the tray on a small side table, she sat next to Lena on the bed.

"Well." She brushed at a grey wisp of hair that clung to her damp forehead. "That was quite the morning, wasn't it?"

Lena chuckled humourlessly. "To say the least. What's happening down there? By the sounds of it I expect someone to be dead soon."

Minna smiled. "I think that they're just about done. Obviously, Simon wasn't expecting you yet. I think he was hoping to have some time to sway Sarah before you arrived. I never met the man, but from what Sarah told me, she believed that she loved him and that he loved her." Minna picked up the teapot and said, "You know that Sarah believed they were going to open a boarding house together. It's obvious, since he's hired you that he has other..." She looked at Lena pointedly "...plans for this business. This must be devastating. God only knows what she's going to do."

Lena coloured slightly as Minna alluded to her profession. She picked a small cookie off the tray but didn't take a bite. She stared at the sweet for a long time before she spoke. "I'm really sorry about all this," she said. "I had no idea that Sarah knew Simon. Had I known..." Lena didn't finish her sentence. They both knew that Lena knew exactly what she was getting in to. It was Sarah who had been blindsided. Lena had chosen this profession but Sarah... well, Lena couldn't imagine how betrayed Sarah must be feeling.

Lena toyed with a strand of hair, twisting it round and round her fingers while she watched Minna pour the tea. The room was silent, save for the sounds of Minna's ministrations; the pour, two plops as she added the sugar cubes, the small tinkling sounds of the teaspoon against the china. Minna picked up one cup and saucer and handed it to Lena, then took a sip from her own. They sat together on the edge of the bed, drinking their tea, saying little. Suddenly a door slammed from somewhere below and they both flinched. The house was instantly and completely silent.

After a few moments, Minna set her cup down and said, "Well, what do you think? Think it's safe to go down there?" She winked at Lena. Lena felt her stomach clench but shrugged noncommittally. Minna smiled and gathered everything back on the tray. Before she left the room, she said to Lena, "I'll let you know how it goes."

Lena only nodded as Minna closed the door. She stood and walked back over to the window. She heard muffled voices coming from the room below. The front door opened and closed, then she watched as Minna walked down the street, presumably to find Sarah.

Lena walked back over to the bed and reached under the pillow. She pulled out an old point blanket, burying her face in its familiar depths. It was rough against her skin and the bright Hudson Bay colours had faded long ago, but it soothed her as it always did. Lena's eyes filled with tears as she cursed her mother for the thousandth time. "Why didn't you keep me?" she whispered. "Was I such a burden?" She wrapped the blanket around her sagging shoulders and lay down on the bed. She was only twenty-two years old and yet she felt ancient. A tear trickled down her nose and she wiped it away with irritation. She was so tired of fighting for everything she needed in this life and she longed for someone to look after her. Pulling the blanket over her face, she closed her eyes and whispered, "Why did you leave me all alone?"

CHAPTER EIGHTEEN

COALMONT, BRITISH COLUMBIA—JUNE 1915

Sarah had never been so angry in her life. Not only was she livid, she was mortified. She had been taken in and duped by a man she thought she loved, a man she thought loved her. She was feeling so many emotions that she honestly didn't know what to think or do first.

Hot tears streamed down her cheeks and she angrily scrubbed them away. She hadn't been in Coalmont for more than two hours when she had stormed into the nearby woods. There was a creek running just out of town, and that's where she plunked herself, on its shores, watching the sparkling water rushing past, on its way to who knows where. The sky was so blue and the creek was so beautiful that the scenario seemed surreal. This picturesque scene didn't coincide with the tumult of feelings careening through her, and for a fleeting moment she imagined jumping in the cool waters of the river and letting it carry her away.

Hearing a sound behind her, she didn't dare turn around. She was afraid that it was Simon and that he had tracked her down. She had no idea what she would say to him and she didn't want his apologies, his declarations of love. She had already slapped him once today, slapping him so hard that his head had hit the wall behind him. She hoped his ears rang for days. It would serve the bastard right.

Minna sat down beside her and put her hand on Sarah's knee. "How you doin' love?"

Sarah couldn't answer; she just shook her head, picked up a rock and threw it into the creek with a vehemence that betrayed her silence.

"Guess this whole thing came as quite a shock?" Minna observed.

Sarah looked at Minna, her eyes filled with so many emotions: anger, bewilderment, and genuine sadness. "How could he have done this to me, Minna? He took all my money. No, that's not true! I gave him my money. I gave it to him! I made him take it!" She spat out the words and they felt like bile in her throat. "How could I have been so stupid?"

Sarah took another rock and hurled it towards the creek. It hit a boulder and split in two. "He told me that we were opening a boarding house together," she exclaimed. "A boarding house!" She stabbed her index finger into Minna's knee with each word. Minna winced, but wisely kept silent, letting Sarah give vent to her anger and frustration.

Standing up, Sarah crossed her arms over her stomach and paced. Walking back towards Minna, she did a very good impression of Simon's swagger and voice. "Oh, my dear," she drawled. "Didn't you know that in these mining towns, well 'boarding house' is just another way of saying 'brothel.' Honestly darlin', I was certain you knew what you were investing in."

Minna kept silent, watching and waiting until Sarah seemed spent. Returning to sit beside Minna, Sarah drew her knees up to her chin and dropped her forehead between them. Minna was not a mother, but from somewhere deep within, those instincts awakened. She rubbed her hand up and down between Sarah's shoulder blades, waiting until Sarah's tears had subsided and her breathing had slowed. After a few long moments, Sarah lifted her head and took a deep, shaky breath.

Taking an embroidered handkerchief from one of her pockets, Minna handed it to her. She waited until Sarah had collected herself and blown her nose, before voicing the words that needed to be said: "What are you going to do?"

Minna waited for Sarah's answer. Sarah took so long to speak, Minna thought perhaps she had no answer to give. But finally Sarah spoke, her voice tinged with resignation, "Honestly Minna, I want to run. Every fibre of my being says run. But I can't. I have no money left. He took it all and spent it all. I sold everything I had in Greenwood and…" she paused, choosing her words carefully. Beginning again, she said, "And even if I could go back to Greenwood, I'm not certain I would be welcome." Sarah coloured. "Let's just say that my reputation has been somewhat tarnished in that town."

Minna nodded. She didn't know everything that had happened between Sarah and Simon but she was beginning to understand the depths of Simon's manipulations and betrayal.

Sarah's sad litany continued. "And then there are these women that are counting on me. Apparently, I am supposed to take care of them. Simon said that I am to be the hostess of our business." She laughed bitterly as she said the word "hostess." "Does he think that will fool anyone? It's all so unbelievable." Sarah sounded so dejected that Minna felt her heart clench.

Sarah looked up at Minna, this woman who had filled such a void in her life in such a short time. "And I can't abandon you. What would you do if I didn't stay? You were counting on this job. He duped you, too."

Minna smothered the instant anger she felt and took Sarah's hand. "Don't you fret about me for one second, you hear? I can take care of myself. You do what you need to do for you."

Sarah thought for a moment, nodded and then stood up, brushing the pine needles and dust from her skirt. She took Minna's hand to help her stand. She had made her decision, though she really didn't have a choice; she would be the newest madam of Coalmont, British Columbia.

Simon was sitting on the front steps when he saw Sarah and Minna approaching the house. He rubbed a palm over his still-smarting cheek. She had slapped him but good, but it was no less than what he was expecting. He knew that she would be angry. What he hadn't anticipated was Madeline and Sarah arriving on the same coach. Madeline had as much sense as a rooster in a hen house. In his last letter to her, he had been very specific of when she should arrive. Her early arrival had nearly ruined everything, but he was fairly certain he had shown Sarah that she had no alternative. He had always been able to make others see reason; it was one of his many gifts.

It had almost bothered him that she had been hurt by his deception; he had to admit he had grown rather fond of her. But Simon's first love was money. It always had been. This place was going to make him rich, he just knew it, but he needed Sarah if he was to succeed.

Simon stood and smiled as Sarah and the old lady walked up to the brothel steps. He opened his mouth to add another apology to the many he had made before, but Sarah held up her hand to stop him.

"Don't speak," she said simply and he closed his mouth obediently. "I will never forgive you for this, Simon Lamont, but you've given me no choice." She shook her head, her voice was filled with hatred. "I will run this 'business,' " her pretty mouth formed a sneer with the word, "as best as I can. And when I feel that I've recouped my losses, we," she said, taking Minna's hand in hers, "will leave. I don't care what you do after that."

She saw Simon's shoulders relax slightly and the smallest smile crossed his face before he could hide it from her. She turned away in disgust. He had known all along that she would concede. He had built a beautiful web and she was the pitiful fly. She loathed him and she loathed herself.

Sarah walked past Simon to the front door but stopped short just before she went inside. She didn't turn. Her soul was beginning to harden, like a mud road in the summer sun, but she allowed herself to be honest with him before the veneer was complete. "You've killed me. You know that, don't you?" She thought of her life with William, the friends she left behind, her lovely yellow house and her grandma's lilac bushes. She straightened with resolve; the time for regrets was over. "Since I'm starting a new profession, I might as well have a new name. From now on you can call me Hattie." And with that, she walked inside and slammed the door behind her.

CHAPTER NINETEEN

COALMONT, BRITISH COLUMBIA—JUNE 1915

HATTIE GRUDGINGLY GAVE SOME credit to Simon for having a lovely place built to conduct their business. She had to admit that he had spent her money well. The house was a large two-storey wood frame construction with a spacious parlour on the first floor, with two bedrooms and a large kitchen in back. The parlour was open to the second floor and a long balustrade ran from one end to the other. A gorgeous wide staircase descended from the second floor to the parlour, turning twice, before it ended at an incredible Turkish rug that Simon had purloined in a card game somewhere along his travels. The girls would conduct business in their bedrooms on the second floor. The largest room, at the end of the hall, was apparently reserved for Hattie. Simon had also purchased the lot next door, which had a small cabin and barn on it. Hattie was relieved to learn that this was where he was planning to live and not in the house with them. Close enough to keep an eye on her and, of course, on all their 'assets.'

Their "upstairs girls" would begin arriving that next week and Hattie found she was so anxious she could barely eat. When Hattie had been married to William, she had handled their financial affairs in Greenwood very efficiently. She had always prided herself on her keen business mind and her ability to handle difficult decisions. But this was unlike any venture she had ever embarked upon. It was beyond her imaginings that she would do something like this and she had no idea where to begin.

It was, surprisingly, Lena who had saved her and guided her through those first few weeks. Hattie knew that she desperately needed some advice, so she invited Lena to join her on the front porch after dinner one evening. Lena, forever an open book, told Hattie and Minna every detail of her sordid life; how she had been abandoned as an infant and how her foster family had betrayed her. She told of being so hungry that she had eaten rotten and discarded food left in the alleys in Seattle. It wasn't until she had found herself in the red-light district of that city that she had first toyed with the idea of selling herself for money.

"It was ludicrous, of course," she laughed without humour. "But then I met a girl named Adelaide. When Adelaide told me how much she made working at Blakeley House, I made up my mind then and there. I persuaded her to introduce me to the madam of the house. Georgina Blakeley, or Miss Georgie, as we called her, took one look at me, asked me how old I was, and if I had any diseases. I told her no, not to my knowledge, and that I was nineteen. She hired me on the spot." Lena wiped away one tear that clung to her eyelashes. "The first time was the hardest." She said it so quietly that Hattie was sure she had forgotten they were there. "But it got easier as time went by. And I haven't been hungry since." She looked at both women, as if imploring them to understand. "It's amazing what a body will endure just for food and a place to sleep."

Hattie and Minna were silent, both listening to Lena's tale with a mixture of sympathy and morbid fascination. Hattie could see now that Lena's laughter and cavalier attitude was a carefully constructed façade. A wall built to protect her from ever being hurt again. Hattie's heart swelled with empathy. *Men*, she thought with bitterness. *They caused nothing but trouble, told you nothing but lies.*

A dove called from the trees somewhere high above them and Lena was lifted from her past. "My goodness!" she said a little too brightly. "How did we get so serious?" She picked up the pad of paper and the pencil that Minna had brought with her. With the pencil poised above the paper, she asked, "You wanted to know what we need, right?"

She began to write, the pencil scratching like a cat's claws on a fencepost. Lena filled out two full sheets with neat and precise notes and when she was done, she handed the first paper to Hattie. "This is a shopping list," she said. Hattie looked it over and most of the things made sense: bed linens, towels, and extra oil for their lanterns. And, Lena explained, they would need cigars and whisky for the men as they waited in the parlour.

There was one thing, however, that Hattie puzzled over. "We need six egg timers? Why on earth would we need…" She stopped in mid-sentence and held up her hand. Lena was about to explain, but Hattie held up one finger to silence her. "Never mind," she shook her head disbelievingly. "I can imagine."

Lena chuckled, then handed Hattie the second sheet. "And this is a menu we may want to try." She said.

"Menu?" Hattie glanced at the words. "I understand selling whisky, but we're not planning on serving food."

Lena snorted. "Look at it again," she said. Hattie read the paper more carefully this time and blanched. The menu had nothing to do with food.

CHAPTER TWENTY

COALMONT, BRITISH COLUMBIA—JUNE 1915

Exactly two weeks after arriving in Coalmont, they were ready to open for business. It was ten to eight in the evening and men were already gathering on the front porch. Hattie looked over "her" girls as she walked into the parlour. They were spread out upon the chairs and divans, like icing spread over a warm cake. She marvelled at their composure. Scanning their faces, she looked for signs of fear or apprehension, but she saw none. What she did see were six young women chatting and smiling and waiting calmly, like they were waiting to attend a meeting at the local benevolent society.

It certainly hadn't been like this an hour before. Then, the entire second floor had been bedlam, six women primping and preening like they were preparing for opening night at the local playhouse. They helped each other with up-dos: French twists and chignons. Each women had liberally used an atomizer, so much that the entire house smelled like a funeral bower.

Of them all, she was obviously the most nervous. For the girls this was thrilling and new and, in some respects, a fresh start. What better place to start anew than here, in the City of Destiny?

"Miss Hattie?"

Hattie jumped, startled to find one of the prostitutes, a young girl named Angel, standing beside her. "Shouldn't we open the doors?" Angel cast her blue eyes over to the front entrance where they could see the men milling in front of the leaded glass windows. "It's after eight o'clock," she said.

Hattie smiled nervously. "I suppose we'd better, before they break it down." Angel smiled, taking a step backward to give Hattie space and Hattie realized, as she looked at their faces, that they were waiting for her. She was, after all, the hostess of this establishment. She had never felt so removed from her element in her life. Steeling herself, she took a deep breath, knowing that opening those doors would expose these beautiful young women to men who wanted them for just one thing. How could she do this? Could she ever live with herself? She certainly hoped so, for she had no choice.

Twisting the cut-glass knobs, Hattie opened the doors but did not move. Her new lavender gown billowed around her, filling the spaces between her and the edges of the door and deterred the men enough that they stood still, unsure of what this new madam expected of them. She said nothing as she surveyed the motley crew, young and old, skinny and large; they waited as if gaining entrance to the Taj Mahal. She wasn't sure why she made them wait. Maybe because she could? This was her place, after all. Or maybe she just wanted to take a good look at what kind of men frequented the red-light district. She suppressed a shudder as one man dug wax out of his ear. Persevering, she addressed the lot of them.

"Gentlemen." She forced a warm smile and with a flourish of her hand, stepped aside. "Welcome to Hattie's Place." They cheered and punched their fists into the air, pouring through the doors like hounds on the hunt.

Hattie did little after that, but entertain. She handed out cigars and served countless glasses of whisky. She laughed at the unending stream of crass jokes and feigned embarrassment when appropriate. Lena had pressed upon her the importance of keeping the men happy as they waited; the last thing they wanted was for the men to take their business elsewhere, but mercy it was difficult. It was incomprehensible how vile men could be.

For six hours Hattie endured and the night seemed interminable. She lost all sense of personal space as man after man pawed at her, hoping to secure some private time with the town's new madam. But Hattie made it clear; her girls had much to offer but she was not for sale.

At two in the morning, Hattie locked the doors, turned, and leaned heavily against them. She had done it; she had worked her first night as a madam. She didn't know whether she should be proud or disgusted, but she did know that she was exhausted. She pressed her palms to her face and massaged her cheeks with her fingertips. Her face hurt from smiling all night long. She couldn't believe how quickly she had transformed herself into an actress.

Hattie longed to lie down and sleep for the rest of week, but she knew that her jangling nerves would never allow sleep to come. So instead, she shuffled down the hall and into the kitchen. She had caught the delicious aroma of coffee at least an hour ago and was dying for a cup. Walking into the warm room, she was caught off guard by the sight of every one of the girls seated round the kitchen table. She had assumed that they were exhausted and had all gone to bed. There was Lena, of course in the thick of things, along with their newer arrivals: Eliza, Nellie, Angel, Lottie, and Josephine. Minna was pouring seven cups of coffee and, from somewhere, produced a pan of fragrant cinnamon buns. Cinnamon buns?

When had this woman had time to bake? She gave Minna a grateful glance and without a word pulled up a chair to join the circle.

Lottie, a dark-haired beauty, wasted no time in taking a bun from the plate. "This is amazing," she said, picking the warm raisins and walnuts from the bun and popping them into her mouth. Licking her fingers, she said, "The last place we worked," she nodded at Angel then, "was a sewer compared to this."

"Where did you two work before you came here?" Eliza asked as she spread butter on a bun.

Lottie thought for a while. "We were working at a small house in Quesnel," she said, not looking up from her cinnamon bun. "Yup. We started working there in 1912, isn't that right Ange?" She shortened Angel's name to rhyme with range and Hattie caught the look of sisterly affection that passed between the two girls.

Angel smiled and answered in a small voice. "Yes. And before that I was working in Fort St. James. That's when Lottie and I met."

Hattie looked at the young Angel seated beside her. She had learned from Lena that Angel was only eighteen years old. She had been fourteen, just a child, when tragedy struck, and she found herself alone. She had been travelling with her family from Alberta to British Columbia when her parents and baby sister were all killed crossing the Rocky Mountains. Angel had no one and nothing in the world.

After a fruitless search for a job, Angel found herself in the red-light district near Fort St. James, lured there by a loathsome company clerk who promised her a job near the Fort. That was when she met Lottie.

Lottie had saved Angel from working in a "crib," a lower form of prostitution often found near mining camps and military outposts. Lottie had told Angel that the only women who worked in cribs were those poor souls who were past their prime and Angel was definitely not past her prime! Lottie and Angel became fast friends that day and it was Lottie who introduced the younger girl to a lucrative career as a high-class prostitute. Angel was perfectly suited to her name, if that was her real name, Hattie wondered. She was lithe and lean with silky blonde hair that hung to her waist. Hattie had watched the men fall all over themselves to be with Angel that evening. They couldn't wait to hand over their money for just a few minutes alone with the divine creature.

Lottie, Hattie had learned, was a few years older than Angel and she watched over Angel like a mother grizzly watches over her cub. Lottie was as dark as Angel was fair and while they were both likeable enough, Lottie had an edge to her that Hattie found a little intimidating. Her face was beautiful, but her full lips were slightly askew, thanks to a small scar that ran from her lip to the edge of her nose. When Nellie had brazenly asked about it, Lottie just shrugged.

"This," she said running a fingertip along the scar, "is thanks to my step-daddy. My mama's fourth husband, I think." She rolled her eyes. "I lost count." She picked up another bun and continued. "I was only thirteen when he took notice of me. That's when I started sleeping with a knife under my pillow. Mercy, but he was a hateful man. When he did show up in my room, like I knew he would, I was ready." She closed her eyes in the telling. "I stabbed him," she said quietly. "I tried to kill him, he was such a cur, but I don't think I did."

Nellie was aghast, "You don't think you did?" She pressed a hand over her heart. "You don't know?"

Lottie shook her head. "When you've wounded a bear, it's not wise to linger. He had locked the bedroom door with the key, so I smashed the window, jumped out, and ran. A piece of the windowpane caught my face on the way out."

Unwittingly every woman touched her own face at the same time and if the story hadn't been so tragic the gestures would have been rather funny. Lottie did chuckle at their reactions and the mood lightened for a moment. "Thank goodness I still have this body," she said, giving her shoulders a little shimmy. "Only good thing my mama gave me."

They all laughed a little and Hattie sensed a nearly imperceptible shift in the room, the lightening of loads. They needed this; Hattie realized. Although not one of them had the right to pass judgment, the need to unburden, to explain why they had chosen this way of life, seemed necessary, integral, before they could continue.

Hattie glanced at the clock on the kitchen wall. It was after three in the morning, but they kept sharing their stories and she didn't have the heart to stop them. She stifled a yawn as she took another sip of Minna's delicious coffee.

Josephine had come from the Yukon, she said, and was so glad that the Similkameen territory seemed a bit warmer. Josephine and her new husband had followed the throngs that streamed from San Francisco and Seattle to stake their claims in the Klondike in 1897. Like so many, her husband never made it. He died of typhoid fever before they even arrived at Dawson City. Josephine had found herself alone and in dire straits; one woman in a dark sea of men. One miner finally offered her a solution; she could travel with him in return for domestic favours. Josephine had naively thought he meant cooking and cleaning, but the miner had different ideas of what domestic meant.

"The old coot finally kicked the bucket," Josephine said with no remorse. "I took the little bit of gold that he hadn't drunk or gambled away and made my way south. She turned to Nellie, eager to turn the focus away from herself. "What's your story Nellie?" She took a sip of coffee before continuing. "Minna said you're from San Francisco?"

Nellie beamed at being singled out and it quickly became apparent that this girl loved the sound of her own voice. Relishing at the chance at a captive audience, she regaled them with many tales of her life in California. Nellie continued to prattle on, without stopping for breath, until Hattie finally interjected with, "What an exciting life you've had!" Then she turned to Eliza and said, "We haven't heard Eliza's story yet and it's getting late." Nellie's face fell but Hattie made it clear that her turn was over. "Where did you come from?" Hattie asked Eliza.

Eliza turned to look at Hattie. She gave a tired smile and Hattie saw one small dimple crease her left cheek. Even at this late hour, Eliza was stunning. Her thick hair was curly and long; it was the colour of the red stone walls that lined the Tulameen River. Her eyes were grass green and just a sprinkling of freckles crossed her nose, enough to make her seem innocent.

But the illusion was quickly shattered when she gave a very unladylike snort and said, "I'm not going to bore you with my life story and all its sordid details. Suffice it to say that it involved a man." They all nodded in commiseration. "I thought he loved me, but I was a fool. Men are incapable of loving one woman."

Eliza's story was so abrupt after Nellie's long monologue, that they were caught unaware. Bitterness saturated the few words that Eliza spoke and permeated the air, dissipating the fragile contentment in the room. Hattie sensed the change with regret. These poor girls, she thought, have been through so much already that she couldn't let them lose what little bit of happiness they had gleaned around this table. She thought back to the day that William walked out on her and to the days that she behaved like an imbecile over Simon. Mortification washed over her and hit her again like an ocean wave. She honestly wished that Simon would walk in at that very moment so she could slap his face one more time.

Hattie spoke, her voice bright with forced cheeriness. "Ladies." She addressed them like they were gathered for afternoon tea. "Seems like we've all been dealt a bad hand, but for whatever reason, fate has brought us together. I can't change the past, but I will take care of you now and together we can take hold of our futures." She looked each one in the eye. "Except for Minna, who managed to snag a good one, we've all been shafted by men." She traced a small knot in the pine table with her fingernail as she formed her next words. "But in this place, we have the power. We have what they want and, as we saw tonight, they are willing to pay handsomely for it." She stood, placing her palms flat on the table. "Tomorrow," she raised one eyebrow, "I intend to start taking my life back."

CHAPTER TWENTY-ONE

COALMONT, BRITISH COLUMBIA—JULY 1915

SURPRISINGLY, IT DIDN'T TAKE long for Hattie's "soiled doves" to settle into their new environs, and the guilt she carried was somewhat assuaged by their gratitude in finding a new, high-class house to work in.

"The most important thing for a prostitute," Eliza explained to Hattie one day, "is to never stay in one place for too long." She darkened her already thick brows with expert precision. "It doesn't take long for your clients to notice that you're getting older and soon they'll start looking for fresh meat." She said the words with such matter-of-factness that Hattie winced. Eliza continued, unperturbed. "When you're in a new house, they have no idea how old you are." She pressed powder to her forehead and nose, smoothing it with her fingertips. Surveying herself in the mirror and deeming her reflection acceptable she stood and turned, checking her gown for flaws. Eliza's dress was the colour of burnished copper and combined with her flaming hair, it gave her the appearance of a hot ember straight from the fire. "Time to open," she said to Hattie. She smiled, but the warmth didn't quite reach her eyes.

Hattie followed Eliza and marvelled at how the woman glided down the stairs, how she beamed at the waiting men below as if she had been waiting all day for this very moment. It hadn't taken long for Eliza to garner a reputation in the district; men came from miles around for a chance to be with her and Hattie soon realized why Simon had asked her to work for them. She was exceptional.

It was then that the realization hit her—these girls were not only her responsibility, they were an investment. The reality of this opened her eyes and, when she really thought about it, made her sick to her stomach.

Hattie watched from the balustrade as Eliza shifted into a different role as each man dictated. She laughed and teased and then, as if choosing which man would fill her dance card, took the next "lucky" fellow by the hand and led him upstairs.

As Hattie passed Eliza and her client on the staircase, she took notice of Eliza's ability to transform, to remove herself from who she truly was. And so, for the first time, it was Sarah who dissolved, as Hattie, the Madam of Coalmont emerged.

"Hello," she said, recognizing many regulars. "I trust you're all having a pleasant evening?" She took a glass decanter from the sideboard and turned to a man, whom she recognized as an owner of a local mining company. "Can I freshen your drink, sir?" she asked, not using his name. Discretion was paramount in this business.

"Yes, please," he said, placing a few coins on the sideboard. While they didn't officially charge for drinks at the brothel, most men gave a tip for the service and the money soon added up.

"Who can I interest you in tonight?" she asked him pleasantly.

"I'd like some time with Lottie, if she's available?" he said, with the eagerness of a boy asking for a bag of penny candy.

Hattie knew, for a fact, that the man was married but she just smiled and, glancing at Lottie's closed door, said, "I'm sure she'll be happy to oblige. She'll be down in a moment."

It turned out to be a long night, but a profitable one. As each girl came downstairs, she marked the transaction in a red ledger that Hattie kept by the kitchen door. Then they deposited the man's payment through a slot in a strong box just beside the ledger. The strong box was locked with two padlocks and only Simon and Hattie held the keys; neither could obtain the money without the other.

"We sure were busy tonight." Minna said, as she placed a cup of tea in front of Hattie. "And we had some excitement, I hear."

"Hmmm," Hattie agreed. "It was payday today for a lot of the men." She shook her head in disgust. "Makes them act like moose in rutting season." She glanced at Minna but didn't apologize for the vulgarity. "Seems the money just burns holes in their pockets and they lose their minds."

"Is Angel all right?" Minna asked.

Hattie nodded. "Yes. Just a little shook up, thankfully." One of Angel's clients had asked for something "off menu" and Angel had refused. When Lottie heard the ruckus in the next room, she had barged in and, seeing her "sister" in distress, promptly hit the man over the head with her shoe. "I think she gave him quite the lump," Hattie laughed. "He won't be trying that again, but it does make me afraid for the next time."

Minna looked at the ledger, trying to find some blue sky, as she always did. "Well, at least we made a lot of money tonight. That's good, right?"

""I suppose." Hattie conceded. "But I just don't see how I can get ahead when Simon takes half the profits."

"It doesn't seem fair," Minna agreed. "When he does nothing around here except to drink whisky."

"I don't think 'fair' is a word used often in Simon's vocabulary," Hattie opined. "Everything he does, he does for himself." She opened the red ledger laying in front of her, running her finger over the countless entries for that night. She sighed. "And he keeps track of every penny."

Minna walked over to the kitchen drawers and pulled out a small wooden box. "That reminds me." She took a large wad of papers from the box and placed them in front of Hattie. "These are the receipts from the mercantile, the livery, the laundry..." She went on, delineating every bill they had collected in the past month. Hattie rubbed her tired eyes. The girls had all gone to their respective rooms and only she and Minna were up, resting their bones in the kitchen.

"What does this say?" she said, holding a paper in front of Minna's face. "It's from the mercantile but I can't read this chicken scratch."

Minna took the receipt from Hattie. "This is from Angus," she said. "He has the worst penmanship I've ever seen."

As Hattie tried to decipher the bill, a thought suddenly occurred to her. Most of the bills were written on ordinary paper and could have come from anywhere. She smiled, an idea taking shape in her mind. She shook the bill in front of Minna's face and exclaimed. "Simon doesn't play fair. Well, from now on, neither will I."

CHAPTER TWENTY-TWO

COALMONT, BRITISH COLUMBIA—AUGUST 1915

THE SUN WAS BARELY over the mountains when Minna padded into the kitchen the next morning. She stoked the fire in the wood stove until the coals glowed red, then added a few small pieces of kindling to catch. Casting a glance at the wood pile against the wall, she sighed. It was getting low and the logs they had stacked outside needed splitting. She was getting too old for such heavy work and God knew Simon wouldn't offer. *That man was about as useful as tits on a boar*, she thought.

When the stove was heating nicely, she took a yellow wire egg basket from the counter and went outside. The morning air was already warm and she took a long deep breath of the summer dawn. She loved this time of day, when the town was still slumbering and the birds were starting to sing. She found herself humming a silly tune when she stopped short. Sitting in front of her was a young man.

He had moved an old crate beside their barn wall and was leaning back, his eyes closed, soaking in the rising sun. Minna regarded him for a moment and debated whether she should say something or leave him be. She made a small sound in her throat and he startled.

"Didn't mean to wake ya," Minna apologized. The young man looked sheepish but remained silent. "Are you all right?" she asked.

He nodded, but at that moment his stomach decided to growl—loudly.

She laughed. "Are you from around here? I don't recall ever seeing you before."

He shook his head. He was always conscious of his accent, so he avoided talking to strangers, but something about this woman garnered trust and he decided he had nothing left to lose. "I'm looking for work," he said bluntly.

Her face lit up and she surprised him when she said, "Stand up for a minute." He did. He towered over her by a good foot and a half and she laughed, craning her neck to look up at him.

"My, you are a tall one, ain't cha?" She sized him up, from his dirty boots to his frayed cap. "You could use a little meat on them bones." She said but noted the muscles in his forearms. "Nothing a few good meals can't cure."

She started walking towards the chicken coop and when he didn't follow, she stopped and turned around. Motioning to him, like she was herding cattle, she said, "Well come along then. Let's gather up these eggs and then you can join us for breakfast." She stopped again, realizing that she didn't know his name. She held out a hand and said, "My name's Minna, by the way." The man swallowed hard and Minna watched his Adam's apple bob. He took her hand and said, "My name is Heinrich Thiessen. After my father." His hand was warm and rough with callouses. "But most people call me Henry," he added.

"Nice to meet you, Henry." Minna prided herself at being an instant judge of character and she knew this was a good one. "Well, soon the girls will be wanting breakfast," she said, glancing to the second floor of the house. Handing him the egg basket, she said, "Let's see if you can make yourself useful."

Henry sat at a large pine table and watched the old woman bustle about the kitchen. She was as round as his Tante Olga and reminded him of the babushka dolls that his sisters played with at home. He was amazed that she could move so quickly.

They had collected at least a dozen eggs that morning and she used every one of them to make scrambled eggs. He glanced around and noted that there were eight chairs at the table. He wondered what kind of family lived here. It must be a large one he thought, judging by the breakfast she was setting out.

Before he could ask, a young woman entered the kitchen. She had long black hair that was plaited down her back and wore a simple dress of blue chambray. She was the most beautiful creature he had ever seen.

She walked over to the old woman and gave her an affectionate peck on the cheek. "Morning, Minna," she said and then stopped in surprise when she saw Henry at the table.

"Who's this?" she said, gesturing at Henry. Her smile was dazzling.

Minna stopped slicing bread for a moment to answer. "This is Henry."

The woman took a chair beside him and said, "Hello Henry. My name is Lena."

Before Henry could respond, Minna interjected. "I was thinking that we might hire Henry to do some work around here," she said, asking Lena: "What do you think? Do you think Hattie would agree?"

Lena stood to take the coffee pot from the stove and poured a cup for herself and Henry. "Mmm," she said. "Especially after last night." When Henry looked at her quizzically, she started to explain but was interrupted by five more women entering the kitchen.

As they seated themselves around the table, Lena introduced each one to Henry. There was Josephine, Angel, Lottie, Eliza, and Nellie. He was still trying to understand why these women were all living under one roof, when the one called Nellie took the other chair beside him and pulled it close. Much too close, Henry thought. When she smiled at him, he felt his face grow hot.

Minna heaped enormous portions on their plates and they began to eat with enthusiasm. There was no prayer over the meal, Henry noted with a prickle of disquiet, but there was an abundance of conversation.

"How are you feeling, Angel?" Lena asked the young blonde sitting across the table.

Angel smiled softly and said, "I'm no worse for wear. Thanks to Lottie." She leaned affectionately on the dark-haired girl beside her. "But Jack sure left with a goose egg."

They all laughed but Lottie frowned, "Hattie needs to tell Jack Thompson that there are other houses in the district he can visit next time. There is just a limit to what a girl will do." She made a face of disgust.

The women all made sounds of agreement and Henry began to feel a growing sense of unease. Suddenly they heard a crash coming from upstairs. For a moment it was silent and then they heard a woman's scream.

Henry followed them through the kitchen door to the most beautiful parlour he had ever seen. At the top of the staircase were many bedrooms and from the last one they heard a man's loud voice.

"Landsakes!" cried Minna. "Go!" she shouted at Henry, pointing to the closed door at the end of the balustrade. Before he could reconsider his actions, Henry was bounding up the stairs, two at a time.

CHAPTER TWENTY-THREE

COALMONT, BRITISH COLUMBIA—AUGUST 1915

Hattie stood in her bedroom trying to concentrate on the dresses that were strewn across her bed. It had been a hot and sticky summer and already the brothel was stifling. Hattie waved a fan in front of her face, but it did little to relieve her discomfort. She hoped that the house would cool off a bit before the evening and before most of their clients arrived, but she wasn't holding out much hope.

She cringed. Nothing was more intolerable or repulsive than dirty, sweaty men, especially when they had their hands all over you! She really needed to speak to Simon about getting a bathhouse built so that she could require that the men take baths before going upstairs to the girls. Hattie snorted when she thought about her "business partner." Just the idea of having a conversation with Simon made her stomach clench, but unfortunately it was inevitable. It had been three months since they arrived in Coalmont, yet she could count on one hand how many times she had had a civil conversation with the man. Hattie had avoided him at every turn, but sometimes it just couldn't be helped. If she was going to get her investment back, she would have to run this place to the best of her ability. But if Hattie had been granted her fondest wish, Simon would be walking down the streets of Coalmont with a knife in his back.

Hattie wiped a handkerchief across her forehead and then turned to focus on the task at hand. She was standing in front of the large oak wardrobe in her bedroom. She could smell Minna's breakfast wafting up from downstairs, but she wanted to pick a dress for the evening so that she could hang it out. The minute the sun went down, business would be brisk and since this was the last weekend of the month, it would be even busier than usual. Many of the men would come with their pockets full, eager to spend their hard-earned cash. Hattie intended to milk them for every penny and in order to do that she needed to look good.

Hattie finally chose a pale peach cotton dress that Simon had ordered for her from San Francisco. The gorgeous fabric was whisper thin and when she walked the dress billowed out behind her like a cloud. The neckline was wide enough that it hung just past her shoulders and the edge was lined with scalloped lace and tiny seed pearls. Hattie loved everything about this dress, except for the fact the Simon had bought it as a peace offering, one of his many peace offerings.

Ever since that first fateful day, when she had told him that she would never forgive him for putting her in this position, Simon had been working hard to gain Hattie's forgiveness. He showered her with gifts and made sure that the brothel was well stocked. He bought her favourite candy and brought her wildflowers. He even purchased twenty hens and a Holstein cow so that they would have eggs, fresh milk, butter, and cream!

Hattie ran her hands over the peach fabric and chuckled to herself. *You just keep buying me gifts, Simon LaMont*, she thought with satisfaction. *I'll take every single thing you buy me, and more, but there is nothing on this earth that you can give me that will buy my forgiveness.*

She was holding the gown in front of her, scrutinizing her reflection in the full-length oval mirror when there was a knock on the door. "Come in," Hattie said absently without turning around. It was probably Minna telling her that breakfast was ready.

"Now that's what I call a welcome sight." A familiar voice filled the room.

Hattie whirled and grabbed the quilt from her bed to cover herself. "Simon! What are you doing up here? I thought you were Minna."

Simon quietly closed the bedroom door and silently turned the key in the lock. He walked towards her, picking up the peach gown that she had dropped. He held it in front of her. "I knew, the moment I saw this dress, that it would look lovely on you. But nothing can compare to seeing you like this." His gaze ran up and down her length and he felt heat spread through his body. He let his eyes linger over her but when he finally looked into her face, he saw only loathing and distaste.

Simon had known that Hattie would be annoyed when she first learned that he had deceived her, but he never expected her to be so angry. He was certain that she would forgive him in time and that they would finally get on with their lives together. He had always been able to manipulate women to see things his way. But Simon had misjudged her. Hattie was beyond angry with him; she was indifferent. She acted like he wasn't even there. And it made him so furious. He was done apologizing and he was done grovelling. It was time that Hattie McBride realized that he would always be a part of her life. Simon reached out to touch her but before he could Hattie jerked out of his reach.

"Don't you dare touch me!" she hissed.

Simon decided to placate her for a moment longer. "Come on, love," he crooned. "What is it going to take for you to forgive me?"

He reached out again and this time she held her ground. He ran the back of his fingers over her bare shoulder and despite the sweltering heat in the room, Hattie shivered.

"Simon." She pushed his hand away, tolerating his touch for only so long. She continued, speaking to him like he was a simpleton. "You don't seem to understand. I will never forgive you for what you've done. You tricked me into giving you everything I had. You persuaded me to leave my husband. You told me we were opening a boarding house. And what did you invest my money in? A brothel! Do you have any idea what you've done to me? You've destroyed my reputation. I can never show my face in polite society again! And on top of everything, you've destroyed my faith in men. As far as I'm concerned, all men are swine." She said the last words with all the contempt that she had bottled inside.

Simon took a deep breath, allowing her this ridiculous tirade, but he was slowly losing patience. She was so beautiful and so desirable and her tenacity just made her more so. His patience gone, he struck then, as fast as a snake, grabbing her by the back of the neck and kissing her hard. Hattie tasted blood as his teeth ground against her lips and she used every ounce of her strength to fight against him. When she finally managed to push him away, he was breathing heavily, lust clouding his eyes and his reason.

Hattie looked at those brown eyes and wondered how she had ever thought they were beautiful? What a fool she had been!

Simon grabbed at her again, this time around her waist, and she raised her hand to hit him. But Simon was ready for her. He grabbed her wrist in a vice-like grip and then, twisted her arm behind her back, causing her to cry out in pain.

"Enough games already," Simon said, his breath hot in her ear. "It's time that we move our relationship forward, don't you think?" He spoke as if they were discussing a bank loan or a train ticket. He spun her around, bringing his face so close to hers that Hattie could smell his breath; she nearly gagged. She struggled against him, her foot catching against the oak mirror and sending it crashing to the floor.

Simon's patience was exhausted. He brought his hand up, slapping her across the cheek.

Her heart contracted with fear, her breath coming in short gasps, and for the first time she was truly frightened. Simon pushed her towards the bed until she hit it with the back of her knees. With one more shove she was lying on the bed and then he was on top of her. Grabbing the neckline of her chemise, he pulled, ripping the bodice down to her waist.

"Simon. Don't," she pleaded.

"Don't what? Come on Hattie," he cajoled. "You've wondered what it would be like to be with me since the first time we met in Greenwood. Admit it." His hand snaked down her stomach. "The time has come, and I've waited long enough."

Hattie's scream filled the room and she braced herself for his attack when the bedroom door crashed open. Hattie watched, terrified, as Simon was lifted from her and his body flew across the room, hitting the opposite wall. He fell to the floor with a thud, his breath leaving his lungs in a whoosh, and then he lay like a rag doll.

Hattie was still lying on the bed, frozen with fear, when a very tall man came and leaned over her, his bulk blocking the sun that streamed in the bedroom window. Before she could say anything, he held out a gentle hand to her.

"You all right, miss?" he asked. There was a soft accent in his words that Hattie could not place. Tentatively, she placed her hand in his and nodded as he helped her sit upright. Who was this man? And where did he come from? She was about to ask when Minna burst into the room, winded from climbing the stairs. She saw the room in chaos, the shattered mirror shards covering the floor, and Simon moaning in the corner.

"Hattie!" Minna cried when she saw her friend and her torn slip. "What on earth?" She rushed to Hattie's side and, taking the quilt, quickly covered Hattie's shivering shoulders.

There was another moan from across the room as Simon attempted to sit up. In just two strides, the stranger was standing before him and with no great care, grabbed him under the armpits, hauling him upright. "Mister," he said, pointing his large finger in Simon's face, "I think it be a very good idea if you leave the lady alone."

Simon opened his mouth as if to protest but then he took a good look at the man's massive forearms. They were like two anvils, scarred and dark from use and abuse. "You catch my meaning?" the man said, folding both arms across his chest and quirking one eyebrow.

Simon cradled his ribs as he straightened and managed a small nod. He shuffled towards the door, taking one moment to gather his coat along with his bruised ego, then walked into the hall and out of the house.

The room was silent now, stark contrast to the cacophony just moments before, until Hattie broke the stillness with a long shaky breath. Minna snapped to attention, tugging the quilt higher around Hattie's shoulders. "Are you all right, dear?" Hattie nodded, grabbing the quilt tight to her chin.

"He didn't hurt you?" Minna was almost afraid to ask but Hattie shook her head.

"No. He didn't," she answered in a raspy voice. She forced herself not to cry. "But I don't know what would have happened if you hadn't come in." She shot a sideways glance at the man who was still standing at the far side of the room.

Minna followed Hattie's gaze and then smiled, holding out a hand and motioning him over to the bed. Walking over to them, the man suddenly remembered that he was indoors and tugged off a ragged tweed cap. He held it in front of him, twisting it like a wash rag as he approached them. Turning to Hattie, Minna said, "Hattie, this is Henry and he's looking for work. What do you think about hiring him as our new bouncer? I think he just proved he's up to the task." Minna smiled at Henry, trying to alleviate the jitters she knew he was feeling. "God knows we could use him."

Henry shoved his cap into his back pocket and then held out his hand to Hattie. "Pleased to meet you," he said, his voice tinged with an accent that Hattie still could not place.

Hattie took his outstretched hand and replied. "I'm am very grateful that you were here today, and I am very pleased to meet you, Mister…?"

"Thiessen," the man supplied. "Henry Thiessen."

CHAPTER TWENTY-FOUR

COALMONT, BRITISH COLUMBIA—AUGUST 1915

"THIS WILL BE YOUR room," Minna said holding the door open so Henry could walk inside. Henry carried his brown leather case into the bedroom that led off from the kitchen and then set it down on the tin frame bed. "I know it's not very big, "Minna apologized, "but I think you'll be comfortable." She pointed to the wood stove just outside the door. "And you're right by the stove so it will be nice and toasty when it turns cold."

Henry smiled and stifled the urge to laugh. For the last few months, he had slept in such abysmal conditions that this room, by comparison, was luxurious.

Minna watched him as he let his gaze wander over the contents of the room; the bed, the nightstand, the rag rug. There were a few hooks on the wall opposite them and one ladder-back chair in the corner. It was a far cry from the opulence of the front parlour, but he didn't seem to mind. "Well!" she said brightly, "I'll leave you to it. Whenever you're ready, you come on out and we'll talk about your job here."

Henry's stomach clenched at the mention of the job but he said nothing. He nodded and Minna smiled as she walked out the door, closing it softly behind her. He sat down on the bed and took a good look at his new home. Other than the bed, there were few items. It was sparse, but at least it was clean. No dust and no cobwebs in the corner. His mother would have approved.

Most days Henry did his best not to think of his family, but it was times like this that the memories came unbidden. It could have been the lack of food in his belly, but he felt a physical stab of pain when he thought of them, especially his mother. She had been so disappointed in him. He could still see her face, her gentle face, on that last awful day before he left the farm. It had been lined with grief, like a worn out road map. Only a mother knows that kind of grief, the pain when your child decides to leave you and chooses his own path.

From the moment he was born, Henry had been a wanderer. His mother often told of when he was just three years old and had gone missing. She found him, thank the Lord, walking calmly down the street of the small town in Saskatchewan where they lived. She knew her boy would never be in one place long. But then the apple doesn't fall far from the tree.

Years before he was even born, Henry's grandfather had been part of the first group of Mennonites to immigrate to Canada. In 1870, concerned that they would lose their religious freedom and military exemption, many Russian Mennonites began to look for a new country to call home. At the same time, the Canadian government, hoping to settle the prairie provinces, began advertising for people, especially skilled farmers, to come to Canada. The promise of land, cheap land, and the promise of religious freedom was irresistible to many of them, including the Thiessen family.

It took the family about three weeks to sail across the Atlantic and another two months before they finally arrived to the Canadian prairies. "The land of milk and honey!" his Gross-Vater had said so many times. Settling in Clair, Saskatchewan, Henry's grandfather grew wheat and a large family. His oldest son, Heinrich, met and married Aganetha Wiebe and they soon started a family of their own.

Life was good. They went to church twice on Sundays and spoke Plautdietsch to their children. Most importantly they lived without fear, content that their sons would never be conscripted and forced to carry a gun.

It should have been enough, and it was until one morning Heinrich saw an ad in the newspaper, *Die Mennonitische Rundschau*. The ad boasted land for sale on Arrow Lake in British Columbia, wherever that was, for an irresistible price! The thought of being a pioneer and going to a place where no one had been before was incredibly tempting to Heinrich.

Henry could still recall the night when his father had gathered them around the supper table. They were going to move to a new province in Canada, he had told them, to a place where they would plant fruit trees and have some cows and chickens. There was timber as far as the eye could see, so much so, that they could build any size house they pleased! The Thiessen children had sat in rapt attention as their father regaled them with the adventure they would have and they were indeed eager to go, but no one was happier than Henry. Henry had been ecstatic!

He had only been nine years old at the time, but by then his own wanderlust was already burgeoning. This was the answer to his prayers. They were going on an adventure. They were going to a new land called the Kootenays and then, his father told them, they would be the first Mennonites to homestead there. It was all that he had dreamed of and more.

Renata—that was the name of their new community—was situated on the western shore of Arrow Lake and it was, indeed, perfect for growing fruit and supporting a young family. For the first few years after they arrived, Henry had been content to explore the mountains, lakes, and rivers near his home and his parents thought that maybe their son's wanderlust had been soothed. But then, just shy of his eighteenth birthday, Henry came home from the general store with a newspaper. A logging company in Boston Bar was looking for lumberjacks. Henry wanted nothing more than to apply for the job.

Of course, his father forbade it. He had shouted that no son of his was going out into the English world alone. Henry reminded him that it was because of his own need to explore that they were in BC in the first place; how had his father conveniently forgotten that? Having his own hasty decisions thrown back at him did nothing but anger Heinrich, but Henry would not take the words back.

It got worse after that. Heinrich would not listen to reason and Henry's resolve remained firm. Their arguments, like a ceaseless volley of ammunition, were a nightly occurrence and each one deadlier than the next. The night before Henry left, they had their worst fight yet. At the end, Henry's father had slapped him. It was so unexpected. Henry knew that his father was angry, but this darkness was something he had never seen before.

And just like that, it was over. Henry packed his suitcase and headed towards the door. His mother had grabbed his arm, pleading that he stay, apologizing for her husband, all the while knowing that her son was leaving. His baby sisters were all bawling, terrified of losing their big brother and terrified of their father's unexpected anger.

As Henry walked out the door, the last words he heard came from his father. They were black, yet tinged with sadness. *"Du bist nicht mehr mein sohn,"* he said. You're no longer my son.

It was hard to believe that nearly six years had passed since that fateful day; he was almost twenty-five now. He had got his wish and had travelled to every corner of the province and had seen its humanity up close and personal. But the joy he thought he'd find in his freedom was fleeting. Yes, the country was beautiful, astonishing if he was honest. But the people; they had been a disappointment.

Henry's first job had been with the logging company and when the men heard his broken English, they teased and laughed. When he brought out his Bible that first night they guffawed. To their credit they did try, inviting him to the local watering hole but when he told them that he didn't drink they were incredulous. "What the hell is there then?" one of the men had asked. Henry had never heard the word "hell" used in any other context but in church and it was usually attached to a sermon warning them about eternal damnation.

He endured the logging camp until winter, then took his considerable earnings and headed north. He went from logging camp to mining camp and everything in between. He even worked at a cannery in Prince Rupert. Slowly, his grasp of the language improved and he made friends here and there, but he grew tired of places quickly. If he was honest, he hadn't found a place where he felt like staying. Henry had been travelling from Cache Creek to Princeton when his wallet disappeared. He was never sure if someone had stolen it or he lost it. In the end, it didn't matter. Every cent of his hard-earned cash was gone. He found himself sneaking into farmyards and orchards. An apple here, a few carrots there, kept him from starving while he looked for a new job. But the longer he spent without a place to stay, the grubbier he got. His clothes were threadbare and filthy and prospective employers took one look at him and decided against hiring a vagrant. When Minna found him this morning, he was on the verge of desperation.

There was a small knock on the door and Henry started at the sound. "*Gott in dein Himmel,*" he thought, chastising himself for regressing into the past. He stared at the door, unaccustomed to having a room to himself. When the door didn't open, he realized that whoever was on the other side was waiting for him to give permission. "Come in," he said hesitantly. The door opened a crack and he saw Minna poke her face into the room.

She smiled. "It was so quiet in here," she said. "I thought maybe you changed your mind about working for us."

He shook his head and cleared his throat to hide his discomfiture. "I was just thinking," he said but didn't elaborate. She glanced at the suitcase on the bed, its contents still untouched. "You about ready for a chat?" she asked. "Or do you need a few more moments to unpack?"

Henry waved at his case, like he was shooing away a pesky fly. "This can wait. It's not so much." He searched his mind for the words to voice his fears. "This place," he struggled but persevered, "is where men come?" He looked ready to crawl in a hole and Minna took pity on him.

"Yes." She sat on the chair in the corner. "Hattie's Place is what you would call a brothel." She watched his face, trying to gauge his emotions. "Trust me. I know what you're feeling, but it's not so bad once you get used to it." She hoped she sounded convincing. "We sure could use you around here."

Henry swallowed hard, weighing his options, and realized he had none. He had been homeless and penniless for months now and he knew he couldn't bear it much longer. He nodded, pushing thoughts of his family aside. He struggled to find the words so he said simply, "I am very grateful."

CHAPTER TWENTY-FIVE

ABBOTSFORD, BRITISH COLUMBIA—PRESENT DAY

ED GUIDED THE PICK-UP truck slowly down Montrose Avenue and muttered under his breath. Two women, ignoring the nearby crosswalk, crossed the road in front of them, their concentration more on the trendy stores and their lattes, than on their safety.

"There it is." Hannah pointed to a small shop to his left. He pulled into an empty parking spot and Hannah immediately jumped out, eager to get inside.

After the excitement of finding the photo in the Bible, the trail to Uncle Henry's past went as cold as it had been before. They had nearly resigned themselves to defeat when the owner of the Vintage Shoppe phoned and told Hannah that she had finished the restoration on the necklace. "I found something really interesting," she had said, sounding rather cryptic. "When can you come in?" Hannah could barely contain herself. The next day they arranged to go to the store as soon as Hannah could close up the office.

The shop was the type that Ed usually avoided and the kind of shop that Hannah loved. A large mural, of a typical Fraser Valley farm, was painted across the false front and the words "The

Vintage Shoppe" were spelled out with small pieces of driftwood above the entrance. Large oak barrels lined the front of the building, each overflowing with bright orange nasturtiums and trailing white bacopa. It gave the shop a nostalgic homey feel, like a visit to Grandma's house. "The owner has a great reputation," Hannah said with enthusiasm. "She's an expert on vintage jewellery and restorations."

An old screen door with an antique push bar advertising "Fresh Up with Seven Up!" creaked as they entered and knocked against a small set of wind chimes, announcing their arrival. The shop seemed to be empty, although strains of the local country music station were playing over the sound system.

"Hello! Be right with you," someone called from the back room. A few moments later a young woman, maybe in her early thirties, dressed in jeans and a vintage peasant blouse, appeared from the back and smiled when she recognized Hannah. "Ah!" she said. "The owner of the necklace!" She had a stained rag in her hands. "Your name is Hannah, right?"

Hannah nodded, impressed that the owner remembered. "Is this a bad time?" Hannah asked, seeing the rag in her hands.

"Perfect timing," the woman said. "I was just about to start cleaning a silver tea set and I was not looking forward to it. You've given me a great excuse to put it off." She held out her hand to Ed. "My name is Victoria."

"Ed," he answered back, shaking her hand, "I belong to her." He pointed to Hannah and both women laughed.

Victoria put up one finger. "Just give me a minute to clean up and I'll be right with you."

As they waited, Ed wandered the shop. It was an eclectic mix of old and new. Royal Albert china cups were tucked in between apple spice candles, first editions of poetry, and vintage crocheted doilies. He chuckled when he saw an old ladder that had been repurposed into a bookshelf. Absently, he turned the price tag over and nearly choked at the asking price.

It didn't take long for Victoria to reappear, the scent of silver polish trailing after her, mingled with the smells of soy candles and old wood. She pulled out a burgundy piece of velvet from under the counter, laid it in front of Ed and Hannah, and then pulled out a small jewellery box. When she drew the necklace from the box, both Ed and Hannah could not keep from expressing their surprise. The necklace sparkled under the store's showroom lights and looked brand new.

"I have to tell you," Victoria said, "that this was one of the most enjoyable restorations I've done in a long time." She picked up the chain and rubbed it between two fingers. "It was so covered in grime that it was like uncovering buried treasure. I had to clean it a few times."

She handed each of them a jeweller's magnifier and then picked up a tiny thin screwdriver. "Look at the engraving on the front," she said, pointing the screwdriver at the front of the heart shaped pendant. The gold heart was covered with clusters of tiny flowers, surrounded by almond-shaped leaves. The stems were gathered at the base and tied together with a ribbon. "The engraving is exquisite." Victoria said. "I've never seen such precise and detailed work on such an old piece."

"It's beautiful. You did an amazing job." Hannah said, but squelched a surge of disappointment. The flowers were pretty, but she didn't see how they were going to lead them anywhere. Her hopes of a new clue were fading fast, like a photograph left out in the sun.

But then Victoria asked, "Who are Jake and Sarah? Are they your grandparents?"

"Jake? And Sarah?" Hannah said. She could feel her heart start to beat faster.

"Yes," said Victoria. She turned the pendant over to reveal more engraving. "Their names are written on the back."

Hannah picked up the magnifier to examine the back. There, in beautiful flowing script, she read: "Sarah & Jake. October 1920."

Hannah looked at Ed and they both smiled. Finally another clue.

Hannah was about to put the necklace into the box when Victoria stopped her. "Wait." She placed her hand over the pendant. "I haven't shown you the best part yet." She turned the heart on its edge. "It wasn't until I started cleaning it for the third time that I noticed them." She pointed to two impossibly tiny hinges and Hannah grabbed Ed's hand. Gently, Victoria inserted the tiny chiselled end of the screwdriver into a groove that lined the sides and exerted a small bit of pressure. The pendant popped opened with a small click.

"It's a locket." Hannah whispered.

Victoria pressed the two sides of the locket flat to reveal two photographs framed inside. They were a bit stained from mould but in remarkably good condition considering. On the left was a beautiful woman with long dark hair and on the right was a man with a very impressive moustache. Hannah caught her breath as she recognized them instantly from the photo in Uncle Henry's bible.

The moment they got back in the truck, Hannah started chattering excitedly. "I can't believe it!" she exclaimed. "I never, for a minute, thought that it was a locket!" She took the necklace out of the box, needing to see it again. Hannah was so lost in her rambling that it took a moment to realize that Ed was not part of the conversation. He was just staring into space.

"What's the matter?" she asked. "Why aren't you more excited?"

Ed turned to look at her. "Don't you get it?" he said. "This means that there is a definite connection between the skeleton in the mine and Uncle Henry. I was hoping that the body had nothing to do with him. That someone left it there after Uncle Henry died. That this was just some awful coincidence." He scrubbed his face with both hands and then leaned his forehead on the steering wheel. "What if my Uncle was a murderer?" He spoke in a soft voice to the floor mats and didn't look at her. "I'm realizing that there are secrets surrounding my family. Dark secrets." He sat up to look at her then. "What if my happy family was nothing but an illusion?"

CHAPTER TWENTY-SIX

COALMONT, BRITISH COLUMBIA—JUNE 1916

HENRY SAT STRAIGHT ON the tall oak stool in the corner of the vestibule, watching the girls and making sure their clients behaved. With his arms folded over his chest, he did his best to look intimidating, but it wasn't difficult anymore. After nearly a year of living in the brothel, Minna had fattened him up and the work he did during the day had added considerable muscle. He had been big to begin with, but now he was imposing.

Surprisingly, the past months hadn't been bad. Hattie was a kind and generous employer and Minna mothered him constantly. He had told himself that he would only work for Hattie until he had enough money to move on. He atoned for his work inside the brothel by taking on all the manual labour that needed to be done outside. He milked the cows, they had two now, chopped wood, weeded the vegetable garden, and did all the household repairs. Neither Hattie nor Minna intended for him to do so much for them, but he thrived and grew even stronger doing honest hard work.

What happened after that, not even he understood. While he loathed what the girls did for a living, he found that despite their unwholesome life, so different from what he knew, he was falling in love with this odd little family. The more he got to know them, the more he empathized, knowing that each one was a victim of their circumstance—just like him. When the girls found out that Henry had four younger sisters, they seemed to forget that he was a man and, except for Nellie, started treating him like their little brother. He was a good foot taller than any of them but that didn't seem to matter. They welcomed him into their home.

But it wasn't home. It was a brothel. The contentment he felt, living at Hattie's was always tempered by the lifestyle he knew he should not be promoting. God, his mother would die of mortification. Shame filled him whenever he thought of returning home. He knew, full well, the story of the prodigal son, but he doubted his father would welcome him home with open arms. He would not subject his sisters to disgrace. Nor would he submit himself to his father's recriminations. The only thing Henry had left was his pride.

The front door opened, and Henry stifled a groan when Simon walked in. Simon nodded in Henry's direction but said nothing. Hanging his coat and hat, he turned and entered the parlour. Simon was truly evil, and Henry felt the man's malevolence to his bones. He came and went with no notice, and his arrivals always put Henry on edge. When Simon was in the company of anyone besides Hattie or the girls, he was charming and magnetic. Henry had heard the phrase "two-faced" before, but he had never understood its meaning till now; Simon embodied the very words.

Henry watched Simon all evening, secretly keeping track of his every step and whereabouts. Simon had been particularly magnanimous that night, handing out free cigars and glass tumblers full of whisky. Revelling in his status as part owner, he strutted around, puffed up with self-importance like a nasty bantam rooster lording over a flock of frightened hens.

But Hattie was not a frightened hen; in fact, she had looked especially confident and radiant that night, Henry thought. She laughed and chatted with all the men, except Simon. She avoided him like he was covered with pox. Her indifference chipped away at Simon's carefully constructed veneer and Henry watched it peeling away as Simon downed glass after glass of whisky, between puffs of his disgusting cigar.

As the evening waned, Henry's apprehension grew. Simon's fixation and his lust for Hattie was barely concealed and, by the end of the evening, he was working the cigar between his lips, like someone would plunge a toilet.

That night, after the house was closed and everyone in bed, Henry lingered in the parlour. It didn't take long, and he wasn't surprised, when the front door opened. With barely a sound, Simon let himself in.

Henry stepped out of the shadows. "Evening Simon," he said. "Did you forget something?" Simon nearly jumped to the ceiling and Henry felt a small surge of satisfaction at the man's startled expression.

"No," Simon blustered, before catching himself. "I thought you'd be in bed by now."

Henry smiled, although his stomach was roiling. "Minna was baking all day, so my room is too hot. I thought I'd sleep out here tonight. It's much cooler."

Simon's eyes flickered for a moment to the second floor and Hattie's closed bedroom door. Returning his bloodshot eyes to Henry, he seemed to be considering the wisdom of his plans. And for a fleeting moment, Henry thought he may have the guts. But Simon was a coward, his spine was as yellow as the mustard weed growing behind the barn. Before the chicken could reconsider, Henry walked over to the front door and opened it, the smile never leaving his face. "I'd like to get a little sleep tonight so if there's nothing else…?" He let the question hang in the air.

Hatred flared on Simon's face for a moment before he replaced it with a smile. Stepping towards Henry, he stopped before him, so close that Henry could smell the stale smoke on his breath. "Take good care of our girls, Henry." He winked at him. "Wouldn't want anything bad to happen to them now, would we?" Taking the sodden cigar that was still in his mouth, he dropped it at Henry's feet and walked out the door.

Watching him leave, Henry stifled the urge to kick the man's backside; instead he kicked the cigar that still lay at his feet, sending it flying over the porch rail. He closed the door, silently locking it, his hands shaking with anger and revulsion. The image of Simon attempting to rape Hattie was burned into his mind and he knew that Simon would not stop until he got his way. The only thing standing in his way was Henry. And so, he stayed.

CHAPTER TWENTY-SEVEN

ABBOTSFORD, BRITISH COLUMBIA—PRESENT DAY

HANNAH PEERED OVER HER menu at her husband and tried to gauge his mood. He had been silent ever since they left the jewellers. She was worried and, although it was killing her, she knew better than to say anything. Thirty-five years of marriage had taught her a few things about him: never touch a man's hat, burgers should be its own food group (apparently the Canada Food Guide had gotten it all wrong), and no amount of cajoling could get him to talk when he wasn't ready. He was avoiding making eye contact with her, instead reading his menu so intently anyone would have thought they had never been there before.

After leaving the Vintage Shoppe, she had suggested that they have dinner at the White Spot, one of their favourite restaurants in the Valley, hoping that a good burger would help him out of his funk. He had grunted, a sound she took for agreement, then didn't utter another word during the twenty-minute drive. They went into the restaurant, the hostess handed them two menus, and he had been staring at his ever since. It took everything she had not to roll her eyes for she could quote, verbatim exactly what he would order.

"Good evening!" the waitress said brightly, recognizing their familiar faces. "What can I get you two tonight?"

"I think I'll try the Toasted Shrimp Sandwich on sourdough and I'll have a coffee with milk." Hannah said. "And can I get a glass of water with lemon, too?"

"Absolutely," the waitress said, jotting down her order. "And you?" she said, turning to Ed.

He handed her the menu. "I'll have the Legendary Burger Platter with fries, large root beer with no ice, a black coffee, and a cheesecake with strawberries."

The waitress nodded and Hannah bit the inside of her cheek to keep from commenting. At this moment, he was not in a mood to be teased.

The restaurant wasn't too busy, so their food arrived quickly. They ate in companionable silence, talking a bit about the weather, their girls, anything but the elephant in the room. The only indication that he was bothered was his fidgeting, but Hannah pretended not to notice. Once their plates had been cleared and their coffees refilled, Hannah decided that he had had enough time to process. Reaching across the table, she covered his hands with her own, stilling the fingers that twisted his wedding ring.

"Ed," she said softly. "I think it's too soon to jump to any conclusions about your Uncle Henry. We don't know anything for a fact yet."

He met her gaze for the first time that evening and then shook his head. "It doesn't look good Hannah, let's be real."

Hannah reached inside her purse and pulled out the old Bible and photograph. She placed the portrait in front of him, turning it so that his uncle's face was right in front of him. "Does this look like a killer to you?" she said, tapping Uncle Henry's young face.

He chuckled, humourlessly. "No," he admitted "But then Billy the Kid was supposed to be a charmer and look how he turned out."

She arched an eyebrow and chuckled. "You're comparing your great uncle to Billy the Kid? Really?"

He smiled and Hannah saw it as a good sign, so she continued. "Let's keep on digging and see if we can't find some concrete evidence before we pass judgment, okay?"

He sighed and nodded, giving in only because it gave him hope.

"You know what I can't figure out?" she said, hoping to get them back on the same page. "Why is the same woman in this photo and in the locket, but the names don't match. The locket says Sarah and the women in the portrait are Minna and Hattie."

Ed shrugged. "Maybe she changed her name? Or it was a nickname?" He took the photo and stared at the woman with the long dark hair. He pointed at her and said, "I think this one is Hattie."

"Why? Why do you think that is Hattie and not Minna?"

Ed shrugged. "I don't know. Just a gut feeling, I guess."

Hannah gazed at the beautiful young woman in the photo and smiled, "Actually I think she looks like a Sarah."

The waitress came and set the cheesecake in front of Ed and refilled their coffees for the third time. Ed scooped a generous portion of strawberries onto his fork and had it halfway to his mouth when suddenly the fork dropped out of his hands. It clattered on the plate, sending bits of strawberry and cheesecake across the table and drawing stares from the nearby patrons.

"Ed! What in the world?" Hannah exclaimed, nearly dropping her coffee cup.

Ed picked up the photo that was laying between them, his face animated and bright. "I don't believe it!" He said, his voice filled with excitement. "How did I not notice this before?"

"What?" Hannah said for the second time. "What do you see?"

He turned the photo towards her, holding it in front of her face. "The boulder!" he said.

Hannah was confused. "What are you talking about?"

Ed jabbed his finger at the photo. "Look in the back, behind them."

Hannah took the photo from Ed and stared at the portrait. In the distance, behind Uncle Henry's left shoulder, was a large boulder. It was as big as a small house and it lay halfway in the stream. It was almost a perfect egg shape except for a large crevice that nearly cleaved it in two.

Ed said excitedly, "Remember when I went to Sam's ranch to help him with his fence lines?"

She nodded, remembering how filthy and exhausted he had been, spending an entire day in the saddle.

"Sam talked about it as we rode by," Ed said, shaking his head. "He told me how they had played on it as children. How they pretended it was their castle." He shook his head again in amazement. "This photo was taken at King Valley Ranch."

CHAPTER TWENTY-EIGHT

COALMONT, BRITISH COLUMBIA—AUGUST 1917

"DID YOU HEAR?" NELLIE asked Henry. "Silver Bill found some pretty good colour on his claim yesterday." Most of the creeks around Coalmont had been panned to the bedrock, so a major find didn't happen often anymore.

Henry grimaced. "If I know Bill, he won't be wasting any time. He and every other miner will be coming to town tonight to celebrate."

Henry was right. The first place Silver Bill went was to the Coalmont Hotel where, feeling very generous, he bought a round of drinks for everyone. Then, after far too many shots, he made his way down Main Street to the red-light district and straight to Hattie's Place.

"Where's Eliza? he demanded, the moment he walked in the door. He swayed and his words were slurred; "Eliza" sounded like "Elisha."

"Eliza is occupied," Hattie said. She knew that it would be sometime before Eliza was downstairs again and Hattie told him so. Would he like someone else? But Silver Bill ever only wanted Eliza.

"Who's she with?" he bellowed. Eliza had an uncanny knack of being whatever a man needed her to be. She was the consummate actress and she could make any man believe that he was the only one for her. Trouble was, Bill believed it.

By the time Eliza came downstairs, Bill was madder than a wet rooster. She was barely down the staircase when he shouted in her face. "How dare you keep me waiting!" he screamed. "Who's taking up all your time while I'm sitting down here, cooling my heels? Huh?"

Henry was there in an instant, but Bill was blind with rage. Imagining her with another man had sent him over the edge. His fists were flying and one connected to Henry's jaw, sending him reeling. Before Henry could right himself, Bill grabbed Eliza by the arm.

"Let go of me!" she screamed as he hauled her back to the second floor. She fought against him trying to pry his fingers loose, all the while screaming insults and obscenities.

"I got gold and I'm gonna show you what it's like to be with a real man," Bill said.

She laughed; a short humourless laugh. "There isn't enough gold in the world for you to buy me tonight." He stopped short and then, without warning, drew back and backhanded her across the face. Eliza shrieked in pain, lost her balance, and tumbled to the bottom of the stairs where she lay still. For a few moments, the room was shockingly silent and then it erupted into mayhem.

Two men who were waiting in the parlour grabbed Bill and one punched him in the face. Angel started to cry and soon all Hattie's girls were screaming for the men to get out.

Amidst the bedlam, Henry herded the men out back onto the street like cattle. He locked and bolted the front doors, strode over to pick up Eliza who was moaning in pain, and carried her up the stairs to her room, all the while Minna clucked around them both like a mother hen.

The next morning was a gorgeous Monday in Coalmont and although it was early, the town was already bustling with activity. Children were playing kickball in the street, Mr. McTavish was sweeping off the front porch of his mercantile, preparing to open for business, and somewhere in the distance a train whistle blew, signalling its imminent arrival to town. Everyone was up and eager to start the day.

Everyone, it seemed, except Hattie.

The sun was over the mountains and shining in her window and Hattie forced herself to sit up and swing her legs over the side of the bed. Her bedroom was a mess. No, that was an understatement; it looked like someone had lit a stick of dynamite in Yin Kee's laundry. Clothes were everywhere and covered every surface. She had been so tired when she had finally gone to bed the night before that when she undressed, she had left her clothes wherever they had landed. Her mother-of-pearl inlay hairbrush was in the corner, on the floor. And her slippers were nowhere to be found. Probably under the bed, she thought. She didn't care.

Hattie stared at her reflection in the bureau mirror. The kohl that lined her eyes the night before had made its way down to her cheeks. Her hair was matted and flattened on one side and she noticed that she hadn't even bothered to take it down before she climbed into bed. Remnants of a bun hung at the back of her neck, listing to one side, and the hair rat showed through in places. Bobby pins made small *tink tink* sounds as they fell on the linoleum when she attempted to stand up. Good Lord, she was a worse mess than her room. Bleary-eyed Hattie surveyed the disgusting lot of it and suppressed a deep desire to crawl back under the quilt and sleep for the rest of the day. But there was a subtle aroma of coffee coming from downstairs and that was just a little more tempting. Minna made the best coffee in the world and Sarah desperately needed a cup.

The linoleum was freezing cold, so Hattie made a feeble attempt to find her slippers. Aha… there's one… poking out from under the rag rug. The other she finally found behind the window curtain. By the time she found her dressing robe and wrapped it around herself, her head was pounding.

Hattie slowly made her way downstairs and into the kitchen. Henry and most of the girls were there, sitting at the table and devouring every bit of food that Minna put in front of them. Fried eggs, bacon, biscuits with real butter, and strawberry jam. Whole milk and coffee. Minna scurried around the table fussing and refilling their plates and topping up their glasses with milk. Most of them grew up without a mother's love, so they gobbled up Minna's attention right along with her delicious cooking. She could not atone for their sins, nor could she erase their pain, but she could ease it a little with good food. Minna made sure of that, so they ate like royalty.

"Hey Hattie," Nellie snickered when she saw Hattie enter the kitchen. "You look like you slept in the stable down the road!"

"Thanks so much," said Hattie sarcastically. "Good morning to you, too."

"Now, now," said Minna, always eager to calm the waters. "Don't be botherin' her Nellie. It was a rough night for all of us." She took Hattie's arm and led her to a chair. "Let me get you some breakfast, love."

Hattie patted Minna's hand, once again thanking God that he brought this woman into her life. "No thanks, Minna. I'm not up to food just yet. But I would love a cup of coffee, please."

"Comin' right up." Minna said. "You just set yourself down there."

Hattie looked at all the girls around the table who were obviously subdued and little shaken by last night's events. "How is Eliza?" she asked Minna when she set a mug of steaming coffee in front of her.

"She's okay but hurtin' a might," Minna said. "I think she has a couple of cracked ribs and her face..." Minna's voice broke and it took her a moment to continue. "You may want to go up and see her soon, I'm thinkin'. "

Hattie took a sip of the hot coffee, her heart heavy. She closed her eyes and nodded.

CHAPTER TWENTY-NINE

COALMONT, BRITISH COLUMBIA—AUGUST 1917

HATTIE TOOK HER TIME with her coffee and lingered in the kitchen long after the girls had gone back to their rooms. Unfortunately, many men mistreated the women in their part of town and what happened to Eliza the night before was not an uncommon occurrence. Henry did his best to protect them, so their house fared better than others, but he could not be everywhere. The attack on one of her girls had left her shaken and unsettled.

She needed to see Eliza. Pushing the chair away from the table, she stood and took a deep breath. Even though Eliza had chosen this profession, Hattie could not help but feel responsible for her and for what had happened. She dreaded seeing what Bill's fury had done to the poor girl.

Before Hattie went to see Eliza, she made her way up to her room to change and clean up. When she opened the door to her bedroom, she could not believe her eyes. The transformation that had taken place was incredible. The bed was made with her beautiful lavender quilt smoothed over the down comforter. The ivory pillow shams were laid perfectly at the head of the bed with

Hattie's matted old teddy tucked between them. The mother-of-pearl inlay hairbrush was lying on top of the dresser, neatly in line with the hand mirror, hair combs, and jewellery. Hattie's dresses were all hung neatly in the wardrobe, her wayward shoes sitting beneath them. Minna. Hattie smiled. Only Minna would have done this. She had been up here and cleaned up the disastrous bedroom before Hattie had even finished her coffee.

She took the brush and attacked her matted hair. Once she had it all smooth and removed all the tangles, she coiled it at the back of her neck and stabbed in a few pins to keep it in place. She noticed that her pitcher had been filled with warm water—Minna again—and so she poured some into the basin and then splashed it on her face. She pulled out her favourite dress from the wardrobe. It was green cotton gingham and it was worn and soft from years of wear, but Hattie loved it like an old friend. It had no frills, no lace, and no embellishments, just a few pearl buttons down the front and one at each wrist. Perfect for the mood she was in today.

Hattie stepped out into the hall and closed her bedroom door behind her. She walked down the hall to Eliza's room and quietly rapped on the door.

"Come in," she heard Eliza say.

Hattie stepped into the room and quickly stifled a cry. Eliza's lovely face was bruised and battered; her right eye completely swollen shut. Her bottom lip was split and puffy and the skin under her right eye was so bruised that it was turning two sickly shades of purple and yellow. Hattie took a deep breath and set a smile on her face although her stomach was trembling.

"Hey sweetheart," she said. How are you feeling this morning?" She took Eliza's hand and fought the tears that were threatening.

"I'm OK," Eliza said through thick lips, "although I'm sure I've looked better."

Hattie laughed softly and squeezed her hand.

Eliza's voice was quiet as she focused her good eye on Hattie. "Where's Bill?" Eliza asked.

Hattie didn't know what had happened to Bill. The closest police were in Princeton and they certainly weren't going to come all the way to Coalmont just because a prostitute was slapped across the face. She was convinced of that. But she was pretty sure that Bill got what was coming to him regardless. "I'm not sure," she answered truthfully, "but one thing I know is that he will never bother you again. Henry will see to that."

Eliza nodded and then turned her head on the pillow to gaze out the window and to the blue sky. Tears pooled in her eyes, then ran down her cheeks and into her hair, turning it into a beautiful shade of the darkest red.

Hattie went downstairs to the kitchen to find Minna already preparing lunch for the girls. She silently slipped behind the woman and kissed her on the cheek.

"What was that for?" asked Minna.

"For my room," Hattie said and squeezed her. "I was dreading cleaning it up."

Minna smiled and shooed Hattie away, like she was swatting away a fly. "Girl, you live like you're in a boar's nest. You need a mama to take good care of you."

Hattie gave her another hug and said, "That's why I have you." She picked up a fresh bun from the counter and took a bite. It was so good and it reminded her of when she was a little girl. How she longed to go back to those days when she carried no burdens and everything was right in her world.

"I think I might go out for the afternoon. You'll be all right without me? You'll check on Eliza?"

Minna turned and took Hattie by the shoulders. "We'll be just fine. You take all the time you need. And I'll make you a lunch to take with you."

It had been a long time since Hattie had been riding. When she and William were first married, they loved to go for long rides on Sunday afternoons. They would take a lunch, Hattie would dress in her riding habit, and they would explore the shores of Boundary Creek. It seemed a lifetime ago.

Hattie didn't own a habit anymore and she wouldn't have worn one even if she did. Instead she persuaded Henry to give her a pair of his old britches. They were enormous on her, but she didn't care. She rolled up the cuffs and used a piece of bailing twine that she found hanging by the barn door as a belt. An old flannel shirt, left behind by one of their customers, completed her ensemble. She was ready.

Walking down to the Livery Stable on Front Street, ignoring the sideways glances from passersby, Hattie made her way inside to rent a horse for the day. She longed to go up into the mountains and clear her head. Mr. Jackson, the owner of the livery, avoided eye contact with her but still gave her a beautiful Appaloosa mare to use. She could hardly wait to get on the horse and ride.

The mare, having been cooped up in the livery for days, seemed as eager as she was to be out. As soon as they left the outskirts of town, Hattie gave the horse free rein. She dug her heels into the horse's flank and whispered in her ear. "Go girl. Just go." They flew down the road that connected Coalmont to Tulameen and Hattie let the horse gallop for as long as she wanted to. It felt so good to feel the wind in her hair and the speed was exhilarating!

As they neared the area called "Old Women's Camp" the horse slowed to a trot and then to a walk. Before Hattie reached Otter Flats, she reined the horse straight north and up the mountain. Soon, they found themselves high in the hills above the small town. Hattie let the horse decide when she wanted to stop and she finally did. The mare chuffed and snorted as Hattie hopped down. Laughing, Hattie rubbed the horse's head under her forelock. "Did that feel good?" she whispered in the mare's ear. In response, the horse bumped up against her for more attention so Hattie obliged, giving her a few more good scratches and an apple that Minna had sent along.

The mare started feeding on the surrounding bunch grass and Hattie smiled, realizing that her appetite had returned. Taking her lunch out of the saddlebag, she sat down on the ground. She found an old stump and leaned against it, raising her face to the sun. Hmm… was all she thought. It was truly beautiful. There were mountains as far as she could see, Otter Lake running from south to north below her on her right, and pungent pine trees were growing all around. High overhead an osprey screeched and soared. It was so peaceful and so beautiful; no sounds but the birds and the wind. She leaned back against the stump, closed her eyes, and felt her tension melt away. The mare was grazing behind her, her rhythmic *chomp, chomp*, a comforting sound in the back of her mind.

Jake Pearson was working his mine, like he did every day, following a promising vein of ore, when he heard something walking outside the entrance of the shaft. Quickly reaching for his rifle, he slowly made his way to the entrance and nearly jumped out of his skin when a large shape passed in front of the mine. Bears often roamed this hillside and he gripped his gun, ready to fire at any provocation. But it wasn't a bear, it was a horse. Jake let out a pent-up breath and then his concern returned. The horse had a bridle and a saddle. The mare's reins were dragging on the ground and Jake took them up to keep her from stepping on them. He looked her over, holding her bridle, and then saw the livery mark on the saddle. "Where's your rider? He asked the mare. She tossed her head, trying to break free to continue grazing but Jake was already looking for her trail. "Come on." He gave her a tug. "Let's see if we can't find who left you out here all alone."

It didn't take much to pick up the horse's trail on the dry hillside. The mare had come over the rise just above his mine and had come back down, following and munching on the luscious bunch grass that flourished on the east side of the mountain. He had led the horse back up and over and was completely shocked to find its rider was just over the ridge and it wasn't a he, it was a she! And not only was it a woman, it was a beautiful woman. She was fast asleep, leaning against an old stump. He stood and watched her for a long moment, marvelling at her complete surrender to sleep and the warm afternoon sun. Her hands lay supine on her lap and her head lolled to one side.

Jake was mesmerized and he was also confounded. He didn't know what to do or say. Should he shake her awake? If he did, would she scream? He could just tie up the horse and leave but that wouldn't do either. She really shouldn't be sleeping out here all alone. She was lucky that it was him that had come along and found her. There were many dangers, both animal and human, in these parts.

"Is this your horse?" he blurted it out.

Hattie was jolted awake and it took her a moment to get her bearings. Did she fall asleep?

"Is this your horse?" he repeated.

"What? Ah… yes." Hattie scrambled to her feet. "She's mine. Actually, she's not mine. She belongs to Jackson's livery. I fell asleep." She was confused and on top of that she was babbling.

When she stood, the man took in the full length of her, his eyes widening at her attire. The corner of his mouth twitched and then he coughed, stifling his laugh with his hand. He cleared his throat and then said, "Well you should have hobbled her or tied her to a tree if you were planning on having a nap." He pointed to the hill to the east. "I found her wandering up over the rise there. That's not safe you know, not for you or her. There are plenty of cougars roaming these hills." He was stretching the truth but the last thing he needed was a woman poking around. His eyes wandered over her britches and the bailing twine holding her pants up. "When I first saw you, I thought you were a boy. But a woman," he lingered on the word, "really shouldn't be in these woods alone."

Hattie's ire rose. She was fully awake now. She had finally gotten some time alone and then this man comes along, ruining her solitude with his loud voice and his attitude. And on top of that, he was telling her how to take care of her horse! Why was it that men were always ordering her around?

She took in the tall length of him, looking him up and down, at his dirty clothes, and his worn and scuffed boots. Had he looked in a mirror lately? "I wasn't planning on taking a nap" she snapped. "It just happened. I came up here to relax. I had a terrible night last night and I needed to get away for a while. Clear my head." She coloured, wondering why she was explaining herself to this scruffy stranger.

His forehead puckered and for a moment Hattie thought she saw a flicker of recognition cross his face, but as quickly as it came, it was gone. He raked his hand through his long hair and Hattie wondered at how long it had been since it had been washed. Or, for that matter, the last time he had shaved? His face was covered with at least two days of stubble and his moustache was badly in need of a trim.

She took a step forward to take the reins from him, but before their hands could touch, he dropped the reins, as if she would give him a disease. Her face burned with indignation and embarrassment, so she ignored the horse and instead turned and knelt to gather her belongings.

He stood there, with his hat in his hands, watching her put her lunch into the saddlebag. Her hair was jet black, as black as the coal they took out of Number 29 and, for a ridiculous second, he wondered what it would look like if it was loose. His Adam's apple bobbed, his mouth opening and closing as he struggled to find the words to say, but nothing came to mind. It was obvious that he had offended her, and he was at a loss as to what to say to make it right.

When her lunch was packed away, Hattie stood to face him. "Thank you, Mister…?" But he was gone. Her words hung in the empty air and she was dumbfounded. First, he insults her and then he vanishes without so much as a by-your-leave? She scanned the mountainside, seeing him just before he went over the rise and was gone.

Jake Pearson sat on top of a crate inside his mine shaft, brooding in the shadows. It was dark, gloomy, and cold down in his mine, which matched his mood perfectly. He pulled out some beef jerky from his stack of supplies and then sat, slowly chewing, ruminating over what had just happened to him in the last hour.

In the end he had blurted out some inane thing and woke her up. He couldn't even remember what he had said to her, but it had made her mad, that was for sure. Oh, he was good at getting a woman riled. It hadn't always been this way. He rubbed his eyes with the heels of his hands. At one time he had been confident around women and enjoyed their company but that was a long time ago.

Jake stood and kicked an old tin can out of his way. The can ricocheted off the mine wall, the sound reverberating down the dark tunnel and echoing for long moments afterward. Sitting back down, he scrubbed his face with his hands, bitter memories filling his mind. The dark-haired woman had been so beautiful, even in her flannel shirt and baggy pants and just thinking about their encounter had rocked Jake to his core. He began to feel an ache grow in the pit of his stomach. Jake had not been so moved by a woman in a long time or so conflicted.

He had recognized her the moment she stood and looked him up and down. He had been in Coalmont enough times to know who the "soiled doves" in the red-light district were, but he had never come face to face with one. He had no interest in visiting the "boarding houses" there and never understood men who did.

He sighed, pushing himself up and walked over to his tools. Reaching for the pickaxe, he hefted it over his shoulder and then swung it with all his might. Pieces of stone and ore splintered from the mine wall, flying in every direction.

CHAPTER THIRTY

GRANITE CREEK, BRITISH COLUMBIA—PRESENT DAY

HANNAH RAN HER HAND over the old log and peered inside the remains of the cabin. There wasn't much left; a couple of walls were standing and there was no roof, but still Hannah did her best to envision this as it once had been—someone's home.

In 1885, Granite Creek had been touted as the third-largest city in the province of British Columbia. In 1886 the *Daily Colonist* newspaper reported that Granite City had "nine general stores, fourteen hotels and restaurants, two jewellers, three bakers, three blacksmiths, two livery stables, a shoemaker, butcher, chemist, attorney, doctor and eight pack trains owned in the city." Hannah stood back from the cabin and glanced to her left and right. There was nothing here now, just pine trees and sage brush. It never failed to astonish her how a once vibrant place, where people lived and thrived, could be so quickly reclaimed by nature. Once the people were gone, the lifeblood of a town always seemed to go with them.

"Hey," Ed said as he came around the corner of the cabin, "are you ready to head up to the cemetery?"

Hannah felt her stomach tighten a tiny bit but took a deep breath and nodded. He took her hand and together they started up the dirt road that led away from the old townsite and to the cemetery on the hillside above it. It didn't take long before the telltale white picket fences came into view. The Granite Creek Cemetery, nestled amongst lodgepole pines, was typical of the many pioneer cemeteries scattered throughout the province. Ornate headstones carved with weeping angels were interspersed among faded wooden crosses and rings of stones. Most names of the dead had been erased long ago by the elements and no longer testified to a person's existence; they told only that someone was buried there, long forgotten by the present. Ed and Hannah hadn't taken two steps towards the cemetery gate when Hannah stopped short.

"Here she is," she said, amazed that they had found her so quickly.

Ed walked to Hannah's side, to a small plot surrounded by a tilting fence. Moss-covered stones were placed around the grave, encircling it. A granite headstone sat slightly askew, with a simple inscription that Ed read aloud: "Hattie McBride, November 1920."

After they had picked up the locket from Vintage Shoppe the week before, Hannah had been infused with new determination. When they arrived home that evening, she had gone straight to her laptop.

"What are you looking for?" Ed had asked.

"Well, I was thinking on the way home about the name Hattie. Have you ever heard that name before?"

Ed shook his head. "No, never."

"Exactly," Hannah's face lit up. "I haven't heard it either. So, it occurred to me to try googling it. Maybe something will turn up."

Ed walked to the desk and stood behind Hannah as they watched the search results appear on the screen.

Hannah eagerly scanned the entries but was disappointed. “The top results are about a professor named James Hattie who teaches at a university in the States,” she said. She leaned back in her chair, her hopes deflating.

“Try adding to it,” Ed suggested. “How about ‘Hattie’ and ‘Coalmont, British Columbia’?”

Hannah smiled. “That’s a good idea.” She added the words into the search engine and pressed “Enter.” This time, at the very top of the results, was an entry for a cemetery. Hannah’s heart leaped. She quickly clicked on the link and a website for the Granite Creek Cemetery appeared. She saw a long list of gravesites on the screen. Hannah ran her finger down the screen and then stopped. “A Hattie McBride is buried in the Granite Creek Cemetery.” Her voice was filled with excitement.

“Granite Creek?” Ed said. “That’s the old ghost town just south of Coalmont.”

Hannah turned in her seat to look up at Ed and, her voice filled with anticipation asked, “When is our next trip back to the cabin?”

Hannah sat down on an old plank bench that was beside the cemetery gate. She shook her head, still amazed. “I can’t believe we found her.”

Ed sat down on the bench beside his wife. “Well, we found a Hattie. You’re assuming this is the same Hattie from Uncle Henry’s photo.

“I know,” Hannah said, “but it’s a pretty big coincidence, don’t you think?” She looked at the tombstone. “If this Hattie died in 1920, that means she lived here when your great uncle was here. And now we have a last name and a death date.” She was already rummaging in her purse for her camera and her ever-present notebook. “I can’t wait to get back to the cabin and do more digging.”

Ed stood, laughing. “You’re like a dog with a bone, you know.”

She laughed, taking the lens cap off her camera. "I do love a good mystery." Hannah stood to take some photos when she turned to look back at the fenced-in graves behind her. "Hmm," she said, turning to look at Hattie's grave again. "That's odd."

"What's odd?"

"Well…" she pointed to the graves within the fence, "every grave here is inside the main cemetery, except hers."

"So?" Ed said, failing to see the significance.

"Well, it's just a little strange that she's buried out here, don't you think?"

Ed shrugged. "Maybe they ran out of room?" He pushed open the cemetery gate, the seldom used hinges creaking in protest. "I'm going to take a look around at the other graves, okay? Let me know when you're ready to head back."

Hannah crouched in front of Hattie's grave and snapped a few photos, making sure she captured every detail and every clue. The date of Hattie's death was inscribed in the centre of the tombstone, but the bottom was covered with twigs and old pinecones. Hannah wondered if perhaps there might be more written at the bottom, so she climbed over the short fence that surrounded the grave.

"Sorry, Hattie," she said as she stepped on the grave, "but I just need to move some of this stuff to take a good picture." She grabbed a handful of pinecones and tossed them over the fence. She was about to grab another handful when she spotted something purple lying in front of the tombstone. "What is this?" she said to herself as she pushed aside a pile of twigs, uncovering the tail of a purple ribbon. Lifting it from the debris, Hannah's heart began to race. The ribbon was tied around the stems of a faded posy of flowers. Hannah stared, transfixed by what she had found when Ed's voice broke the silence.

"Are you ready to head back?"

"Almost," Hannah said absently, still looking at the flowers. "Look what I found." She turned and held the tiny bouquet up to his face.

Ed glanced at the dried plants in her hand. "Flowers?" He wasn't that impressed. "You found flowers on her grave? It's a cemetery, Hannah. People leave flowers all the time."

But her hands were shaking now. "I realize that," she said, thrusting the bouquet closer to his nose. "Don't you see?" She pointed at the grave. "She died more than ninety years ago, Ed. These flowers can't be more than a few months old." She fingered the edges of the ribbon. "This ribbon is wired and they didn't make wired ribbon a hundred years ago, trust me." Hannah walked over to Hattie's grave and lay the brown flowers on top of the headstone. "Someone came to this tiny cemetery to bring these to her. Someone out there still cares about this woman, whoever she is." She turned to look at her husband. "Someone out there has our answers."

CHAPTER THIRTY-ONE

COALMONT, BRITISH COLUMBIA—NOVEMBER 1917

"Hi, Henry." Nellie strolled up to Henry doing her best to look coy and demure.

"Hey, Nellie," Henry said, nodding his head to acknowledge her presence. He did his best to sound pleasant but not overly so. Nellie was wearing a long gown of pale blue satin that emphasized her alabaster skin. She was rail thin, without a curve to be seen. Henry supposed that some men liked skinny women; he was just not one of them. She was also one of the nosiest people he had ever met. She was always digging for tidbits and gossip and wanting to know things that were none of her business.

"Quiet night," she said, feigning a yawn.

"Mmm," he said.

She sidled up to him, placing a hand on his thigh. "Maybe we'll have an early night for a change and you can join me upstairs." She looked up at him through pale lashes and added, "No charge, of course."

Henry gritted his teeth and removed her hand. Nellie was about as subtle as a runaway mule. Merciful heavens, how many times could he say no to this woman?

"Henry?" Hattie came over and took Henry's arm. "Could I steal you away for a minute?" She gave Nellie a glowing smile which Nellie did not return. "Minna has a little emergency in the kitchen."

When they entered the kitchen, Minna was there but there was no emergency.

"Danke," he said, sitting down on one of the kitchen chairs and rubbing his forehead.

"You're welcome," Hattie laughed. "I could see you squirming over there and thought that maybe you needed rescuing. Nellie will get over her crush soon, you'll see."

Henry shook his head dubiously.

"Actually, I wasn't quite lying," Hattie said. "I need this month's receipts before Simon comes for the latest tallies." Shortly after they had hired Henry, Hattie had explained how she was skimming from the profits. Henry had been honoured that she shared the confidence but, whether she knew it or not, his protective instinct for his new family grew tenfold. Henry had been both proud and terrified. They all knew full well what Simon would do if he found out.

Henry said, "They're in my room. I'll get them for you." He was gone a moment and then came back with a stack of papers. Handing them to her, he chuckled, "My little sister prints better than this."

Hattie agreed. "Good thing, too. Makes it very easy to copy. Oh, I almost forgot," Hattie said, "I have something for you." She picked up an envelope from the kitchen table, handing it to him.

"For me?" he said, incredulous. The address on the front of the envelope was simple. It read, "Mr. Henry Thiessen, Coalmont, British Columbia." He recognized his sister Nettie's writing immediately and instantly he felt his pulse begin to race. He tore the envelope open and quickly read the short letter inside. He sat back, the letter falling to the floor.

"Henry?" Hattie's voice was filled with concern. He had turned pale. "What is it?" She picked up the letter and scanned the contents. There were a few short lines written in beautiful slanted script, but it was not English. She knelt in front of him, truly worried now, for tears had filled his eyes.

"Mein Vater ist gestorben." In his grief, he had slipped back into his mother tongue. When he saw the confusion on her face, he repeated it in English. "My father has died."

CHAPTER THIRTY-TWO

COALMONT, BRITISH COLUMBIA—NOVEMBER 1917 TO MAY 1918

THE NEXT FEW MONTHS were hard on everyone in the house. Shortly after receiving his sister's letter, Henry left for the Fraser Valley. He said his goodbyes and promised to return, but they all worried that once he was back home with his family, he would forget the ties he had made in Coalmont.

Christmas came and went and Hattie did her best to make it special. Of course, Minna prepared a feast for Christmas Day. They exchanged small presents but, if they were honest, the day felt hollow.

Then, just after spring arrived, everything went sideways. A placer miner visiting the red-light district brought a nasty bug with him. At the time, he was already coughing incessantly and had a fever high enough to fry bacon. And even though he could barely stand, he insisted on paying for Ruby, one of the girls who worked next door. Within two days Ruby couldn't get out of bed she was so ill and it didn't take long until everyone else in the district had contracted the illness. Hattie finally closed her doors and hung a sign out front that read, "Closed due to illness."

Hattie and every one of the "doves" came down with the fever, Lena worst of all. Minna bustled from room to room, playing nursemaid to her "girls." She ran herself ragged and just when they were starting to feel better, Minna came down with a fever, too.

Poor Minna. She fought it for as long as she could and for days insisted that she wasn't sick. But when she nearly toppled over in the kitchen when making their dinner, Hattie forced her upstairs and into bed. Minna was bedridden for more than two weeks. She slept fitfully, tossing and turning as her fever rage. Hattie started to fear for her life. When the old woman's fever finally broke, they all breathed a sigh of relief, knowing she had finally turned the corner.

Carrying a tray with some broth and tea, Hattie quietly peeked into Minna's bedroom. As she stepped inside, Minna managed a weak smile.

"How are you feeling this morning?" Laying the tray on the bureau, Hattie came to sit on the edge of Minna's bed. "I brought you some chicken broth. Help you get your strength back up."

Minna's only thought was, *I hope it doesn't kill me.* But, as Hattie propped her pillows, Minna only smiled and whispered in a raspy voice, "Sounds wonderful." They sat in silence as Hattie fed Minna the broth until Minna asked, "Has Simon been around?"

They were both worried that with Henry gone, Simon would cause trouble but the epidemic in the district had been a small blessing in disguise. Hattie shook her head. "I haven't seen him. My guess is that he's staying as far away as possible till this thing blows over."

"We must be getting low on supplies," Minna said, with worry in her voice. Henry had been going to McTavish's every Monday to pick up their weekly order. When Henry went home, Angus had kindly offered to have their order delivered, but he had put a stop to all deliveries when the epidemic hit the district.

Hattie knew what Minna was thinking. "Henry's been gone for months now and we can't last much longer." Minna's voice was barely a whisper. She made a feeble attempt to prop herself up on an elbow. "I need to go to McTavish's to stock up or soon we'll have nothing left." She ended the sentence with a cough loud enough to wake the dead.

Hattie grimaced. "You can barely make it through a sentence, let alone down the road," she said, pushing her gently back into the pillow. "You need to concentrate on getting well. I can pick up our supplies this week." She got up and walked over to the dresser. Minna looked at her dubiously, watching as Hattie moved about the room, tidying it unnecessarily. "I can do it," Hattie reiterated, looking over her shoulder at the old woman. "I'll just go as quickly as I can and get it over with."

Hattie brought the tray down to the kitchen and then fixed herself a cup of tea. She had hidden her apprehension well, but honestly, she'd rather do almost anything than go to McTavish's.

She washed the dishes, tidied the kitchen and then, deciding she had stalled long enough, she finally went up to her bedroom to change. Hattie put on her best afternoon dress and hat and, with a deep breath, and Minna's shopping list in hand, she was off to the respectable part of town.

Coalmont, British Columbia, was like every other mining town in the West. Built in haste to provide supplies, entertainment, and comfort to unending fortune seekers, the town seemingly materialized overnight. Naturally, most of the businesses catered to men and rarely, if ever, did they think of the necessities and challenges for the few women who braved life in the West.

Hattie picked up her skirts as she made her way down Main Street. Passing by Johnson's Dairy and the Miller's Brothers

Restaurant and Confectionary, she looked for the nearest boardwalk. An accumulation of mud, rain, cow, and horse dung had made Main Street nearly non-negotiable. A few businesses had built boardwalks in front of their establishments, but there still weren't enough of them. Her skirts got so grimy and she went through so many packages of skirt protectors; well, she could almost buy a new dress with the amount of money she spent keeping her hems looking new.

Sidestepping around two fresh horse piles, one of them still steaming, she finally made her way onto the boardwalk of McTavish's General Store.

The Coalmont general store and post office were owned by a Mr. Angus McTavish. When Coalmont was in its infancy, McTavish sold goods from a tent and as the town grew, so did his business. He sold everything from sugar and coffee to stove lids and dynamite.

Mr. McTavish had hung a string of sleigh bells above the store entrance, and when Hattie walked in, their gentle tinkling sound signalled her arrival. There were three other women milling inside and although they all looked up to see who had arrived, not one of them acknowledged her presence. They pretended like she wasn't there. Hattie seldom left the red-light district, but when she did, she mentally steeled herself for the inevitable icy reception.

A woman nearest the front door took one look at Hattie and turned her back, seemingly engrossed in a package of laundry soap flakes. Hattie could feel a physical ache in her heart and bit the inside of her cheek to keep from crying. *I will not cry*, she thought. *I will not give them the satisfaction.* She knew who she was. She was not evil. She was not repugnant. Did they think they would go to hell because their skirts brushed against hers? She was strong, but sometimes it hurt so much she could barely breathe.

Hattie took her time looking around the store. Mr. McTavish had some new readymade dresses on display and she could not help but linger over them. They were so beautiful. There were also some new hats and shoes. A lady could never have enough shoes! Finally, after all the other women had left, she made her way to the front counter and the oak cabinet of skirt protectors, which was full of an assortment of coloured packages. Hattie was choosing which colours went best with her day dress when Angus McTavish made his way over to her.

"Needing some skirt protectors, Hattie?" he asked.

She made a face. "Unfortunately, I do, and I also have an order from Minna."

"She's still sick then?" Angus asked.

Hattie nodded. "Yes, but in her mind, she's right as the mail." Angus laughed. Hattie handed him Minna's list. "I practically had to tie her to the bed to keep her from coming here today. We're nearly out of everything."

Angus slapped the counter with a meaty hand and, turning to fetch a pencil and pad, said "Comin' right up, just give me a moment." McTavish was one of the few people in town who had never treated her with contempt. He had come to the brothel on occasion but only to bring Minna some groceries or to pass on the latest gossip. For some reason those two got on like a house on fire.

Angus was a portly and jovial bachelor with flaming red hair. Whenever he saw a pretty woman, he would remark, "She can leave her slippers under my bed any time." Everyone around him would laugh when he commented on a beautiful girl, but the truth was that Angus McTavish had as much chance of those slippers being left under his bed as Hattie had of becoming the next mayor of Coalmont. But the man was generous and honest and Hattie appreciated his self-deprecating sense of humour. His acceptance of her and all those in Coalmont who weren't exactly "model" citizens was heartening.

Angus wrote Hattie's entire order on the scratch pad and then tallied it up. When Hattie paid for it, she gave him a small smile.

He winked and then said, "Andy will be along sometime today to deliver it."

Hattie was grateful. "I appreciate it," she said, but felt she needed to assure him. "I think the worst of the epidemic is over."

Angus flapped a hand, brushing away her concern. "I'm glad to hear it," he said. "And you tell Minna that I packed some special peppermint tea in the box just for her. Help her get over that cough right quick. Okay?" Hattie nodded, smiled again and turned to leave.

Stepping out of the store and onto the boardwalk, Hattie took a deep breath. *Well, that wasn't so bad*, she thought. She made her way down the street as far as she could until the boardwalk ran out and then, lifting her skirts, she got ready to brave the muck and the filth once again.

"It is just deplorable isn't it?" Hattie was caught off guard and spun to see a woman, about her own age, standing just behind her.

"What?" Hattie was taken aback and at a loss for words. It had been a long time since she had conversed with anyone in town, especially another woman, so she found herself struggling to say something intelligent. "Deplorable?" was all she managed, repeating the woman, and could have kicked herself.

"Yes," said the woman, laughing. "The streets! They're barely fit for sheep and cows, let alone the women of town and their long skirts! I can't tell you how many dresses I've had ruined by these muddy streets." She lifted the skirt of her day dress to show Hattie its hem, already stained with mud. The dress was royal blue, simple, and functional, yet Hattie recognized the quality of it. Hattie took in her dark hair, very similar to her own, which was drawn up in a tidy chignon at the base of her neck. Two elegant gold combs were tucked behind each ear and Hattie noticed the subtle streaks of grey at her temples. The woman smiled widely, her grin lighting up her blue eyes.

Hattie couldn't help but laugh. "I know. I just ordered three more packages of skirt protectors from Mr. McTavish. Not that they help much." The woman beamed at Hattie and, shaking her head, said, "I know what you mean."

The two regarded each other for a long moment and then the woman, looking Hattie straight in the eye, held out a gloved hand and said, "I'm Rose Hawkins. Emmett Hawkins' wife. We have a ranch just west of Tulameen."

Hattie stared at Rose's outstretched hand and nodded, dumbstruck. Never in all her time in Coalmont had another woman introduced herself, let alone offered her a hand in greeting. She finally took the proffered hand and managed. "I'm Hattie. Hattie McBride. Nice to meet you."

Rose smiled at Hattie and then, looking up at the sun and the blue sky, said, "It's a beautiful day, isn't it? Much too lovely to be indoors. How about you and I go for a little stroll?"

CHAPTER THIRTY-THREE

COALMONT, BRITISH COLUMBIA—MAY 1918

HATTIE AND ROSE WALKED down Front Street and made their way slowly to Upper Town. Hattie was at a loss. She had absolutely no idea what to say or how she had found herself taking a walk with this lovely, upstanding woman. She, of course, knew who Rose was. Everyone in Coalmont knew who Rose Hawkins was. Rose was a regular attender of the Coalmont United Church, an active participant of the ladies sewing circle, and she was a Vancouver socialite. The rumour was that she had left her affluent family to marry a rancher who stole her heart.

"What a lovely day." Rose said again. She looked over at Hattie and smiled. "I'm so glad I ran into you at the mercantile. I have wanted to meet you for a long time now."

Hattie looked directly at her, measuring the sincerity of Rose's words, but Rose did not falter. Her smile remained as she waited for Hattie to respond.

"Why?" It was the first thing that came to Hattie's mind and Rose burst out laughing. Hattie watched her, fascinated. She had never met a person with such an infectious laugh or such an open demeanour.

"Well," said Rose, "I have to admit that I have always been just a bit curious about you. Emmett always tells me I'm too nosey. But I like to meet people. I like to hear about their lives." She gazed at the mountains and was quiet for a moment. "Quite often I've found that what we believe about a person doesn't even come close to the truth. I like to make up my own mind when I meet someone, don't you?"

An hour later, Hattie stepped up onto the front porch of the brothel. She had just spent the most extraordinary afternoon wandering the streets of Coalmont. The two women had drawn many stares, but Rose seemed not to care, so Hattie decided she didn't, either. They had talked about everything, from dresses to the weather. Surprisingly, they found that they had more than a few things in common; their ancestors had come from Scotland, they both abhorred cooked peas, and the lilac was their favourite flower. Even more surprising was that Rose never once asked about the brothel, never even hinted that she knew what Hattie did as a profession. When, an hour later, Rose said that she had to get home before her children arrived home from school, Hattie had been keenly disappointed.

"I left our two youngest, Thomas and Ida, with Jack's wife, Lucy," Rose said. When Hattie looked at her blankly, she amended her statement. "Lucy is married to one of our ranch hands and she helps me out whenever I need to run some errands."

Hattie listened to Rose's talk of simple domesticity and was keenly aware of how much she missed a "normal" life. It was the first time, in a long while, that she had felt like she was Sarah again.

The willow rocker on the porch looked very inviting so she sat down, unwilling to have the pleasant afternoon come to an end. The lilacs that Henry had planted behind the house were just starting to green up and she anticipated their arrival this summer. Leaning back into the chair, she closed her eyes and allowed herself to imagine a friendship with Rose.

"There you are," Simon said, shattering her reverie.

Hattie sat up abruptly at his appearance, gritting her teeth with forced civility. "Hello Simon," she said with a sugary voice. "We were beginning to think you'd disappeared."

"Wishful thinking?" His toothy grin reminded her of the Cheshire cat and she resisted the urge to spit in his face.

He glanced at the door and the closed sign still in place on the glass. He shuddered. "I take it that the plague isn't over?"

Hattie sighed heavily. "It wasn't a plague. But thanks for your concern." Her voice dripped with sarcasm. "The girls are much better, but Minna is still sick. I think we'll be able to open next week." She was done talking. "What is it you want?"

"I came for this month's take and, well, I just had to hear it for myself, I guess. Someone told me that they saw you walking with Rose Hawkins this afternoon," he snorted with derision. "I told them they had to be mistaken," he sneered. "There's no way that Rose Hawkins would be seen with the likes of you."

Hattie stood, unwilling to be cowed any further by this loathsome man. "First of all," she said, "we were closed all month so there is no money. And, secondly… did it ever cross your addled mind that I am what I am because of you?" She was toe-to-toe with him now. "Not that it's any of your business, but I was walking with Rose this afternoon. It might surprise you to know that some people in this world are honest and kind." She glared at him. "Present company excluded, of course."

Rose Hawkins hadn't had such a lovely afternoon in a long time. She smiled at the memory, while she scrubbed potatoes in her kitchen sink. Meeting Hattie McBride had been a revelation and honestly, the woman had been a breath of fresh air! The few women who were in Rose's social circle were, unfortunately, staid and stoic. Rose did her best and tried to connect with them, to find some common ground, but they were about as exciting as watching bread dough rise.

Rose had always thought that there was much more to Hattie McBride and, after chatting in town with Minna a few times, she knew she wanted to meet Hattie for herself. This whole town had Hattie painted black with broad brushstrokes, but that had never set right with Rose's innate sense of fair play. She was determined to get to know Hattie for herself, to form her own opinions. And she was determined to prove this town of uptight know-it-alls that they didn't know everything. This morning, when she had spotted Hattie leaving McTavish's General Store, well... she knew right then and there that God does work in mysterious ways.

Rose was jolted from her thoughts when the screen door on the back porch slammed and Emmett Hawkins strode into the kitchen. He glanced over at his wife but said nothing as he stomped over to one of the straight-back chairs that encircled the enormous kitchen table. Making an irritated huffing sound, he sat down to take off his muddy boots.

Emmett Hawkins was a bear of a man who had carved out a life for himself in this unforgiving country. He had left Tucson, Arizona, in 1897, at the ripe age of seventeen, swept along with the hoards flocking to the Klondike. But Emmett never discovered gold; he didn't even come close. What he did discover was that there was wealth to be made in beef. While passing through the Similkameen Valley, Emmett fell in love with the wide-open country. Instead of staking a claim, he found work as a ranch hand in Princeton on the Lucky Creek Ranch.

The owner of Lucky Creek, Elias King, was a kind man and he took young Emmett under his wing. Emmett saved every cent he could and whenever he had enough money, he bought a calf. It didn't take long before he had an impressive herd of his own

Herefords. When Elias passed away, Emmett was shocked to find that he had been named in Elias's will. With the money Elias left him, Emmett bought some land in the hills west of Coalmont and named it the King Valley Ranch in honour of the man who had become his surrogate father.

Emmett met Rose in 1903, married her in 1904, and their first son, Jesse, had been born a year later. Over the next twelve years they had five more children—two more boys and three more girls— Emma, Clarence, Hazel, Thomas, and Ida. Building a life on their ranch had been all that Emmett had ever dreamed of. He loved working this land, he loved their brood of children, and still adored his wife. Most of the time.

Rose peered over her shoulder and bit her tongue as she watched huge clumps of mud drop onto her clean kitchen floor. She turned back to the mound of potatoes facing her and bided her time. She had suspected that this was coming and she was ready for it. The best way to deal with Emmett and his opinions was to let him say his piece. When he had the opportunity to get his thoughts off his chest, she would get her say. And she intended to have her say.

"So," he finally managed. "Heard today you went for a bit of a walk around town. Make any new friends today, Rose?"

Rose swallowed a sigh of exasperation and threw a half-peeled potato back into the sink. "Honestly, Emmett, you know I hate it when you patronize me! You know perfectly well that I went walking with Hattie McBride this afternoon or you wouldn't be acting as surly as a mule and be tracking mud into my kitchen! Why don't you just come right out and say what's on your mind? It's obvious that you've got a burr under your saddle."

Emmett rubbed a hand across his forehead. "Rose!" he pointed a finger at her. "You just can't go traipsing around town with the local madam and not expect some talk! She runs a brothel for heaven's sake!"

"I'm well aware of who she is, Emmett Hawkins, and don't you dare point your finger at me! What happened to 'love your neighbour as yourself' or 'judge not lest ye be judged? Or did I just imagine those parts of the Bible?" She crossed her arms and raised one eyebrow at him.

Emmett threw his hands up in the air and stood, knocking the chair to the floor. "I'm not saying that you shouldn't be kind to the woman, but do you have to spend the whole afternoon with her? What will people think? Don't you care what people will say?"

Rose sighed and walked over to Emmett. She and Hattie had been together for no more than an hour, but Emmett always exaggerated when he was frustrated. She reached out to touch his forearms that were crossed defiantly over his chest. "Emmett," she said his name softly to sooth him, like she had done a thousand times before. "Hattie McBride is a victim of her circumstances. I am certain of it. Do you honestly think that the women in those horrid places choose to work there willingly? How many times have we heard those words – 'There but by the grace of God go I' - spoken from the pulpit?"

Emmett ran his fingers through his hair, walking across the floor to look out the kitchen window. He made a small grunting sound that seemed just a bit like an acquiescence.

Rose continued. "Remember when you met my parents for the first time?" Emmett snorted derisively. "My father was positive that you were a bum and a good-for-nothing and that the only reason you were courting me was for my money. Was he right?" She walked up behind him and wrapped her arms around his waist, resting her cheek between his shoulder blades. He didn't answer, so she answered for him. "You didn't care what my father thought because you knew you loved me, and you were determined to marry me. What would have happened to us if I had chosen to believe my father?" She paused to gather her thoughts and when she spoke her voice implored him to understand. "I knew that I loved you from the first moment we met and despite what everyone else told me, I followed my heart. I know what Hattie is, but my heart is telling me that she's also a woman in desperate need of a friend. What kind of person would I be if I disregarded her just because I was worried about what others thought? Even Jesus had friends who were prostitutes," she cajoled.

Emmett turned and took Rose in his arms. They rocked from side to side, letting the heat of their argument dissipate, the tension falling to the floor like petals from a wilting flower. He kissed her temple and grunted. "I know you're right," he admitted grudgingly, but he couldn't resist teasing her when he added. "Just promise me that you won't be taking up any new professions, okay?"

CHAPTER THIRTY-FOUR

TULAMEEN, BRITISH COLUMBIA—JUNE 1918

McTavish's Mercantile, like so many general stores of its era, was the hub and heart of the town. Townsfolk went to McTavish's for their mail, their weekly supplies and, most importantly, they went to catch up on the local gossip. If anyone knew what was going on in town, it was Angus McTavish.

Angus was unpacking a crate of cast-iron stove lids that morning when he heard the sleigh bells above the front door chime. He stood up and leaned over the counter to see Rose Hawkins enter the store.

Angus grinned broadly. "Hey there, Rose. How are you on this fine mornin'?"

"I'm doing well, Angus. Thank you. And you?"

"Oh, can't complain, can't complain." He tugged on his suspenders and hitched his pants up a few more inches to cover his ample girth. "What can I get for you today?"

Rose let a small giggle escape before she could stifle it, covering it with a small cough. "Oh, I just need a few things. Most importantly, I need some coffee beans. Emmett nearly bit my head off this morning when he saw that the coffee tin was empty." She nodded towards the crate that Angus was unpacking. "And I see you have a new shipment of stove lids. I'll take two of those too while I'm here. Seems like, just when I replace a lid, the next one starts to warp."

Angus nodded. "Yup. This Blakeburn coal burns hotter than a French… "Angus suddenly realized that he was in the presence of a lady and cleared his throat. "Sorry," he said, turning crimson." He took two lids out of the sawdust in the crate and carried them to the counter. After he laid them by the cash register, he grabbed a burlap sack for the coffee beans. Their rich aroma filled the store as Angus shared all the latest Coalmont gossip with Rose. She hadn't asked, but he was happy to volunteer nonetheless. Rose nodded and smiled at the appropriate times but mostly she just listened. Angus McTavish was one entertaining man. She was listening with half an ear when a movement through the window caught her eye. Letting out a small sound, Rose realized that it was Hattie McBride walking past the store.

Angus looked up at her quizzically and then looked out the window to where her gaze was drawn. He looked back at Rose confused. "You acquainted with Hattie?"

Rose nodded slightly. "Only a little. We had a lovely walk and visit one afternoon, a few weeks ago." Angus raised one eyebrow, trying not to show his surprise. Rose knew that she had shocked him, but she decided to throw caution to the wind. She leaned forward and said, "Would you mind holding those things for me Angus? I'll be back." With that, she turned, hurrying out the front door, leaving Angus McTavish scratching his head in bewilderment.

Hattie was walking down Front Street, deep in thought, when she heard someone calling out her name. Her name? Who would be calling after her? She stopped and turned and was pleasantly surprised to see Rose Hawkins hurrying down the street to catch up with her.

"Hello, Hattie," Rose said breathlessly. "I was just in McTavish's store when I saw you walk past and I just couldn't let you go by without saying hello!"

Hattie smiled. "Hello Rose. It's nice to see you again."

Rose opened her mouth to say more and then realized she didn't know quite what to say next. A small awkward silence hung between them as they both groped for the right words, but what was right and what was proper were two different things.

Rose cleared her throat and did her best to continue their conversation. "I so enjoyed our walk the other day. Do you have time for another now?

Simon's last words to Hattie came flooding back to her and so she decided to be frank. "Honestly Rose, I would love to spend some more time together. But you shouldn't be seen with me! You know what I am. I don't want your reputation to suffer because of me."

Rose sniffed. "You know what? I've spent my entire life being what others needed me to be. I've been the good daughter, the loving wife, and the doting mother. I've done everything that was expected of me." She grinned sheepishly. "Well, almost everything. But I'm tired of people telling me what is right and what is proper. Today, I've decided, to hell with conventions."

The women decided to walk the road that connected Coalmont to Granite Creek. Not only was it a quiet and beautiful forest road, but it afforded them some privacy from the curious onlookers they knew would be watching. It was a gorgeous morning in June, the perfect season in Coalmont. The forest was coming alive, bursting with new growth and yet it was too early for the bugs to be a nuisance.

Rose and Hattie walked in silence until they crossed the bridge over the Tulameen, rounding the corner towards Granite. When they entered the forest, Rose let out a deep sigh. She said, "You know, it's times like this that I miss home. The smell of wet earth and all the green reminds me of when I was growing up in Vancouver.

"What is Vancouver like?" Hattie asked.

"Oh, it truly is a beautiful city," Rose sighed. "Like a jewel between the mountains and the ocean. The forests are emerald green and covered in moss. I've seen the moss so thick that you would swear you were lying on a feather bed. And the trees! Some of the trees are so big you just can't believe it. You know, there's a hollow tree in Stanley Park that is so big that they had an elephant stand inside it."

Hattie was fascinated and tried to picture a tree that large. She couldn't. "You're joking," she said.

Rose covered her heart with her palm and said, "No word of a lie. My mother sent me a postcard of it. I'll show it to you sometime."

When Rose alluded to a future visit, Hattie couldn't help but feel pleased. "I'd love to see it," she said and then pressed Rose for more. "What was it like to grow up there?"

"Honestly, I had an idyllic childhood," Rose said. "Daddy was in shipping and he did well. We had a large house in Point Grey, which is near the ocean, but we weren't too far from the forest either. Oh, the days we had." Rose smiled in memory. "We enjoyed exploring the beaches, but it was the forest we loved best, especially in the summer. We had trails everywhere and we knew them all by heart. We built forts and played hide and seek and when the huckleberries were in season, we'd eat them until we were sick to our stomachs!"

"How many siblings did you have? "Hattie asked.

"There were just the three of us. I was the oldest, my brother Owen came next, and then about seven years later, my baby sister

Amelia was born. After Amelia, I think that they would have liked more children, but they never came. I suspected that my mother miscarried numerous times, but you know such things were never talked about. But I was old enough to see the signs. I knew when my mother had been crying. And the way they doted on us, especially Amelia. Every now and then I'd catch my mother just staring at my baby sister with a sad smile on her face. I guess that would explain why they spoiled us so." Rose stopped to pick a yellow arnica and held it to her nose.

They walked in silence for a few minutes more when Hattie spoke softly. "I know how your mother must have felt. My husband and I tried for years to have a child, but it never happened." Her voice trailed off.

Rose was stunned. A husband? Hattie had a husband? She squelched the overwhelming desire to ask a thousand questions but instead held her breath, hoping that Hattie would continue of her own volition.

"We were very happy at first," Hattie said. "William was his name. He was good to me. But then, when I couldn't conceive, well, I think it just wounded his pride. He was demoralized. There was nothing William wanted more than to be a father."

"What happened?" Rose asked quietly.

Hattie sighed. "He started drinking. At first, I laughed it off, teased him about it, but soon it became all he ever did. He stopped working and stopped meeting his friends. It made me so angry. We couldn't say two words to each other without fighting. I think he thought I blamed him, but I never did. Truth is, we don't know whose fault it was: his or mine. In the end, it didn't matter."

Hattie sounded so dejected that Rose couldn't help the tears that welled in her eyes. She thought of their large ranch house, full of the sounds of laughter and life. Sometimes it was sheer bedlam, but she wouldn't have wanted it any other way. She couldn't imagine their home without their children in it. She blinked away her tears and managed to say, "Hattie, I'm so sorry."

Hattie stopped to look at Rose. After a moment she walked to the side of the road and sat down on an old log. Rose slowly followed, sitting down beside her. Hattie was staring at her hands and then said, "What you're wondering now is how I ended up here? Aren't you?"

Rose coloured slightly. "Well, I have to admit that I have wondered that. Now I'm even more curious. But you don't have to tell me if you don't want to."

Hattie smiled. "No, it's okay. I don't mind. You know, I haven't told anyone this story, except for Minna. I don't trust people much." She picked at the lichen growing tenaciously on the log. "Not anymore."

Twenty minutes later they were still sitting on the log. Rose was listening in stunned silence and trying to keep her mouth from dropping open. She had done her best to abandon any preconceived notions of who Hattie McBride was; but this? She hadn't come close to knowing who this woman was. Poor Hattie had been abandoned by her husband, conned and nearly raped by a man she thought she loved, swindled of all her money, and forced to run a brothel. Rose couldn't fathom what Hattie had been through.

"So," Hattie was finishing her story, "that's how I ended up in Coalmont."

Rose didn't know where to begin. "How are you coping?" she asked. "It can't be easy."

Hattie shook her head. "There are days when I can't believe that this is my life, but it could be worse. And you know, it hasn't been all bad. I would have never met Minna if I hadn't come here. She is so dear to me. And now I've met you." She glanced over at Rose and smiled. Hattie stood. "I guess we should start back," she said but stopped abruptly when she saw a horse and rider trotting towards them.

As they neared, Rose's face lit up and she held up a hand in greeting. "Jake!" she said, obviously delighted at the man's appearance. The rider tugged on the horse's reins, bringing it to a stop and swung a leg over his saddle, landing on the ground with the lightness of a cat. He smiled, tugging on the brim of his hat and Hattie's heart plummeted, recognizing him immediately. It was the scruffy man she had met on the mountain.

CHAPTER THIRTY-FIVE

TULAMEEN, BRITISH COLUMBIA—JUNE 1918

"Rose," Jake smiled broadly in greeting, revealing beautiful white teeth, "I haven't seen you in a long while. How are you and how's that husband of yours?"

"Oh, he's fine," Rose said, waving a hand in the air. "As ornery as ever, but I'm used to him after all these years." They both laughed.

Hattie heard their laughter but did her best to look anywhere but at the two of them. She twisted the edge of her shawl and examined its hem, knowing all the while that he hadn't recognized her yet. Of all the people they would meet it would be this man? She had never wanted to disappear more than at this moment, but she knew that at any time Rose would realize they had not been introduced. She steeled herself for the inevitable.

As if on cue Rose said, "Oh, my goodness. Where are my manners?" She turned to Hattie. "Hattie, this is Jake Pearson. Jake, this is my friend Hattie."

Jake looked at Rose's friend for the first time and his eyes widened. She was wearing a dress today, her hair was tidy, and the enormous britches were nowhere to be seen. But it was her, the woman with the lost horse: the Madam of Coalmont. He replayed Rose's introduction in his mind. Did Rose just introduce her as "my friend"? Jake took off his hat to cover his discomfiture and holding out his hand said, "Hattie. It's a pleasure to meet you." She took his hand for the briefest of moments before dropping it and returning her attention to her feet. He cleared his throat and decided to be honest.

Looking at Rose, he said, "Actually Rose, Hattie and I have met once before." He looked at Hattie and smiled sheepishly.

"Yes." Hattie interjected; her voice uncertain. "He helped me with my horse the other day when I was up on Otter Mountain."

Rose raised an eyebrow at Hattie. "Really?" she said, tilting her head to one side to look at Jake. "This is news."

Hattie couldn't help the flush that crept up her face. "Yes," she admitted. "I fell asleep after my ride up the mountain and my horse wandered off. He," she pointed at Jake without looking at him, "brought her back to me." *He was also condescending and rude*, she thought, but she kept those opinions to herself.

Rose expected Jake to respond to Hattie's explanation, but he said nothing, only nodded in agreement. An awkward silence fell between the three of them, settling over them like a damp fog. Rose decided that maybe she should change the subject.

"Where are you headed to Jake?" Rose asked.

"I needed some dynamite, but Angus is fresh out." He pulled a short rod that protruded from a saddle bag. "So, I thought I might as well do a little fishing in Granite Creek while I'm here." He smiled. "It's been a while since I've had fresh trout."

Rose smiled in return. "Save one for us, will you?" Jake nodded and said, "Hopefully they're biting, but I'll be sure to bring one by if I get extra."

Glancing over at Hattie, Rose was surprised to see that her friend was staring at her feet, clearly uncomfortable. "Well," Rose said, "I think we best be getting back, don't you Hattie?"

Hattie's relief at the reprieve was clear. "Yes, I do." Before Rose could say another word, Hattie nodded politely to Jake, then set down the road towards town.

What on earth? Rose thought. She hurried after Hattie, shooting a confused backward glance at Jake who was standing with his mouth hanging open, with a fishing rod in his hands.

Rose and Hattie walked along in silence for a few moments until Rose could wait no longer. "So, are you going to tell me what's going on between you and Jake Pearson? Because I can fairly see the steam coming out of your ears. I've never felt so much tension between two people in my life!"

Hattie kept tromping down the road. "It's nothing," she said.

Rose managed a snort. "Ha! Well, if that's nothing then I'm the King of England. What on earth happened between the two of you?"

Rose reached out to touch Hattie's arm and she finally stopped walking. Turning to face Rose, she said, "He's rude and arrogant."

Rose laughed. "Oh, my goodness, Hattie. If there is one thing Jake Pearson isn't, it's rude. He's one of the kindest men I've ever met. And arrogant? Whatever gave you the impression that he was arrogant?"

Hattie made a *hmph* sound, but Rose persisted. "What exactly happened between you two?"

Hattie threw up her hands, relenting. "It happened a few months ago," she started to explain. "We had had a terrible night and one of my girls was badly hurt." Rose grimaced but said nothing as Hattie continued. "Minna sent me away for the afternoon so I could clear my head. It was so warm and sunny," she said, remembering the day. "I rode up Otter Mountain, sat down to have my lunch, and fell asleep."

Rose couldn't help but giggle. "You fell asleep?"

"Yes." Hattie's smile was rueful. "I was exhausted, so I forgot to tie up the horse. She wandered off, Jake found her, and brought her back to me."

"That's it?" Rose asked. "That's all that happened?"

Hattie shook her head. "He gave me lecture on how reckless I had been. It was humiliating."

Rose was confused. "Well, you have to admit that he was right, but that can't be all that happened?"

Hattie coloured. "I haven't told you the worst part yet," she said, "I was wearing Henry's britches and a shirt I found in the brothel." She stared at the gravel beneath her feet. "I looked like a fool. And when he saw me, he started to laugh. He said he thought I was a man! And then when he recognized me, he just walked away. Not another word, like I was a nobody. The whole experience was humiliating."

Rose bit her lip to keep from smiling. "What did you expect him to say, Hattie? Oh hello! I recognize you. You're the town madam, aren't you? And you must realize how unexpected it must have been to see you there. And wearing britches?" Rose chuckled again.

Hattie managed a regretful laugh, admitting that Rose had a point. She added, "They were so big on me that I tied them up with a piece of twine."

This time Rose laughed out loud. "I would have given anything to see you that day."

She thought for a moment and then decided to confide in Hattie. "Let me tell you about Jake," she said. "He came here about four years ago after the relationship he was in ended badly." Hattie stopped walking to stare at Rose. *Well, that got your attention,* Rose thought. She continued, "That's not even the half of it. The man she left Jake for was apparently Jake's brother." Hattie gaped at this revelation while Rose continued. "When he came to Coalmont he lived mostly up on the mountain, holed up in that wretched mine, eking out a living. It's only been in the last year or so that he's started coming to town, going to church, getting to know the locals. That sort of thing. So, you can understand if he seems a little brusque and awkward around women. He's out of practice. He truly is a wonderful man. He's just a little gun-shy around the opposite sex and I don't blame him."

Hattie's pace had slowed considerably. She felt much of her ire and irritation towards Jake evaporate with Rose's words.

Rose took Hattie's hand, looping Hattie's arm within the crook of her own. "Jake has become a good friend to our family and we consider ourselves lucky to be part of his small circle of friends. You could do worse, having a man like Jake Pearson call you his friend."

CHAPTER THIRTY-SIX

TULAMEEN, BRITISH COLUMBIA—AUGUST 1918

HATTIE CLUCKED TO THE mare, urging her up the mountain. For the thousandth time she considered turning around, seriously doubting the wisdom in what she was doing. But she pushed her misgivings aside. It took almost two months to get up the courage to do this and she was going to before she lost her nerve. Allowing the rhythm of the mare's gait to sooth her nerves, she concentrated on the back of the horse's head as they rode towards Jake and his mine.

As they approached the familiar clearing, Hattie saw the stump where she had fallen asleep and where she had met Jake for the very first time. She looked past it to the rise just beyond and thought of the man who was on the other side. Her heart started pounding in her chest and when she let out a shaky breath the horse turned an ear to listen, anticipating guidance from her. Hattie pressed her heels into the horse's flank and leaned forward. "Come on girl," she whispered in the mare's ear. "Let's get this over with."

The unmistakable sound of steel against stone reverberated from deep within the mountain. Hattie drew the mare up in front of the mine shaft and then stared down into the dark depths of the mine and listened to the ringing. The blows landed with precise timing and only stopped for a few moments before starting over again. She stayed on the horse, uncertain of what she should do, all the while chewing on her bottom lip. Finally, with a sigh of exasperation she jumped off the mare.

Hattie tied the horse to a nearby tree—she wasn't about to make that mistake again—and walked towards the mine entrance. She placed a hand on one of the large timbers that framed the opening and leaned in.

"Hello!" she cried into the depths. The rhythm of the hammer continued without a break and she blew out a breath, wondering once again at the wisdom of this endeavour. She waited and waited and when the blows stopped, she yelled again. "Hello!" This time the ringing did not continue. Hattie stood aside, holding her breath, wondering if he had heard her. She waited for a few moments until she saw a light coming towards her. It swung back and forth as she watched it getting nearer.

When Jake stepped out into the daylight, a look of puzzlement crossed his face. But as quickly as it came it disappeared and then he smiled, a broad smile that made Hattie's heart skip a beat. Hattie felt an unfamiliar flutter in her stomach and she was uncharacteristically flustered.

"Hattie?" He said. "Well, you're the last person I expected to see up here."

Hattie hid her nerves by turning her attention to the mare, scratching her under her forelock. "Yes, I'm sure." There was an awkward pause, so she blurted out, "So this is your mine?" The minute the words came out of her mouth she wanted to kick herself. Of course, this was his mine. How stupid could she be?

Jake smiled and ignored her embarrassment. "Yup. This is my mother lode."

She laughed and raised an eyebrow. "Really?"

He shook his head and chuckled. "No, this mine will never make me rich, but I'm doing better than some. I bought it from three fellows who had much bigger dreams than me. They put in the tracks, but they invested far too much." He shook his head. "They were positive they were sitting on a fortune, but they didn't last long."

Hattie peered into the dark depths and then at the large timbers framing the entrance. The words, "The Linnea" was carved into the wood. She wondered if Linnea was a love interest and was surprised at how much the thought bothered her. She ran her fingers over the letters but didn't ask. Watching her, Jake explained. "Linnea was my grandmother."

Setting his pick down, Jake asked. "So, I have to know. What brought you up here?" He smiled. "I know you didn't come all the way up here to look at my mine."

Hattie said, "Honestly, I never expected to come up here again. But then, well Rose can be rather persuasive."

"Rose?" asked Jake. "Why would Rose want you to come up here? To see me?"

Hattie smiled sheepishly. "Rose didn't ask me to come here but she did tell me what a great friend you've been to them." She focused her attention on the mare and conceded, "I came here to apologize. I'm sorry I was rude to you when we met you on the road the other day."

Jake stood poleaxed. When he finally found his voice he said, "I'm the one who should be apologizing," he said. "I'm not used to talking to women much anymore. I was so surprised when I saw you up here. I can't even remember what I said but I know that I wasn't exactly at my best."

Hattie shrugged. "I have to admit that I hadn't been very responsible that day. You were right; I just didn't want to own up to it."

Jake shook his head, "I should have kept my opinions to myself."

She shrugged again. "Don't worry about it. I'm a lot tougher than I look."

Jake contemplated her beautiful face and thought, *Yes, I'm sure you are.*

They stood on either side of the mare, neither sure of what to say next, both uncertain of this unexpected turn of events. Hattie brushed a leaf from the mare's mane and Jake watched as an errant strand of black hair blew across her face. She absently tucked it behind her ear and when she looked back at him, she found that he was staring. God knows, in the past year, she had more than her share of men ogling her, but this was different. She felt her pulse quicken. The desire to flee overwhelmed her and she reached for the mare's reins. Jake saw her growing unease, like a bird ready to take flight. He knew that if he didn't say something at that moment it would all be over. She would be gone and he would never have this chance again.

He put his hand out to touch her, to stop her, but thinking better of it, brushed the velvety nose of the horse instead. "Thank you, Hattie, for coming up here and saying the things you did. I'm sure it wasn't the easiest thing to do." She felt her cheeks warm and an unfamiliar ache grow in the pit of her stomach. Jake decided to press his luck. "What do you say? I'm about due for a coffee and some lunch. Would you care to join me?"

"I'd like that," she said, surprising herself, but then added, "but not for too long."

"Good," he said, smiling and taking the reins from her hands before she could change her mind.

They turned, Jake leading the mare and Hattie following behind. They walked to a small clearing just east of the mine. A tiny cabin sat on the edge of the clearing, nestled within the lodgepole pines. Two chairs sat on the front porch like they were waiting for someone to sit and visit. A smouldering campfire ringed by some blackened stones was in front, the smoke curling to wind its way through the trees.

Jake led the horse to a small corral, putting her inside the enclosure. "Can you stir up the fire?" he asked Hattie.

"Sure," she said and grabbed a charred stick laying on the ground by the stones.

He turned to the cabin. "I'll see what I can find for our lunch." Moments later he emerged, his arms overloaded.

She laughed, hurrying towards him. "Let me help you." She said reaching to relieve him of some of his burden. She took a cast iron frying pan, a tin of coffee, and a well-used coffee pot.

Jake held up a brown wrapped package and a bowl of eggs. "Bacon and eggs?" he asked.

"Sounds perfect," she said, realizing that she was famished.

Jake tended to the bacon while Hattie made the coffee, claiming it was the only thing that she couldn't burn. When the food was ready, they took their heaping plates to the chairs on the porch. They ate in companionable silence and when their stomachs were full, talked of little things: Emmett's new horse, an unusual bird he had seen, a funny story that Angus had shared.

Jake took her plate and disappeared within the cabin. When he reappeared, he was carrying two large chocolate-chip cookies. He handed one to her. "Rose knows I have a sweet tooth," he explained. She laughed and took the offered sweet. He tapped his cookie to hers in a salute. "To old friends." He said, smiling at her.

Her heart flipped like a fresh-caught trout, but she managed to answer, "And to new ones."

CHAPTER THIRTY-SEVEN

TULAMEEN, BRITISH COLUMBIA—MARCH 1919

"HENRY SEEMS HAPPY TO be back," Hattie said to Minna.

"Yes," Minna said as she scattered flour on the table. She threw a large lump of dough in the centre and started to flatten it with a rolling pin. "I was surprised he came back here, actually. After months away, I was certain we'd never see him again."

Hattie took a sip of her tea, thinking of Henry's sudden arrival back in Coalmont. The girls had been overjoyed to see their "little brother" again, and although she'd never admit it, Minna was elated. When Henry walked into the kitchen that day, he had scooped the old woman into a bear hug. Hattie's relief at Henry's return had been palpable. While he was gone, she lived each day, ever vigilant to Simon and his whereabouts. She knew she couldn't trust Simon, so she gave him no opportunity. She made sure she was never alone and slept in Minna's room at night.

"I'm so glad he's back," Hattie reiterated. "I think we all missed him more than we care to admit." She watched Minna expertly roll the dough thinner and thinner. "Has he said anything to you about what happened between him and his family?"

Minna spread melted butter over the dough and shook her head. "No. Not a word except to say that his mother and sisters were moving to a place called Yarrow. Apparently, his mother's brother lives there and they're going to live on the same farm together." She scooped some brown sugar from a large tin and began to sprinkle it over the butter.

"Well, that's good then. I know he's worried about them," Hattie said.

Glancing up at Hattie, Minna said, "He's been spending a lot of time with Jake since he got back." She watched for Hattie's reaction, but Hattie only said, "Yes. I think Henry is quite taken with him."

Minna refrained from replying and instead picked up the cinnamon and sprinkled it liberally over the brown sugar. "I think Henry is missing his father," she mused. "I don't think he could find a better man than Jake to help him through this."

Hattie knew Minna was fishing, but she kept her voice even, deciding instead to change the subject. "Rose is going to love these cinnamon buns," she said. She took another sip of tea, trying to settle her stomach. "But I still can't believe I agreed to this."

Minna chuckled. "When is the last time you've spent an evening away from this place?" She waved her dough covered hand around the kitchen. "It's time you got out and got back to doing things with regular folk. Rose has invited us to dinner and Lena and Henry can manage things here for one night." She placed the pan of buns into the wood stove with finality and Hattie knew there was no arguing with her.

Hattie drew up a small rig in front of the large farmhouse on King Valley Ranch. Rose was out the door before Hattie could even apply the brake. "Welcome!" she said with arms outstretched. "I'm so glad you made it." She looked over the two horses and the small four-seater. Running a hand over the gleaming leather harness, she asked, "Is this new?"

Hattie nodded. "Yes, well, it's used but new for us. Henry bought the rig and horses from Jackson's livery." She jumped down and walked in front of the team, giving them both affectionate pats. "This is Dan," she said, rubbing the glistening coat of a chestnut Morgan gelding. "And this is Dolly." She gave the Appaloosa mare an affectionate kiss on the nose. "We've a few adventures together, haven't we girl?"

Minna harrumphed. "When you're done kissin' the horses, do you mind helpin' an old woman down?"

Hattie laughed. "I'm coming," she said as she walked to the other side of the buggy. Minna handed a cheesecloth covered pan to Rose and then took Hattie's hand to step down to the ground.

Rose peeked under the cheesecloth and saw the fresh cinnamon buns within. She kissed Minna on the cheek and then gave her a sly smile. "This will put you in Emmett's good books, you know that, right?" Rose turned to Hattie and then gave her a hug, whispering in her ear. "I'm so glad you decided to come."

Hattie couldn't remember the last time she had enjoyed herself this much. They sat, all ten of them, around the largest kitchen table that Hattie had ever seen. Rose made roast chicken with dumplings, creamed corn, and glazed carrots. It was delicious.

The chatter around the table was incessant and Hattie didn't know how Emmett and Rose kept their brood straight. There were so many of them. The excitement of the smaller ones at having visitors was infectious. When they found out that Minna had been born in Tennessee, the barrage of questions was endless. They listened to story after story of slavery, growing cotton, and the start of the Civil War. It was certain that they learned more listening to Minna in those two hours than they did in the years they had spent in a school room.

Hattie soaked in the laughter of the room but wondered if any of the children knew that she ran a brothel. She expected that the older two, Emma and Clarence, were aware since they seemed a bit more subdued towards her. They were old enough to hear gossip and Rose must have given them fair warning. And Emmett, God bless him, was doing his best. It couldn't have been easy for Rose to get him to agree to this dinner.

But Rose was determined. Despite facing censure and obstacles, over the past few months their friendship had blossomed. Rose was positive that Hattie would someday find her way out of the brothel and return to proper circles. And Rose knew it wouldn't be easy. Not many were as understanding or open-minded as Rose Hawkins, so she took it upon herself to set an example. Hattie loved her with all her heart.

There was a knock on the back-porch door and Emmett bellowed, "Come on in!" Jake Pearson walked into the kitchen.

"Uncle Jake!" the children exclaimed, jumping up and pulling him towards the table.

"Come sit," said little Ida, patting a chair beside her. "Minna was just telling us about weevils!" She made a disgusted face and they all laughed.

Rose got up. "I was just about to serve Minna's cinnamon buns, so your timing is perfect," she said.

Jake looked at her in confusion. "I came to pick up some eggs. Remember? You said that you'd be home tonight."

Rose looked at Jake with innocence. "Oh, I did, didn't I? I completely forgot." She poured some coffee grounds into the percolator. "Well, now that you're here you might as well stay." The children cheered and Hattie watched Jake turn about thirty shades of red. She glanced over at Rose, but her friend's back was turned.

Walking over to her, Hattie asked, "What are you up to Rose?"

Rose pressed her fingertips to her chest. "Me? Up to something? I have no idea what you're talking about." But her smile was as wide as the Tulameen River.

CHAPTER THIRTY-EIGHT

COALMONT, BRITISH COLUMBIA—APRIL 1919

"Hold still, you mangey thing!" Hattie slapped the hide of the Holstein and wondered again how the milking had become her job this morning. The cow, who Henry lovingly referred to as Lucy, turned her head to glance back at Hattie with large brown eyes, contentedly chewing her cud and seemingly unperturbed that she was causing a problem.

Lucy shivered as another pesky fly landed on her backside. Flicking a tail to remove the annoying creature, she nearly sent the milking pail flying again and Hattie caught it just in time.

"Grrrr." Hattie let an exasperated growl escape her throat. She righted the bucket and replaced it back under the cow's udder. "I can do this," she said through gritted teeth. Grabbing a teat, she pulled, just like Henry had shown her. Nothing. He had made this look so easy. What was she doing wrong? Sighing, she rested her forehead on the cow's warm flank and tried again. "Grab from the top," she repeated Henry's instructions to herself, "squeeze and pull down." She stared hopefully. Not a drop.

"Have you ever milked a cow before?"

Hattie jerked and knocked the pail over herself this time. "Jake," she said, pressing her hand to her throat. "You scared me!" He was leaning against the door post of the barn, his hands tucked into the front pockets of his Levi's. She felt her heart begin to race and she knew it had nothing to do with being surprised.

A grin spread across his face. "Sorry," he said. "I wasn't trying to sneak up on you but there was a lot of talking going on in here." He quirked an eyebrow. "I'm not surprised you didn't hear me."

She was embarrassed at being caught talking to herself, but he pretended not to notice. Instead, he walked down the alleyway to the stall where Lucy was tied. Running a hand over her sleek black-and-white coat, he spoke into her doleful eyes. "Hey, Lucy," he crooned. "What's she doing to you?"

"I'm not doing anything to her." Hattie picked up the empty pail and turned it upside down, shaking it for him to see. "How do people do this twice a day? I'll be here till midnight at this rate."

He laughed. "Why are you doing the milking, anyway?" He looked around the small barn. "Where's Henry?"

Hattie stood, brushing hay from her skirt. "He's picking up lumber to build us a new corral, so I said I would do it."

"Oh, I thought he'd be back by now. I'm here to help." He held up a wooden box laden with carpentry tools.

Hattie smothered a momentary feeling of envy at the amount of time Henry and Jake spent together. You should be thankful, she chided herself, that Henry's made such a good friend.

Jake considered her and the poor cow for a moment before asking, "Would you like me to milk her? It looks like I've got some time to kill."

Hattie smiled with relief. "Would you?" She passed him the pail. "That would be great." Suddenly she was very aware of how confined the milking stall was. She took a step backwards and then, sidling up to the stall wall, she skirted both him and the cow and stepped back into the alleyway. “If it’s not too much trouble,” she added.

Jake took the pail from her and set the milking stool to an upright position. “No trouble at all.” He stroked Lucy to settle her. “Besides, looks like poor Lucy should have been milked a while ago.”

As Jake set to milking, Hattie stood, unsure if she should go or stay. When she had gone to see him at his mine, he seemed to enjoy her company, but since then something had shifted. His visits were always like today, with a reason attached. He made sure she knew he wasn’t coming to see her, only to help Henry with a new project or some such excuse. Over the months his visits came with amazing regularity and, much to her dismay, she found herself looking for him. If he saw her, he was sure to say hello. He wasn’t unkind, yet she could feel his quiet censure as sure as if he had built a wall around himself. Her disappointment was keen, filling her with fresh regret for an impossible situation. What did you expect? She chastised herself. Did you expect him to forget who you are? What you do for a living? She disgusted herself; why would she expect differently from him?

The sharp tang of fresh milk permeated the air, bringing her out of her thoughts, and she was surprised to see the bucket was already half full. No sense making him carry the bucket to the house, she reasoned. Sitting down on a nearby bale of hay, she leaned back against the rough wood of the barn wall. The barn was filled with the pleasant smells of animals, milk, and fresh hay and she felt herself relax, enjoying a rare moment of quiet. A large orange barn cat came up to her, rubbing against her skirts. She leaned forward and scratched it affectionately between the ears. “Hey, Rusty,” she said.

Jake shot a glance over to where she was sitting and watched her lavish attention on the cat. “Rusty?” he asked.

"Mmm," she said. "Henry named her. He seems to think that every animal needs a name around here."

Jake laughed and Hattie continued. "Rusty just showed up one day and we've been feeding her." She scratched her under the chin. "She's a good mouser." Hattie glanced around the barn. "And, from what Henry told me, a good mom too. She had kittens a few weeks ago." At that moment four fluffy kittens emerged from behind another bale of hay, mewing for their mother.

Jake grinned as they stepped out on wobbly legs, tentatively into the bright world of the cow barn. He looked around and then said to Hattie, "Pass me that tin up there on the windowsill." Hattie turned to find an empty sardine tin and handed it to Jake. He placed it under the cow and filled it with warm milk. When he set the tin by the kittens they were unsure as what to do with this new discovery. Hattie giggled as they sniffed and sneezed at the white liquid, spraying it all over themselves. But it didn't take long and the kittens were all enthusiastically licking at the milk until the tin was dry.

Jake pulled the bucket out from under Lucy and Hattie was amazed to see that it was full, a thick layer of froth edging the rim and spilling over the sides.

"Wow," she said. "That was fast."

Jake rubbed his forearms to lessen the ache. It had been a long time since he had milked a cow and it hurt more than he cared to admit, especially to her.

"You seem to know your way around animals," she ventured, hoping to connect with him again.

He nodded. "I was raised by my grandparents who owned a dairy farm. They came from good Swedish stock as my grandfather would say."

She laughed. "Why did your grandparents raise you?" The question was out of her mouth before she could stop it and she could have died of mortification. "I'm sorry." She put a hand up to stop him from speaking. "Don't answer that. It's none of my business."

He picked up a black-and-white kitten and placed it on his lap. "It's okay. I don't mind." He stroked the kitten absently. "My father died shortly after I was born and I guess my mother didn't handle it well." He was silent for a moment before continuing. "She left me with my father's parents. I've only seen her about three times in my life."

Hattie was truly sad for him. "How tragic," she said.

He shrugged. "It really wasn't. I think they missed my father so much that they heaped all their love on me. I was all they had left of him."

She watched him carefully, wondering if he would mention his brother. "Do you have any other family?" she asked softly.

He didn't look up, instead focusing on the kitten. "I have a brother but we were never close. The only time I see him is when he's out of money," he said, his face darkening. "Or when he's bored."

Hattie waited for him to elaborate but he didn't. The subject of his brother was obviously very painful for him and she was sorry she had mentioned it.

Jake set the kitten down and said, "For whatever reasons my mother chose to raise him but not me." He looked at her. "We didn't have the same father," he said, as if that explained it. "To tell you the truth, I'm certain that the best thing my mother ever did for me was to leave me with my grandparents."

He gave her a small smile and she marvelled at his lack of bitterness. Despite all that life had dealt him, he looked for what was good. Her heart began to soften, like butter left out in the sun. One of the kittens jumped off a hay bale in attempt to catch a dust mote floating in the sun and they both laughed at its valiant attempts. He had a wonderful laugh, the kind that came from deep within his belly and you could not help but laugh with him.

Hattie began to feel a tightness form in the pit of her stomach and the realization hit her with the force of a lightning strike. *I'm falling in love with him*, she thought. How had this happened? She barely knew him, yet she knew her feelings as sure as she knew her own name. I am falling in love with this man. Jake smiled at her and she looked down, focusing instead on the kittens, afraid that he would see the revelation on her face.

"I've been meaning to tell you how grateful we've been for the time you've spent with Henry," she said, eager to hide her feelings. "We've been so worried but your friendship with him has seemed to help a lot."

Jake gave her a humble smile. "I honestly love spending time with him and I'm so glad that Minna introduced us. I've never met a man so eager to learn about the land and so willing to work. He's insatiable."

"Has he said anything about his family to you?" Hattie asked.

Jake shook his head. "No, not really. I know he's very worried about them." He looked at Hattie and decided to be frank with her. "Honestly, I think he's more worried about protecting you."

"Me?" Hattie's face searched his. "Why?" But she knew why. She knew it the moment the words left her mouth.

His face clouded and the tenuous thread that connected them seemed to snap. Hattie felt him pull away. The futility of their situation flooded through her and she started to stand, not knowing what else she could do except go back to the brothel.

It was his warm fingers on her hand that stopped her, sending a current through her body and she paused for a moment.

"Hattie," he said her name so quietly that she thought maybe she had imagined it. But then his fingers tightened around her wrist and he pulled her gently back to sit beside him. Before he could reconsider, and before she could protest, he leaned over and kissed her.

The kiss was warm and soft, lasting for only a moment and when he pulled away a small "oh" escaped her lips. There were a thousand reasons that she should stop him, a thousand reasons why this was a bad idea. But each one evaporated, as quickly as dew evaporates on a sun-kissed windowpane.

Her hands seemed to slide up his chest of their own volition and she lifted her chin in invitation so that he would kiss her again. As the kiss deepened, she wound her arms around his neck, running her fingers through his hair. It was soft and thick and she relished the feel of it, losing herself in sensations she hadn't felt since her first years with William. Jake was as lost as she, running his hands down her ribcage, marvelling at the feel of her, like she was made for him and he was overwhelmed.

Hattie was the first to pull away, pushing at him slightly to end the kiss.

"Jake. Stop," she said, breathlessly.

He did, although he did not move away, instead he rested his forehead on hers, his fast breath mingling with hers. "I'm sorry," he said.

"Don't." She pressed a finger to his lips to silence him. "Please, whatever you do, don't apologize." Her finger traced his moustache and then along his rough cheek. "I've wondered what it would be like to kiss you since that day at your cabin."

He took her hand from his face and placed a kiss in her palm, smiling when she shivered at the touch. "Really?"

"Yes." She said, a sad smile on her face. Pulling her hand from his grasp, she pressed it to her heart. "Jake." Her voice was low but filled with emotion. "I haven't felt like this for a long time." She shook her head, reason returning to her. "But nothing can happen between us. How can it?"

He was silent and when he didn't answer, she understood that he knew it, too.

Standing, she said, "I need to get back to the house." She looked at him and then nodded to the brothel. "Minna needs the milk to make butter today and Henry will be back any minute." She kept her voice bright, but it sounded brittle to his ears.

Taking the milk pail from her hand, Jake followed her out the barn and into the dewy morning. They walked in silence until they reached the back door.

She stopped, turning to take the milk from him. "Hattie…" he started, but then the words failed him. Waiting for the length of a heartbeat, she felt herself break in two, a burning rising in her throat. To her horror, she knew she was going to cry. The sound of a wagon reached their ears. Leaning down from the porch, she kissed him quickly on the cheek, stepped inside the brothel and closed the door.

CHAPTER THIRTY-NINE

COALMONT, BRITISH COLUMBIA—APRIL 1919

Rose Hawkins sighed, revelling in the momentary silence of her home. It had been the usual chaos that morning: packing lunch pails, missing primers and lost shoes but as she reminded herself daily, what else did she expect? She had given birth to six babies in just ten years and it was a wonder that she hadn't lost her sanity or, for that matter, one of her children.

During a momentary lapse in judgment, Emmett had agreed to drive Emma, Clarence, Hazel and Thomas to school. Ida, who was extremely vexed for not being old enough for Grade 1, begged to go along for the ride. Emmett relented. Rose smiled and shook her head. That child had her daddy wrapped around her little finger. Rose pulled back the kitchen curtain to peer out in the yard. Jesse, who was turning sixteen next year, was heading to the barn and would be helping his father with calving today. She knew that there was a mountain of laundry waiting for her, but it wasn't going anywhere; she was going to enjoy a well-deserved cup of tea.

Throwing a few extra logs on the fire, Rose grabbed an afghan and pulled her favourite armchair closer to the stone fireplace.

Inspired by the cosy nest she had created, she rummaged through a stack of mail until she found the latest copy of *Ladies' Home Journal* that her mother had sent her from Vancouver.

Tucking her feet under her and covering herself with the afghan, she sighed, filled with utter contentment. She took one sip of the delicious orange pekoe and reached for the magazine, then nearly jumped out of her skin when someone knocked on the back door.

"Lord, have mercy," she muttered under her breath. For a fleeting moment she considered ignoring whoever it was at the door, but quickly dismissed the idea. It was probably one of their ranch hands looking for Emmett and it could be an emergency.

The knocking came again, more insistent this time, so Rose quickly disentangled herself from the afghan and went to see who it was. Opening the door, she was shocked to see Hattie standing there.

"Hattie!" Rose exclaimed. "What on earth are you doing here this early in the morning?"

Hattie looked chagrined. "I'm sorry Rose, but I didn't sleep much last night and I wanted to leave the brothel before anyone noticed." Rose observed the dark circles under her friend's eyes and was immediately concerned. Hattie said, "I need some advice and you're the only one I can talk to about this."

Rose stepped back, to wave Hattie inside. "Of course. Of course," she said, taking Hattie's wrap. "I was just about to have a cup of tea, so let me fix you one too and we'll talk."

Hattie sat in silence by the fireplace until Rose joined her. Rose set a steaming cup of tea beside Hattie on a side table and sat across from her.

"So, tell me," Rose asked, "what it so concerning that it's brought you to my kitchen before the sun's barely up?"

"Jake kissed me." Hattie said the words so abruptly that Rose jumped, her tea sloshing over the rim of her teacup.

"He what?" Rose put the cup down before she spilled again.

Hattie stood, ignoring her tea, and crossed the room to one of the large living room windows. "I don't know how it happened." She pressed her arms against her stomach, trying to ease the ache that refused to go away. "One minute we were talking and the next minute he was kissing me." She turned around expecting to hear Rose's recriminations. But instead Rose was grinning. "Why are you smiling?" Hattie asked. She came back to stand in front of Rose.

"Why shouldn't I smile?" Rose asked. "It's what I've been hoping for."

Hattie was dumbfounded. "Rose." She sat down with a plop. "You have got to be the most exasperating person I've ever met." She took a deep breath. "I came here because I need someone sensible to tell me why this is a bad idea. I need you to tell me that he's better off without me."

Taking a sip of her tea, Rose smiled slightly. "Why on earth would I do that? Jake is one of our dearest friends. He deserves someone to make him happy."

Hattie waved both hands in front of her, like she was trying to stop a runaway horse. She said, "Jake is a good and decent man. How can I possibly make him happy?" With those words, her eyes suddenly grew bright with tears. She looked down at her lap and said quietly. "All I will bring him is shame and regret."

Rose took another long sip of her tea, watching a flood of emotions play havoc with her friend's heart. She wondered at the wisdom of saying what was on her mind. Setting the teacup down, she leaned forward and gently touched Hattie's knee. "Are you falling in love with him?" Hattie's eyes shot up, colliding with Rose's intense gaze. She opened her mouth to respond but the denial never came. When Hattie remained silent, Rose knew that her suspicions had been correct. "I thought so." Rose said.

Still staring at her friend, Hattie asked. "How did you know?"

Rose shrugged, "Anyone can sense the chemistry between you two. Even when you claimed that he was…" She paused and arched one eyebrow, "Rude? Wasn't it?" Hattie's smile was rueful, remembering that day when they'd met Jake on the road. "And," Rose added, "if you didn't care about him so much, you wouldn't be acting this way. You're trying to protect him."

Hattie took a deep breath and a sip of the now tepid tea.

"What are you going to do?" Rose asked.

Hattie laughed, a short humourless laugh. "What is there to do?"

Rose was confused. "Well, to begin with, you could tell him how you feel."

Hattie sighed, the hopelessness of her situation overwhelming her. She pressed her fingertips to her lips, recalling their kiss in the barn. "When we kissed it felt so right. So perfect. But it's ridiculous!" She shook her head with vehemence, as if she could dislodge the tumult of feelings. "How can we have a future? It's bad enough that he spends so much time with Henry at the brothel. I'm sure people are already starting to wonder. Any relationship between the two of us would ruin his reputation."

Rose snorted. "I doubt that Jake gives two figs about his reputation." She threw her hands up in frustration. "And do you honestly think that Jake is spending so much time at the brothel because of Henry?" Hattie shot a glance at her friend. Rose smiled and said, "My guess is that if Jake wants to be with you, he'll move heaven and earth to make it happen."

Hattie smiled, despite her reservations, but continued her reasoning. "Even if I disregarded all that stands between us, there's still the money to consider. I haven't got the money back that Simon stole from me. I promised Minna that when I did, we would leave. Leave together. I can't abandon her, Rose. After all she's done for me these past years. I owe her that much and more."

Rose considered the bond between Hattie and Minna and knew, from watching them together, that Hattie loved Minna like she was her own mother. She would never knowingly hurt her.

"Actually," Hattie said suddenly with forced cheeriness. "I don't know why I'm bothering you with all this." She waved a hand in the air. "After Jake and I kissed, I think he came to the same realization."

"How do you know?" Rose asked.

"Because," Hattie said, with a hint of peevishness in her voice. "He said nothing." She set her cup down so forcefully that it rattled in the saucer. "He left without a word." Hattie brushed an imaginary piece of lint from her skirt. "So, you see, it doesn't matter how I feel, he knows just as well as I do that we have no future together. If he has any sense at all, he'll stay away from me."

There were so many things that Rose wanted to say but she knew that Hattie had already convinced herself that she had no future with Jake. Hattie had come to the ranch claiming to be looking for advice, but it wasn't advice she was seeking. She was looking for absolution.

The room fell silent, the unspoken words hanging in the air like the early morning mist over Otter Lake. Hattie picked up her tea and grimaced when she took a sip. "I've been prattling on and on and I've let my tea go cold." Holding the cup and saucer out to Rose, she spoke with cheeriness that Rose knew she didn't feel. "Could I have some more hot water, please?"

Rose took the cup from Hattie and left for the kitchen. When she returned, she had full intentions of convincing Hattie to talk to Jake, but Hattie had already moved on. The moment Rose settled back into her armchair, Hattie asked, "So, tell me, how are your anniversary plans coming?"

CHAPTER FORTY

COALMONT, BRITISH COLUMBIA—JUNE 1919

EMMETT HAWKINS CURSED UNDER his breath as the silk caught on his calloused fingers. He had spent a lifetime in the saddle, could lasso a wild calf in under seven seconds, but he could not manage to knot a tie with any semblance of skill.

Watching silently, Rose stood at their bedroom door as her husband attempted the Windsor knot. When she decided that he had tortured himself long enough, she stepped forward, reaching to take his rough ranch hands away from the tie.

"Let me do that for you," she said, touching his cheek lightly before fixing the knot. "Fifteen years of marriage and I'm still tying your ties for you," she teased. He made a sound resembling a disgruntled bear and she laughed, saying, "Maybe if you wore them more than once a year you'd be a bit better at it."

He shook his head. "I am only doing this for you, you know. As far as I'm concerned ties should be worn only for marryin' and buryin'."

Rose laughed at this sentiment although she had heard it many times before. Never, in all her years had she met a man who disliked dressing for a party as much as her husband. She tugged on the tie and then centred it over his Adam's apple.

He immediately pulled at it to loosen it. "That's too tight," he complained. "How's a man supposed to breathe with this frippery?"

She smiled at him indulgently. "I tell you what," she soothed, running a hand down the now perfect tie. "If you keep this on until dinner is over, I'll pretend not to notice if it disappears after that."

Emmett eyed his wife, contemplating her compromise, and then smiled. "Deal." Pulling his pocket watch from his vest, he asked, "When are the festivities to begin?"

"Six o'clock," she said, rolling her eyes. "We've only been planning this party for two months, Emmett." She wagged a finger in his face. "Don't pretend you don't remember."

Rose walked over to their bedroom window to view the party from above and took in the beautiful tables with their white table clothes and the Mason jars overflowing with cherry blossoms. Every tree in the Hawkins' yard was festooned with white crepe flowers, so much so that the yard looked like it had been sprinkled with crumpled hankies. Hazel and Ida had gone a little overboard with the flowers, but they were so excited to contribute to the decorations that Rose hadn't had the heart to tell them to stop. "Everything is ready I think," Rose said brightly but Emmett heard the hitch in her voice. Rose had tried all week to disguise her worry, but they knew each other too well. Looking at the back of her, concern filled him and so he followed her, doing the only thing that he could. Wrapping his arms around her waist, he kissed the back of her neck. She leaned her head against his strong shoulder, relishing in the comfort she always found in his arms. "Do you think Hattie will come?" She whispered the question as if afraid of the answer.

"I hope so," he said honestly. "I know it means so much to you that she's here."

Rose smiled, knowing how hard that answer was for him. He had fought her friendship with Hattie from the very beginning but over time had slowly changed his mind. He saw how much the two women had grown to love each other and he honestly wanted the best for Hattie.

Emmett placed his hands on her shoulders and turned her to face him. Cupping her face in his hands, he kissed her softly on the lips. He felt powerless to do anything about the situation but tried to reassure her. "She'll be okay," he said, although he wasn't sure he believed it. They stood together for long moments until the sound of horses, rigs, and even a few automobiles could be heard coming down their long drive. Emmett peered over his wife's shoulder to look out the window. "I think our guests are arriving," he said, taking her hand to lead her downstairs. "Let's get this shindig started."

The anniversary party of Emmett and Rose Hawkins was a lovely affair and, despite Rose's slip in social stature, was still considered a coveted invitation. Guests dined on braised carrots, roasted potatoes and, of course, the best beef that King Valley Ranch had to offer. Emmett had his ranch hands turning it on a spit all day and it had been roasted to perfection.

Emmett walked over to Rose, who was visiting with a group of their friends. "The cook says that dinner is ready to be served," he said. "We should sit down soon."

Rose glanced down the gravel drive in hopes of seeing Hattie and did her best to hide her disappointment. "Yes," she said, taking his hand and smiling broadly. "We might as well get started."

"Everyone!" Emmett shouted over the din of children, friends, and family and waited until they were reasonably quiet. "Let me take a minute to welcome you all…" He stopped short when the sound of a lone buggy came from the road. He felt Rose squeeze his hand.

"They're here," she whispered into his ear.

He smiled as he watched Henry expertly guide the buggy between two other rigs and then help Hattie and Minna disembark. Emmett started again, ignoring the whispers and glances from the other guests. "Thanks again for coming." Grinning slyly at his wife he said, "I want you to know that this is a very special day." Long pause. "Because, I'm telling you that, this is the one and only time you will see me wearing a tie!" Everyone laughed, knowing it was true. "Seriously," he went on, "Rose and I are so fortunate to be celebrating fifteen years of marriage. And God only knows how we made it this far." He squeezed Rose's waist, hugging her to his side. "No, that's not true." He smiled over the sea of happy faces. "We are here today because of each one of you. No one can make it through this life without friends."

Rose's eyes searched the crowd and found Hattie, Minna, and Henry standing on the edge of the gathering. She beamed, trying to convey a thousand words with one smile.

CHAPTER FORTY-ONE

COALMONT, BRITISH COLUMBIA—JUNE 1919

Once the anniversary feast was over, the real party began. Rose and Emmett had hired some musicians from Princeton to play for them all night. There were musicians playing guitar, accordion, banjo, and a decent fiddle player, too. The music was celebratory and infectious. Even Hattie began to feel her cares ebb a little.

She hadn't been asked to dance, but that was only what she expected. What respectable man would ask her? But she was happy to sit on the edge of the dance floor, watching everyone else having a good time. The Hawkins children were dancing with each other and Minna was attempting to teach Henry the two-step. Watching Minna and Henry, it was very apparent that Henry had never danced before in his life and the steps were far too much for him to master. Finally, in frustration, he picked Minna up and swung her around the dance floor, her feet dangling at least a foot off the ground. The sight of it was so comical that Hattie couldn't help but burst out laughing.

"It's good to hear you laugh." Hattie looked up and smiled to see Rose standing beside her. "Scooch over," Rose said, sitting down when Hattie made room on the bench. She leaned against her with affection. "You doing okay?"

The two friends sat in silence, watching the guests twirling around the dance floor. Jake passed by them with a beautiful young blonde in his arms. A stab of jealousy shot through Hattie and surprised her with its intensity. Rose felt Hattie stiffen and suppressed a knowing smile. Hattie asked, "Is Jake seeing that woman?"

Rose laughed. "Margaret Evans?" She looked at Jake and his partner. Shaking her head, she said, "They are just friends, although I know she would like it to be more."

Hattie scrutinized the woman dancing with Jake. She was very pretty and obviously enamoured with him. She was gazing up at him with large doe eyes and Hattie suppressed a very childlike urge to stick her tongue out at both of them.

Jake may have appeared indifferent to Hattie, but nothing could have been further from the truth. He had been keenly aware of her presence from the moment she, Minna, and Henry had arrived at the party. He could feel her eyes on him as he danced with Margaret and, as they passed by Rose and Hattie, he had to force himself to not look in her direction.

He had resolved to stay away from her, as she had asked, but as the evening waned, he felt his determination crumbling, like the banks of a raging river. He could think of nothing, except holding her in his arms again and so, when the music ended, he escorted Margaret back to her family and then, walked straight to where Hattie and Rose were sitting.

Hattie's heart skipped a beat when she saw him approaching, smiling that dazzling smile of his. How could one man have the ability to affect her so?

"I haven't had a chance yet to give you my well wishes, Rose," Jake said, kissing Rose on the cheek.

"Thank you, Jake," Rose said. "Emmett and I are so glad you could come." She eyed Margaret, who was watching them intently from across the dance floor. "I hope you're enjoying the party?"

Jake nodded. "Absolutely. I can't remember the last time I've been dancing." Then, without warning, he turned to Hattie and asked. "Would you care to dance?" He held out his hand and she flushed, staring at his upturned palm.

When she didn't respond, Rose nudged her in the ribs. "Go," she urged. "Enjoy yourself."

Hattie placed her hand in his, feeling its familiar warmth and his fingers squeezed hers. She knew she should resist and glanced nervously at the crowd that surrounded them. Tugging on Jake's hand, she offered a token resistance. "Jake," she hissed.

But he ignored her protest. "Don't worry about them," he said, turning her into his arms.

The fiddle player began a rousing rendition of "I Love the Ladies" and Hattie and Jake found themselves in the fray of twirling couples. Jake was an excellent partner and Hattie let herself be led around the dance floor. It was incredibly freeing to lose herself to the music and for a moment she imagined that she was just like every other woman there and that Jake was her beau. All too soon, the song ended and Hattie moved to return to the edge of the floor when the music started up again playing a soft ballad.

"Don't go," Jake whispered into her ear.

Surrendering, she stepped back in his arms, forgetting the stares and whispers. The moment she felt his warm chest under her cheek, she lost all reason. Hattie breathed in deeply to take in his scent and to fix it in her memory. It was a mixture of unique smells: wood smoke, Ivory soap, leather, and pipe tobacco. The scents combined were intrinsically Jake. Closing her eyes, she gave into her feelings, knowing that she couldn't ignore them anymore.

When the song ended, she opened her eyes, and saw Henry and Minna approaching. Minna had a pained look on her face and her hand was pressed to her belly.

"Minna's not feeling so good," Henry said as soon as they were near. "She wants to go home."

Hattie gathered her scattered thoughts, hating to leave Jake but, knowing that Minna needed her. "Yes. Of course. Let's go."

But Minna held up her hand immediately. "No. I don't want to spoil your evening," she said, turning to Jake. "Jake do you mind bringing Hattie home?"

Hattie's heart lurched at the thought of spending time alone with Jake and was about to protest when Jake quickly answered, "Of course. I'd be happy to." And before she knew it, Henry and Minna were walking away, Henry's arm protectively over Minna's shoulders.

Glancing back at the retreating ranch house, Minna chuckled and pulled out two cakes from the basket she had with her. She handed one to Henry and took a big bite of the other.

"Wedding cake?" Henry asked, taking the cake.

"Well, I couldn't very well eat it there, could I?" she said smiling. "That wouldn't have been very convincin'."

"Do you think your idea will work?" Henry asked.

Minna shook her head growing sombre. "I don't know but we need to do somethin'. I'm so afraid for all of us. Hattie needs to move on, and I don't think she's going to do that without Jake in her life. They need to get things settled between them."

As the party was winding down, Hattie revelled in the anticipation of spending time alone with Jake. Despite the censure from some guests, he had not left her side for the remainder of the evening and the effect of his nearness was intoxicating. Finally, he asked her if she was ready to leave and she nodded, her mouth going dry.

They found Emmett and Rose to say their goodbyes. Jake shook Emmett's hand and Hattie held out her arms. "Congratulations to you both," she said, giving Rose a hug. "Everyone should be as lucky as you two." Rose hugged her back and silently prayed that her friend would find the same happiness.

Jake and Hattie rode in the moonlit silence for a while until he spoke. "Well, I think we've given the town enough to talk about, don't you?" He meant it to lighten the mood, but she didn't laugh.

"Jake," she said, not looking at him, "I need to tell you something." When he didn't answer, she forged on. "I'm in love with you." She hadn't meant to blurt it out so pragmatically, but it could not be undone.

Jake stared between the horses' ears for a long while and then, without warning, pulled the rig to stop at the side of the road. She thought that maybe he was angry, but when she turned, he was already reaching for her. Their kiss was immediate and intense, full of feelings that had been bottled away for far too long.

When he finally pulled away, he said, "I love you too, you ornery woman." She laughed through her tears and kissed him again. This time they kissed with exquisite slowness.

"I'm sorry," He said, nibbling the corner of her mouth. "I should have said it first."

"It doesn't matter," she said. Knowing that he loved her was a miracle.

"I wanted to," he admitted, "that day in the barn." He shook his head, angry at himself for the time they had lost. "There have been so many things in our way, haven't there?" He took a deep breath and said, "There's something I need to tell you too—"

"Jake," she interrupted him, "when I came to Coalmont, I thought it was to start a new life, but I was betrayed by a man who I thought loved me." She shuddered, remembering those first horrid days. "It's important to me that you know that I didn't choose this life. Simon's betrayal forced me into this existence." She continued, "I was so bitter. And I thought I would never trust a man again." She took his face in both her hands and kissed his beautiful lips. "But you changed all that. You are my miracle and I can't imagine my life without you." She buried her face into his neck as he pulled her close. "What are we going to do?" she asked, her words muffled by his coat.

Jake felt dread seize him, but he fought to keep his voice even, squeezing her tighter. "Don't worry. We'll figure it out."

They rode in silence until they reached the red-light district. As they neared Hattie's Place, it took everything Jake had to stop the team and pull into the yard. He hopped down from the rig, holding out his hand to help her down. When she was on the ground, she stayed in his arms and waited for his kiss. It didn't take long. "Tell me I won't have to stay here much longer," she breathed into his mouth when the kiss ended.

"I promise," he said, with more conviction than he felt. "I will take you away from this."

She held his hand for a moment, before going into the brothel, and believed that it was true.

A cough came from behind Jake and he whirled.

"Well, well, well. This is unexpected," Simon said, stepping out of the shadows.

Jake gritted his teeth. "Hello Simon."

Simon smiled, like a cobra ready to strike, "It's been a long time. Too long." He walked over to stand in front of Jake. "If I didn't know better, I'd think you've been avoiding me." He glanced at the new corral. "Although it seems you've been coming around a lot more of late."

Jake sighed, exasperated. "I've helped Henry with a few projects. And you're never around during the day. You are the last person I want to see." He stared at the brothel, terrified that someone would hear them. "Why on earth would you choose to come to Coalmont, Simon?" He hissed. He walked over to the horses and began to remove their harnesses. "You must have known I was here."

Simon licked his thumb and then smoothed his moustache with it. "I had heard you were here and I just couldn't let you be in the City of Destiny alone."

Jake snorted, "You mean, you thought I might have some money you could borrow?"

Simon feigned surprise. He gestured at the brothel, the sounds of boisterous men still coming from inside the house. "Does it sound like I need money?"

Jake fought every urge to punch the man in the face. Instead, he said, "The brothels are going to be a thing of the past, Simon," he chuckled. "It won't be long, and you'll be out of business."

Simon was on him in a moment, like a viper in a basket. "Is that your plan?" he hissed. "You're going to take Hattie away from all this? You're going to live happily ever after?" He pressed his forearm to Jake's windpipe, but Jake was strong; years of swinging a pickaxe had seen to that. He broke out of Simon's grasp easily and quickly turned him, pinning his arm behind his back.

Simon struggled until Jake pinned him against the barn wall. Jake's voice was ominous as he spoke quietly into Simon's ear, "Listen to me. I'm only going to say this once. Stay away from me and stay away from Hattie. If you don't, I promise you will regret it."

CHAPTER FORTY-TWO

COALMONT, BRITISH COLUMBIA—SEPTEMBER 1919

IDA HAWKINS WAS SETTING the table for dinner with her usual precision, laying the fork exactly one inch from the plate with the sharp edge facing the plate. She was just five years old but was astute and wise beyond her years. Of all their children, Rose was the most careful of what she said around Ida, for the child never missed a thing. So often, Emmett or Rose would find their daughter sitting quietly on a rock or the back porch. When they would ask her what she was doing she'd smile and say, "Just lookin'."

When Ida was satisfied with the placement of all the cutlery she, turned to her mother. "Mama?".

"Hmmm?" Rose said, concentrating to finish the lattice top of an apple pie. "What is it, sweetheart?"

Ida walked over to watch her mother work and asked, "Is Uncle Jake in love with Miss Hattie?"

Rose nearly tore the delicate pastry but managed to answer calmly, "Why do you say that?"

Ida thought a while and then answered. "Well, he used to come for dinner by hisself, but now every time he comes, Miss Hattie comes, too."

Rose smiled, relieved. "That doesn't mean they're in love."

Ida gave her mother an exasperated look and said, "I know that. But it's not just that. It's how he looks at her."

Rose stopped her work to look at her daughter. "How does he look at her?"

Ida rolled her eyes to the ceiling doing a very good impression of a lovesick swain.

Rose couldn't help but laugh. "I don't think I've ever seen Uncle Jake look like that." She wiped the flour from her hands and knelt in front of Ida. "How did you get to be so smart?" She tweaked Ida's nose, making the little girl laugh. "Who's your very best friend?" Rose knew the answer before Ida replied.

"Betsy," the little girl said without hesitation.

"Well, I feel the same way about Miss Hattie as you do about Betsy."

Ida seemed to mull this thought for a while; the idea that her mama had a friend besides her papa. Rose continued, "Did you know that tomorrow is Miss Hattie's birthday? That's why she's coming with Uncle Jake today. So that we can celebrate her birthday together." Rose contemplated a moment and then continued, taking her daughter's little hands in her own. "I'm going to tell you a secret, but you must promise not to tell a soul. Can you do that?" Ida nodded; her face solemn. "You are right. Uncle Jake is in love with Miss Hattie, but no one can know yet. Do you understand?"

Ida was perplexed. "Why not?" She thought that love was a good thing.

"Well, sometimes grownups have problems that they have to sort out." Rose explained. "They have to work them out and fix them before they can be happy."

Ida seemed to be working this through her mind. "Are you and papa helping them sort their problems?" Rose marvelled again at her wise little girl. She kissed her on the forehead and said, "Yes, we are."

After dinner, Emmett suggested that the adults move to the parlour while the children cleared and did the dishes. Without so many extra ears in the room, Rose could finally ask what had been on her mind all evening. The moment they sat down she said, "So tell me what happened last week."

Word was spreading that the "boarding houses" in the province's red-light districts were not enjoying the freedom as they had in years past. Pressure from groups such as the Purity League and the Women's Temperance Union were pressing local governments to do something about the flagrant disregard for the law. They said that it was high time that law enforcements stopped looking the other way. Last week, Hattie's Place had been raided and six men fined for "visiting a bawdy house." Hattie herself had been given a warning for running a house of ill repute.

Hattie blew her nose. "It was awful, Rose," Hattie said, dabbing at her eyes, "and so humiliating."

Jake took Hattie's hand and said. "I know this was such a bad week for you, but at least it got Simon to wake up to the changes going on." He turned to Emmett and Rose, explaining, "The lawmen that visited the red-light district were pretty clear. Soon they'll be shutting everything down; Hattie and Simon could go to jail if they don't close."

"Has Simon left Coalmont?" Rose asked hopefully.

Jake shook his head, "No, but he hasn't lived in the cabin for quite some time. I think that the rumblings of prohibition and temperance were a little too close for comfort."

Hattie frowned and shook her head. "Simon would never leave for good without his share of the brothel." She twisted the hankie in her hand and said, "But at least he may see reason now when we tell him what our plans are."

Rose sat up straighter. "You have a plan?" she asked expectantly. "What are you going to do?"

Jake answered, "We are going to make Simon an offer. It seems that he has incurred quite a few gambling debts." His voice took on a hard edge. "I doubt that, in his estimation, what we have will be enough to buy him out, but if he doesn't pay his creditors, he'll be in serious trouble. He'll have to accept our offer."

"Once you buy him out what's going to happen to the brothel then?" Emmett asked clearing his throat. "And all your girls?" he added, colouring slightly.

"Lena is running it for now," Hattie said, "But we're hoping to turn it into a legitimate business, a real boarding house." Her voice took on a wistful tone. "Any of our girls can stay and work there if they choose."

Emmett was impressed. "That sounds like a fine plan. There are plenty of coal miners looking for a place to stay and three good meals."

Hattie smiled at Emmett, realizing how far the two of them had come. "Thank you, Emmett."

Rose's emotions swelled at seeing Emmett's heart softening towards Hattie. Standing, she said, "Well, on that note, I think this is the perfect time to give you your birthday present."

Hattie chided her friend. "I told you not to make a fuss."

Rose laughed and gestured to the empty room. "Does this look like I made a fuss? She held out her hand to Hattie and said, "Come with me."

Rose led Hattie, Jake, and Emmett out of the house and together they began to walk towards the river. As they turned a corner of a well-worn trail, Hattie was surprised to see Henry, Minna, and a man she didn't recognize, standing beside a very large boulder.

"What are you two doing here?" she asked with a delighted smile.

Rose replied before either could. “I asked them to come.” She turned to the stranger who was unpacking some equipment. “This is Mr. Laurentson.” The man smiled at the group that had gathered. Hugging Emmett’s arm with excitement, Rose continued. “Mr. Laurentson is an exceptional photographer and he is going to take some portraits of all of us today.

CHAPTER FORTY-THREE

COALMONT, BRITISH COLUMBIA—PRESENT DAY

ED TURNED HIS TRUCK onto Parrish Street and slowly drove up to the Coalmont Hotel, peering at it through his windshield and the driving rain.

When Ed had called Sam last week and asked him if they could meet for coffee, Sam had readily agreed. There was nothing that old Sam loved more than to sit around chewing the fat with his buddies.

Ed noticed that the "Open" sign was lit and then he saw the familiar old Ford pickup parked beside the hotel. Ed laughed. Sam was here already and probably at least two cups of coffee ahead of him. Anticipating a good visit with his friend and maybe getting a few answers, he pulled to the side of the road. Turning up his collar, he ran across the street, taking the hotel steps two at a time.

Sam was sitting at the bar, already visiting with a few of the regulars. He turned towards the door when he heard it open and his face lit up when he saw Ed. "Hey Ed!" he said, waving at his friend. "We're over here."

Ed's heart sank when he saw that half of Coalmont was in the hotel. "Afternoon, Sam," he said, shaking the old man's hand and nodding at Sam's cronies. Sam waved a hand at the empty bar stool beside him. "Well, take a seat and sit a spell. We haven't really had a good chat since you were up at the ranch.

Ed hesitated. "Actually, I was hoping we could talk alone for a bit." He nodded towards an empty table.

"Sure," said Sam, a little surprised. He grabbed his coffee cup, nodded at his compatriots, and followed Ed to the table. *What was this all about?* he wondered. Ed slid in beside the table and Sam sat across him. While Ed ordered a cup of coffee, he wondered at where he should begin. In the end it was Sam who spoke first.

"So, what's on your mind? I know you didn't come in here just to see my pretty face." Sam's eyes wrinkled up when he smiled. His face was like leather from years of working on the ranch in the elements, the creases that lined it like a road map.

Ed laughed, taking a sip of his coffee and decided to get straight to the point. He reached into his inside jacket pocket and drew out the old portrait, laying it on the table between them. "This photo belonged to my great uncle," he said. After Sam looked at the portrait, Ed turned it over so that Sam could read the back. Sam read the inscription, then turning the photo back over to look at the faces, Ed saw the recognition begin to cross Sam's face.

"Wait a minute," Sam said. "This is our ranch." He lifted the photo to look at it closer. "This was taken by the river that cuts through our property."

Ed nodded. "I know. I recognized that big boulder from when I went to help you with your fence line." Ed put his cup down and asked. "Sam, have you ever heard of Hattie McBride?"

The older man lifted his ball cap, revealing a thatch of white hair and scratched his head. "Hattie McBride?" He pointed at the woman in the photograph. "You think this is Hattie McBride?" He let out a slow, long breath. "As far as I know, there's never been a photograph found of her."

Ed felt his pulse quicken.

Sam never took his eyes off the photo. "You say this photo was your uncle's?"

"Great uncle, actually," Ed corrected. "He was my grandmother's brother and apparently lived in Coalmont for a number of years. That photo was hidden with a number of other things." Ed wasn't ready to tell Sam about the mine yet.

Sam chuckled and nodded. "Well, your great uncle must have lived a very colourful life if he knew Hattie."

"Really?" Ed asked. "Why would you say that?"

Sam was quiet for a minute, then grinned. "Because she was Coalmont's madam. She ran a brothel."

Ed sat in stunned silence and Sam could see that his friend was truly shocked at this revelation. He again looked at the photo of the four people with the familiar river and stones and suddenly asked, "How did you know her last name was McBride?" He turned the photo back over. "It just says 'Hattie' here."

Ed was still processing but managed to answer. "Hannah googled her name. Eventually we found a website for the Granite Creek Cemetery that listed a Hattie McBride who was buried there. We drove to the ghost town and went to the cemetery to see it for ourselves. We're assuming this is her," Ed pointed to the photograph. "There aren't too many women named Hattie, it seems."

Sam contemplated for a while. "Hattie was buried outside the cemetery grounds, you know. I remember once, when I was about eight, we were at a church picnic at the old townsite and some man joked that Hattie should have been buried up in the mining camps, which was where she belonged. They thought it was a great joke until my grandma blew up in the man's face. I had never witnessed anything like that before. Grandma Rose was always so calm and kind but that day she was madder than a hornet." He shook his head, still perplexed. "I always wondered why that comment made her so mad, but she never said anything about it after that day."

Ed asked, "But why wouldn't they bury her in the cemetery?"

"Because," Sam answered, "the church wouldn't allow a prostitute to be buried on consecrated ground. Seems silly, but I guess that's how things were done back then."

The waitress came by and refilled their mugs. Sam grew silent as he stirred some sugar into the fresh brew and Ed could see that he was turning things over in his mind.

"Hattie died before I was born," Sam said, "but as I was growing up we heard the stories. Not from Grandma Rose mind you, she never talked about Hattie much, but my Aunt Ida, she was my father's youngest sister, she loved to tell us stories of Coalmont's glory days and we paid attention.

Ed said a silent prayer, thanking God for Aunt Ida. "What did she tell you?" He tried to keep the excitement from his voice.

Sam leaned forward to lace his fingers around the mug of coffee and began. "Coalmont was a big town back then. Hard to imagine this sleepy place full of saloons, the trains coming and going. And like any old town, there was a red-light district. That's where Hattie started her..." He raised an eyebrow and chuckled, "...business."

Ed smiled. "And how did her 'business' go?"

Sam shook his head and grinned. "Apparently, it was a lucrative one. Hattie had a reputation for being smart and there were a lot of lonely men out here in those days, working the mines, far from home."

Sam leaned back in the booth, fingering the handle of his mug. "But what I never did understand is that apparently, she was also my grandmother's good friend. Grandma Rose was a church-going woman. Never drank or swore, never did anything unseemly. The only thing she ever did that raised eyebrows was to call Hattie McBride her friend, a woman who was, what would have been called at that time, a 'soiled dove.' "

Sam paused, took a long sip of his coffee and stared out the old hotel window towards Main Street. He waited so long before continuing that Ed started to wonder if that was the end of the story. "Something happened to Hattie, didn't it?" prompted Ed.

"Yes," Sam said. He turned and looked Ed straight in the eye. "Hattie was murdered."

"Murdered?" Ed stared at Sam. "Are you kidding?"

"No, I'm not kidding. There was a fire; a cabin next door to the brothel, I think. It was burned to the ground. The next day they discovered her remains inside."

"Murdered?" Ed repeated. He was still in shock. "Why? Who?" he stuttered. This was not what he was expecting.

"No one knows," said Sam. "They never did press charges or carry out much of an investigation. There was an inquisition, but the police never came up with any concrete evidence and, to be honest, it seemed that no one cared much. She was only a prostitute, after all."

Ed shook his head, gazing at the woman in the portrait with Jake, Minna, and Uncle Henry. That photograph had been so important to his uncle that he had kept it for decades and had hidden it away. And no one cared that she was murdered? He didn't believe it and he didn't buy it for a second. Sam pondered for a while and then asked, "Why are you so interested in Hattie, Ed?"

Ed thought for a while, wondering how much he should tell his friend. He shrugged. "I don't know. I guess it bothers me that we never knew Uncle Henry and…," he held up the old photo, "she obviously meant something to him." Ed stared at his uncle in the photo. "We're finding out that he lived this adventurous life but never shared it with his family. He was a miner and was friends with a prostitute. He had quite a past, yet we know nothing about him."

"A miner?" Sam asked, intrigued. "Where did he mine? In Blakeburn?"

Ed shook his head and, without thinking he said, "No, he had a claim on Otter Mountain."

"Otter Mountain?" Sam questioned. "Are you sure?"

Ed could have kicked himself for saying more than he had intended. "Pretty sure." He shrugged. "We have his mining certificate and I think that's where it is." He hoped he sounded nonchalant, but his heart was thudding against his ribcage.

"Have you gone up there?" Sam asked. Ed was about to lie but before he could, Sam continued. "Because you shouldn't. The LL Ranch runs their cattle on that mountain. They have for years."

Ed was confused. There were no cattle on Otter Mountain. When they found the mine, the grass had been as high as their knees in places. He had spent enough time hunting on Crown land to recognize if there were cattle around. Either Sam was misinformed, or he was lying. Ed feigned disinterest and smiled. "Good to know." He needed to change the subject. "So where was the red-light district?"

"Just down there." Sam pointed a thumb to the east. "Right at the end of Main Street. Hard to believe it, seeing as there's nothing there now." He paused for a moment, shaking his finger in the air. "You know, if I remember correctly, the lady who owns the motel here in town had a plaque made and placed it somewhere near Hattie's Place. I haven't seen it, but I remember someone telling me about it."

Ed drained the last dregs of his coffee and stood. He shook Sam's hand. "Thanks for all the information Sam. I really appreciate it." Ed walked out onto the front porch of the hotel and stood for a long while trying to assimilate all that Sam had told him. Hattie was a prostitute. Hattie had been murdered. Someone else owned the land where Uncle Henry's mine had been. He felt like he was staring at a hundred pieces of a puzzle, but he didn't know where to begin to make them fit.

Turning towards his truck, Ed was intent on heading back to their cabin, when he glanced to the east. He looked down Main Street to where Sam said the red-light district would have been. The sky was clearing, the rain had stopped, and before he knew it, Ed was walking in that direction. He wasn't sure what he expected to find, but he knew he needed to go there and see for himself the place where Hattie had lived and died.

A few minutes later, he arrived at the area where he assumed all the brothels and saloons began. Ed tugged his collar higher, trying to deter the mosquitoes as he surveyed his surroundings. He walked down the dirt road for a short distance and tried to picture this street during that era, alive with loose women and bawdy men. It was so quiet and deserted, he just couldn't imagine it.

Turning back, Ed walked over to a large pile of lumber and debris, small testament that someone had once lived there, and saw a small white plaque attached to one of the grey wooden planks. This must be the plaque that Sam mentioned. Ed read it out loud:

> "Beneath this pile of rubble lie the burnt ruins of Hattie McBride's house. Madam of Coalmont from 1915 to 1920, Hattie was murdered here when her house was set ablaze. No one was ever convicted of her murder. Hattie was laid to rest in the Granite Creek Cemetery."

Ed straightened. That was it? He thought. That's all that can be said to sum up this woman's life? A surge of anger ran through him as he thought of the injustice. He stood, staring at the plaque, ignoring the mosquitoes that buzzed around his ears, when a mourning dove cooed somewhere high above him in the pines. Ed's gaze was drawn to the sound and that's when he caught a glimpse of purple behind the rubble. He walked around the remains of Hattie's house towards the edge of the woods and stepped into a grove of lilac bushes. They were a scraggly lot and obviously hadn't been tended for a long time, but they were lilacs, he was certain. Standing there, he took a long look around and started to notice more than just bushes. There was an old fence that looked like it may have been a small farm pen. When he stepped into the woods, he found what remained of a small outbuilding. A rusty pump stood to one side of the building and an old rotting harness was on the ground, overgrown with mustard weed and sage.

This was where she lived. This was where she died.

The dove called again, its mournful sound like a lament that sent a chill through Ed, deep into his soul. Uneasiness came over him as the breeze blew through the trees, filling the twilight air with a heady perfume. Ed glanced around, half expecting to see Hattie walk towards him through the trees. He turned and hurried back to his truck.

CHAPTER FORTY-FOUR

TULAMEEN, BRITISH COLUMBIA—PRESENT DAY

A WEEK AFTER ED'S CONVERSATION with Sam, he got a call from the Land Title office that confirmed what Sam had told him; the land no longer belonged to his uncle. Ed suppressed a stab of disappointment. "When did he sell the land?" he asked the clerk. He could hear a few clicks of a computer at the other end of the line.

"There is no bill of sale attached to the property," the clerk said. "Just a transfer of title to an Isaac Pearson."

Ed was confused. "What does that mean?"

The clerk said, "Well, it looks like he gave it to him. Was this man related?" he asked. "He could have bequeathed the property to anyone in his will."

Ed had a sudden thought. "What's the date on the transfer?" he asked.

A few more clicks and then the clerk answered, "January 5, 1968."

"January 1968." Ed repeated the date. Just a few months after Uncle Henry died. "Would it be possible for you to email me a copy of the transfer document?"

"Certainly."

After giving him Hannah's email address, Ed said, "Thank you. You've been very helpful."

Ed put his phone down and rubbed his forehead. He could feel the beginnings of a headache coming on. Hannah had gone to Princeton to buy some groceries, so he was alone in the cabin. "I need to get out of here," he said to himself. Grabbing his truck keys and jacket, he headed out the door.

He didn't plan to drive up Otter Mountain, but he found himself navigating the gravel road about fifteen minutes later. He always felt he could think better in the mountains. He was nearing the spot where they had first hiked to the mine when he slammed on the brakes. There, nailed to a tree, was a brand new, bright red "No Trespassing" sign. He parked the truck on the shoulder and got out and walked over to the tree. The grass under the sign was newly trampled and Ed could see fresh boot prints under the tree.

Confused, he continued walking down the road. He didn't have to go far, maybe about a hundred metres, when he saw another sign posted. He shook his head. When he and Hannah had come here there had been no signs posted. He was very careful to respect private property whenever he was hunting. He was dismayed. Someone was making sure they didn't return to the mine and the only person he told about the mountain was his friend, Sam.

Ed got back into his pickup but didn't start the engine. He stared at the No Trespassing sign while a swirl of unanswered questions tumbled in his mind. After his conversation with Sam, he couldn't shake the feeling that Sam knew more than he was letting on. Why did he lie about the cattle on Otter Mountain? There was something else, too, but he couldn't put his finger on it. It was like a dream that he couldn't quite remember.

And hour later, he parked the truck in front of their cabin and went inside. Hannah had returned and was making supper in their cosy kitchen.

"Hey," she said when he walked in. "Where have you been?"

"Just went for a little drive."

Hannah could hear hesitation in his voice. "What?" she asked, already bracing for some bad news.

Ed sat down on one of the bar stools at the kitchen island. "Well, I went back up to Otter Mountain and it's all posted."

Hannah said, "What do you mean, 'posted'?"

Ed poured himself a glass of wine. "I mean, there are brand new No Trespassing signs posted all along the road right where we started our hike."

Hannah was thoughtful. "You think Sam contacted LL Ranch, don't you?" Ed had told her about the conversation he and Sam had at the Coalmont Hotel, including Sam's remark about LL Ranch running cattle on the mountain.

He was so disappointed and confused. "I don't know what to think, Hannah."

"Why would Sam lie?"

"I don't know. I'm hoping it's just a mistake."

Hannah said nothing as she stirred the spaghetti sauce on the stove. Suddenly she turned and asked. "How old is Sam?"

Ed was surprised by this question. "Sam? Um. I guess he'd be about seventy. Why?"

She furrowed her brow. "I guess I'm just surprised that he knows anything about Hattie. She died before he was even born."

"He told me that his Aunt Ida knew Hattie's history."

Hannah walked from the stove and went to the bookshelf. She brought back a large hard cover book entitled *The History of Tulameen* to the kitchen island. After thumbing through a few pages, she came to the photo that she had been looking for. "What did you say Sam's grandmother's name was?"

Ed answered, "Rose."

Hannah eyes lit up as she turned the book towards Ed. She pointed at a black-and-white photo. “These are Sam’s grandparents,” she said.

Ed read the caption under the photo, “The Hawkins Family. Circa 1918. Emmett and Rose Hawkins with their six children: Jesse, Emma, Clarence, Hazel, Thomas and Ida.”

Hannah moved to stand beside Ed so that they could look at the photo together. She read the small paragraph about the family; there were a few sentences regarding each Hawkins child, the last about Ida. She read, “Ida Pearson (née Hawkins) died in Princeton in 1994.” She ran her hand over the picture. “What a beautiful photo, don’t you think?”

It was then that the realization hit Hannah, like a bolt from the sky. She ran to get her laptop and brought it to the kitchen island. Scanning quickly through her email, she found the one from the land title clerk. “Uncle Henry transferred his land to an Isaac Pearson,” Hannah said, her voice rising with excitement. “Ida’s married name was Pearson.”

That evening, Ed asked Hannah to see what she could find out about LL Ranch. After a little web-surfing, the only item she found was a listing for a Jim Pearson in Princeton.

Ed came to stand behind her. “No luck?” he asked.

Hannah glanced at the notes that Ed had taken from his conversation with the Land Title clerk and at the office. She shook her head. “There is no Isaac Pearson listed in this area, just Jim,” she said.

Ed pointed to the listing. “Is that his address?”

Hannah clicked on the address and instantly a map opened to show the location. “Isn’t the internet amazing?” Hannah asked. Ed grimaced. He hated how much information was available on the web and she knew it. But in this case, it was working to their advantage.

He gazed at the map. "Can you click on the satellite view?"

Hannah did and instantly the map changed, showing a blue lake at the back of the property and many green alfalfa fields.

"That's a ranch," Ed said, looking at the image on the screen. The view was grainy, but it was obvious that there was a large house near the main road. Outbuildings and vehicles dotted the landscape and a stock yard full of cattle was visible.

"I have an idea," Hannah said excitedly. She moved the mouse to the right of the screen and click on a small icon, dragging it to the road in front of the house. Instantly the screen zoomed in to show the street view. Hannah moved the mouse to the left of the screen to view the house and then scrolled back. Two large timbers stood sentry on either side of the drive with an enormous log spanning the width of them. Carved into the log were the words, "Welcome to LL Ranch."

"Bingo!" Ed exclaimed. "We found them."

Hannah asked, "What are you going to do?"

Ed smiled. "I'm going there to pay them a visit. I think the Pearsons owe us a few answers."

CHAPTER FORTY-FIVE

PRINCETON, BRITISH COLUMBIA—PRESENT DAY

ED STOPPED HIS TRUCK to gaze at the LL Ranch. It was impressive. A large log house sat at the end of a long gravel drive. The driveway was lined on both sides with split rail fencing and wildflowers bloomed in profusion along the way. He whistled in appreciation. The Pearsons, whoever they were, were doing well.

With a little apprehension, Ed turned onto the gravel and made his way to the house. He was barely parked when a young man, working on a John Deere tractor, came over to greet him.

"Hey there!" the man said.

Ed held out his hand. "Hello. Sorry for barging in on you like this. My name is Ed Janzen and I was hoping to talk to the owner of LL Ranch."

The man smiled, wiped his greasy hands on a rag and then shook Ed's hand warmly. "Levi Pearson. My family has owned LL for generations, so I guess you can talk to me. What is it you'd like to know?"

Ed took a deep breath. "I own a cabin in Tulameen." He saw that Levi relaxed visibly, which Ed took as a good sign. "And I'm a pretty avid hiker and hunter. I was hoping to do some scouting on Otter Mountain and someone told me they thought LL Ranch owned some of that land. I came by to ask permission."

He braced himself for a refusal, but surprisingly Levi just smiled and said, "The land on Otter Mountain belongs to my grandfather actually and we barely use it. I don't see what harm it would do if you wander around."

Ed was about to ask about the No Trespassing signs when Levi suggested that they go inside. "I have a map somewhere of our property lines that I can give you and then you'll know for certain where you are.

Ed let out a shaky breath. "Thank you. That would be great." Ed was confused. He was expecting pushback and he was ready to confront these people. He had a copy of the deed and mining certificate in the truck to show them. But Levi seemed oblivious. It was very possible that this family knew nothing of the body in the mine.

Levi led Ed into the ranch house through two massive wooden doors with cast iron fixtures. The entrance of the home had a vaulted ceiling and antiques from western pioneers were artfully exhibited throughout. The display rivalled any museum Ed had been to.

"Wow." Ed couldn't help but voice his appreciation. He walked over to a framed set of arrowheads. "Are these replicas?"

Levi shook his head. "Nope. Those are real and most were found by family. We've lived in this area for over a hundred years." He made the statement with a great deal of pride. Levi motioned for Ed to follow him. "Come on in the study. I think the maps are in there."

Ed followed him into an impressive study panelled in oak. Overstuffed leather couches were on either side of the room and at the end was an enormous stone fireplace. Hanging over the mantel was a large portrait. Ed stopped abruptly when he saw it.

Levi saw Ed looking at the photograph and said, "That's my great-grandfather. Pretty impressive, wasn't he?"

Ed felt his mouth go dry but managed, "Yes, he sure was." He kept his tone indifferent and asked, "What was his name?"

Rummaging through a pile of papers on the desk, Levi answered without looking up. "Jake. His name was Jake Pearson."

For a moment, Ed toyed with the idea of coming clean and telling Levi Pearson who he really was. To tell him that he recognized his great-grandfather, that his great uncle Henry was connected to the Pearson family in some way. But before he could even question the wisdom of a clean slate, another man walked into the study. His resemblance to Jake Pearson was startling and Ed could barely cover his astonishment.

The man stopped short when he saw Ed. "Oh, I'm sorry. I didn't know we had company."

Levi turned to face the older man. "Oh, hi Dad. I didn't know you were in the house, or I would have called you." He gestured to Ed. "Dad, this is Ed Janzen. Ed, this is my father, Jim Pearson."

Jim held out his hand, "Nice to meet you."

Ed was amazed at how welcoming both men were to a complete stranger and he warmed to them immediately.

"Ed has a cabin in Tulameen," Levi explained. "And he heard that we have some land on Otter Mountain. He came by to ask if he could do a little scouting on it." Levi held up some loose papers. "I was just about to give him a map to show him what land is ours." Ed watched the older man's face. Was it his imagination, or did he see Jim's lips tighten for a moment?

"I'm sorry," Jim said, "I'm afraid we can't let anyone on that land at the moment." He walked over to a small bar at the side of the room and poured himself two fingers of Jack Daniel's. "We're running cattle on it at the moment."

"Really?" Ed asked innocently. *Two can play this game,* he thought. "I drove up the mountain not that long ago and I didn't see any cattle. The grassland looked pretty healthy. That's why I thought I'd check it out for deer sign."

Jim was silent for a moment and then threw back the whisky in one shot. "Sorry. I meant we'll be running cattle on it soon." Levi looked perplexed and opened his mouth to speak, when a little girl came running into the room. "Grandpa!" She hurled herself at Jim and he picked her up, kissing her on the cheek.

"You home already?" he asked.

She made a face. "The bus just dropped me off."

Levi asked her, "How was school today, Minna?"

Ed was so surprised at hearing the same unusual name from the photo, that he jerked his head to stare at the little girl. She was adorable, with long dark hair in two ponytails and enormous brown eyes. Tearing his gaze away, he looked back at Jim, but he knew he hadn't caught his reaction in time. Jim was eyeing him with suspicion, all warmth vanished, like a fire gone cold. He set his granddaughter down and turning to Ed he said, "I need to get back to work. Sorry we couldn't accommodate you." He tugged on the brim of his hat and, with that, he was gone.

CHAPTER FORTY-SIX

FRASER VALLEY, TULAMEEN, AND PRINCETON, BRITISH COLUMBIA—PRESENT DAY

Ed and Hannah had been home, in the Fraser Valley, for just over a month. The deadline they set to tell the police about the skeleton in the mine had come and gone. Neither had brought it up. But a day didn't go by that Ed didn't think about the situation and what to do. The answer came quite unexpectedly when Sam phoned them from Tulameen.

Ed recognized his friend's number on the call display, so he did his best to hide his surprise. He hadn't talked to Sam since their conversation at the hotel and Ed was sure he was avoiding him.

"Sam?" he said when he answered the phone. "Is that you?"

There was a long pause and then Sam's unmistakable gravelly voice came on the line. "Hey, Ed," Sam said. "Yup. It's yours truly." His voice was cheerful, but it sounded forced.

"What's up Sam?" Suddenly Ed was worried. "Did something happen to our cabin?" Sam was always kind enough to check on their place when he drove through the small community.

"No, no," Sam said. "Everything's okay… That is… well…" He tripped over his words. He paused again and then asked, "When's your next trip to Tulameen?"

"Well, I don't know," Ed said. "Why?"

"Well, the next time you come up I'd like to come to your cabin for a visit." He cleared his throat, then added. "Come up soon if you can. It's pretty important."

It was two more weeks until Hannah could take some time off from the office and they could go back to Tulameen. Ed phoned Sam when they arrived and Sam said he'd be over in the morning.

Neither Ed nor Hannah slept well that night and they were up with the sun. When Sam walked into their warm kitchen, he shook Ed's hand and Hannah gave him a kiss on the cheek, but she could see that both men were subdued, their usual banter gone.

"Sam," she said, "it's so good to see you." Trying to relieve the tension in the room, she gestured to one of the kitchen stools. "Have you had breakfast yet?" She got out an extra mug and plate and poured Sam a cup of coffee.

"That sounds great, Hannah." He looked at Ed who had yet to say a word. "But I think we need to talk first." Hannah refilled both her and Ed's mugs and they sat. Sam took a deep breath and began.

"I was just wondering," Sam started and looked at Ed, "how you broke your leg?"

"What?" Ed felt his stomach drop. "Why do you want to know?"

Sam took a sip of his coffee. "Well, you never did say how it happened. Seemed to be a pretty bad break from what I remember, but no one I've talked to can recall how it happened."

Ed looked at Sam for a long while and then said, "Why are you asking me this?" Sam didn't answer, so Ed answered for him. "Because you already know, don't you?"

Sam took another sip of his coffee and then looked at Hannah who was avoiding his eyes. Turning back to Ed, he said. "I asked you if you went up to the mine and you never did tell me." Sam looked Ed straight in the eyes. "You fell into the old mine on Otter Mountain. That's how you broke your leg, isn't it?"

When neither Ed nor Hannah answered, Sam knew he was right.

It was Ed's turn to ask the questions. "You went to the Pearsons and told them about my Uncle Henry, didn't you? Why?"

Hannah touched Ed on the hand. She could see that he was getting angry and frustrated. "Sam," she said, trying to diffuse the situation. "We know that you're connected to the Pearson family in some way."

"You do?" Sam couldn't keep the surprise from his voice.

Hannah smiled and said, "Your Aunt Ida. The Tulameen history book listed her married name. It was Pearson."

Sam stood suddenly. "I actually came here to take you somewhere. There's someone I'd like you to meet. As soon as you're ready, let's take a drive."

Two hours later, Sam drove up to LL Ranch, but instead of pulling into the main drive, he took a spur road that led into the foothills behind the large log house. Stopping the truck in front of a small cabin, Sam parked next to a lake.

"Whose place is this?" Ed asked, looking at the ranch house in the distance.

"Come on," Sam said, motioning to the cabin. "He's waiting to meet you."

The three of them walked into the small log cabin to find Jim Pearson inside, along with an old man sitting in a leather recliner. An oxygen tank was on the floor next to the recliner, the hose from the tank connected to two prongs in the man's nostrils. He looked like he was nearly a hundred years old and Ed wondered, for a ridiculous second, if he was still alive. But that doubt was dispelled the moment after they walked in. He rapped his cane on the empty chairs across from him and said, “Sit down. Sit down.” They all did as they were told.

The old man held out a hand to Ed first. His voice was like grit and sand. “You must be Henry’s great-nephew,” he said. “Is that right?”

Ed was startled at the man’s firm grip and voice. “Yes, sir,” he managed. “I am.”

The man smiled. “I’m so glad to meet you. Your great uncle was a good friend of mine.”

Ed was trying to catch up. “I’m sorry sir, but who are you?”

The old man laughed, the sound escaping him like an ancient accordion. “Of course. Introductions should come first.” He placed a hand on his wheezing chest. “My name is Isaac Pearson. And Hattie McBride was my mother.”

CHAPTER FORTY-SEVEN

COALMONT, BRITISH COLUMBIA—MARCH 1920

MINNA CRACKED AN EGG on the side of a cast-iron skillet, emptying the contents in the pan and then scrambling it with the dozen eggs and bacon that were already frying. She sprinkled a little salt over the cooking eggs and it sizzled and popped.

"Smells good in here!" Henry said as he entered the kitchen.

Minna chuckled, "You always think it smells good in here."

He gave her a wide smile as he took a stack of plates from the cupboard and set them on the table. After all this time, Minna still couldn't get used to a man helping in the kitchen, but Henry ignored her protests. "My *mutti* would box my ears if she saw me sitting around watching you work," he had once said, so Minna had long since given up arguing with him. "Grab some forks too, will ya?" she asked, and Henry obliged. "Is everyone coming down to breakfast?" she asked him.

"Lena said she'd be down shortly," he said, setting the forks on the table. "And Angel and Lottie, too." Henry pulled two pine chairs next to the table. "I don't think Nellie's coming." He shook his head. "She's got her nose bent out of joint again."

Minna looked up from the eggs she was scrambling. "What about Hattie?"

Henry shrugged. "Haven't seen her yet this morning."

Just then, Lena came in and went directly to Minna, planting a kiss on the old woman's warm cheek. Minna beamed but then feigned consternation, flapping her away with her faded apron. "You do beat all child… fussin' over an old woman."

Lena snatched a piece of warm bread from the counter and laughed. "Good morning to you, too!" She sat next to Henry, giving him a warm smile and said, "Can I help it if I'm in a good mood?"

Lottie and Angel joined them, laughing about something they had observed in town the other day. They sat together at the table and Minna placed heaping serving plates of food in front of them: eggs, bacon, toast, jam, and honey. As they filled their plates, Minna watched them, marvelling at this happy ragtag family that God had given her. Truth was that, except for Nellie, they were all in a good mood.

Five days ago, Hattie had officially closed the brothel and, for better or worse, had set her and Jake's plan into motion. Angel and Lottie happily agreed to stay and help Lena with the boarding house but, sadly Josephine and Eliza had moved on. They were going to miss them both. The only one who wasn't happy with the new plan was Nellie. But then, when was she ever happy? Minna had never met a more exasperating creature. She was just pouring the coffee when Hattie came into the kitchen. She sat slowly in an empty chair that Henry provided and let out a shaky breath.

Lena took one look at Hattie and exclaimed, "Lord, Hattie. You look as white as a ghost."

Running her fingers through her tangled hair, Hattie said, "I'm exhausted. I could barely get out of bed this morning."

Minna set an empty mug in front of Hattie and filled it to the brim. "Well, a cup of my fresh coffee will do the trick. Perk you right up."

Lena took an empty plate and scooped a large portion of eggs onto it. Placing it in front of Hattie, she said, "Try some eggs, too." Winking at Minna, she said, "They're delicious as usual."

Hattie picked up her fork and put a tiny portion of eggs into her mouth. She chewed for a few moments and then abruptly stood up. Placing a hand over her mouth, she turned and ran from the room.

Minna knocked softly on Hattie's door and then let herself into the bedroom. Hattie was sitting on the side of the bed, a basin balanced precariously between her knees. The miasma of the room quickly reached Minna's nose and she grimaced. "Looks like you brought them eggs up for a second look," she said, smoothing Hattie's disheveled hair.

Hattie quirked one eyebrow and tried to smile. "I must have the flu," Hattie said. She wiped her mouth with a handkerchief. "But I can't seem to shake it. This is the fifth day in a row that I've felt terrible."

Minna took the bowl from Hattie and set it gingerly on the floor. Sitting next to Hattie she said, "There ain't no way to ask this easy." She smiled and took Hattie's hand, "Do you think you might be pregnant?"

Hattie's eyes widened and she shook her head. "No, I can't be."

Minna coloured but she forged ahead. "So, you and Jake haven't been together that way?"

Now it was Hattie's turn to look chagrined. "Well, yes we have, but…" Her voice got quiet. "I always assumed I couldn't get pregnant." She pressed a hand to her flat belly. "William and I tried for years." She gripped Minna's hand like a vise. "Oh Minna, do you think I could be?"

Minna smiled. "Of course you could be. How long has it been since your last monthly?"

Hattie shook her head. “I really don’t know. My flow hasn’t been regular for a long time and I stopped keeping track years ago.”

Minna squeezed her hands and said, “Let’s wait and see how you feel in a week or two and if your monthly comes or not.” She stood and walked to the door, miming a kiss before closing it behind her.

Hattie stared at the closed door for a long time, afraid to move or breathe. She looked down at her stomach, imagining the life that might be growing there. The dream of having a child was something she had given up long ago. Her mind told her it couldn’t be true. But her heart was beating wildly. Pressing her hands over her stomach, she held them there, as if to keep the dream from escaping.

CHAPTER FORTY-EIGHT

TULAMEEN—PRESENT DAY

"Your mother?" Hannah spoke for the first time since entering the cabin. She felt her heart begin to pound with anticipation.

Isaac turned to her and nodded. "And who might you be?"

Hannah answered, "My name is Hannah. I'm Ed's wife." She pointed to her husband who was still gaping at the old man in the chair.

"Very nice to meet you, young lady," Isaac said.

Hannah grinned. She was by no means young, but she would take the compliment. This man was a charmer. Probably had been all his life.

He eyed her astutely, "Now," he said in his raspy voice, "you're wondering how old I am, aren't you?"

Hannah nodded, surprised. It was the first thought that came to her mind when he said he was Hattie's son. "We've been researching your mother a bit," Hannah admitted. "She died in 1920."

Isaac nodded. "November 1920. I was barely a month old when she was murdered."

Hannah laid a hand on the old man's arm. "I'm so sorry. When we heard that she had been murdered, well, we were just shocked."

Isaac smiled and patted her hand that still rested on his arm. He said, "Sam has told me that you and your husband were asking about my mother." He paused for a long moment and then, as if he was afraid to continue, he said quietly. "He said you might have a picture of her?"

Ed suddenly looked at Sam. That's what had been nagging at him all this time. When he had shown Sam the photo from Uncle Henry's bible, Sam had said that he thought there were no photos of Hattie. He couldn't have known that unless Isaac had told him.

Hannah picked up her purse and pulled out the old Bible. "We found it in here." She showed Isaac the old book. "Uncle Henry had hidden it inside the back cover." Carefully, she extracted the photo from the pages and handed it to Isaac. *He took it with such reverence*, Hannah thought, as she watched his face, like a child receiving a special present.

"Oh, my," he said, his eyes suddenly bright with tears.

"Dad." Jim jumped to his feet immediately. "Are you all right?"

The old man shooed him away. "I'm fine." He fished for a hanky from his pants pocket. "Just a little overwhelmed." He dabbed at his eyes. "My father always told me how beautiful she was, but I never realized it until now. It was one of the greatest regrets in his life that he didn't have a photograph of my mother. He said that they had taken some at the Hawkins' ranch, but he never knew what became of them."

Hannah glanced at Ed. They were both thinking of the locket. Should they say something about the mine? But before they could contemplate the answer, Jim cleared his throat. "So, I'm thinking that maybe we need to talk about the mine on Otter Mountain?" Ed was suddenly gripped by a small feeling of panic. Was this family caught up in some murder?"

When did you fall into the mine?" Jim asked simply.

Ed looked at Sam. "Sam told you, I guess?"

Jim smiled wryly, but shook his head. "All Sam told me was that you had broken your leg quite badly. You just confirmed it though." Jim chuckled. "I found a wrapper from a protein bar and a plastic bag that had the words, 'tensor bandage' on it."

Ed looked sheepish and then explained how they had found the mining certificate in the old suitcase. "We never knew anything about my great uncle," He explained. "I was just curious to see where he had been." He looked at Hannah. "We never imagined that I would fall in." He paused before continuing. "Or what we would find."

Jim eyed him carefully and then spoke with great care. "Yes, I can imagine that it must have been pretty frightening to find some old bones."

Hannah was almost afraid to ask. "So you knew they were there?"

Jim nodded. "They've been there for nearly a hundred years now.

Ed said sheepishly. "I tripped over them."

To everyone's amazement, Isaac began to laugh; a deep belly laugh. Wiping his eyes, he said. "That's the funniest thing I've heard in a long time. It's about what he deserves."

"He?" Ed asked. "You know who that is in the mine?"

Isaac nodded and gestured to the empty chairs beside him. "Why don't you sit back down and I'll tell you what my father told me."

CHAPTER FORTY-NINE

COALMONT, BRITISH COLUMBIA—MARCH 1920

To SAY THAT HATTIE was preoccupied for the rest of the week would have been an understatement. Her mind jumped from one scenario to the next and played havoc with her thoughts.

How will I tell Jake? What will he say? Will he be happy?

Although they had professed their love for one another, the subject of marriage had not yet come up. To complicate things, Hattie wasn't sure if she was even free to marry. Over the years she had written several times to William to finalize their divorce, but she had never received a response.

To keep her mind occupied and between bouts of nausea, Hattie worked together with Lena to transform the brothel into a boarding house. There had already been numerous enquiries as to when they would open, and Lena was anxious to get started and run a real respectable business. Hattie was dusting for cobwebs, reaching high into the corner with a broom when there was a pounding on the front door. Dread seized her. She knew only one person would demand entrance like that. Henry was the first to reach the door and, seeing Simon's livid face through the leaded windows, he turned and told them all to stay upstairs. Unlocking the door, he feigned a smile as Simon stormed in.

"Where is she?" Simon yelled as soon as he entered the parlour.

Henry stood his ground. "She?" he asked innocently. "You'll have to be more specific, Simon. There are a few 'shes' in this house." Henry motioned to all the women who were now gathered on the second floor.

Seeing Hattie at the balustrade, Simon turned to rage at her. "What is this?" He held up the closed sign that Hattie had hung on the front door only a few days before.

Hattie raised an eyebrow and couldn't resist in replying, "I'm quite certain you can read, Simon. What does it look like?" Lottie sniggered, which enraged him further.

He took a step towards the staircase, but Henry quickly blocked his way. "You can say your piece down here, Simon," Henry said, placing his large bulk between the angry man and the second floor. Simon seemed to consider it for a moment but then took a step backward.

"I came here to collect the brothel money from the past month." He glared at Hattie. "Imagine my surprise to find my business closed without my knowledge.

Hattie walked to the top of the staircase and said, "We planned on discussing this with you, but you were gone. We didn't even know when, or if you were coming back." She shook her head. "You have this way of disappearing, Simon."

Simon looked at her for a while, obviously unsure of how to respond. "Well, I'm here now." he blustered. "And I'm telling you right now that we are not closing this place."

Lena interjected, hoping to diffuse the situation. "We're not closing permanently, Simon. We're just making it into a real boarding house."

Simon snorted. "Do you really think that a boarding house will make money like Hattie's Place did?" He tore the sign in two and threw the pieces on the floor.

Hattie sighed. "Simon, I really did want to talk to you about this first, but we didn't have a choice." She walked down the stairs and stood beside Henry, who had not moved. "We were raided again last week and they made it quite clear that we had to close permanently or face the consequences. They said that was our final warning." Hattie looked up at her girls who were still watching from the second floor. "I wasn't willing to risk that."

Simon pressed his clenched fists to his temples, pacing the room in frustration. "We could have kept running if you really wanted to. Grease a few palms with enough cash and anyone would be willing to look the other way." He looked around at the parlour, now devoid of the garish furniture. The menu no longer hung on the wall. "And what do you expect me to do?"

Hattie walked to the strong box they had installed when they first opened. "Give me your key," she said, holding out her hand. Reluctantly Simon gave her his key for the box. After opening it, she withdrew all the cash and counted it. She placed a large portion in an envelope and handed it to him. "Here. I've gone over the books in the past week and that's what's left. I kept what you stole from me and half of what this place is worth." Her voice was cold. Then she added. "Plus interest. The rest is yours, which is more than you deserve."

Simon opened the envelope and thumbed through the contents. He growled, "You must be joking." He slapped the envelope with the back of his hand. "I can't live on this. It's worth twice this amount." He leered then, "And I never stole anything from you. You gave that money to me quite freely, if I recall."

Hattie winced and then turned, walking back to Henry. "Don't remind me of how gullible I was." She pointed to the envelope still clutched in his hand. "That's all there is left. Business was pretty slow after the law showed up. They scared most of our clientele away." She crossed her arms in front of her chest. "Our "partnership…" she spit out the poisonous word, "is over. We think it's time you move on permanently."

Simon ignored her, like she hadn't spoken, "You keep on saying 'we.' Who is this 'we' you keep referring to?" He swept his hand up to the women on the second floor. "Your prostitutes?" His gaze swept to Minna. "Or your old maid?" Looking at Henry, he sneered, "Or your farm boy?" Gazing around the room, his eyes narrowed. He tapped a finger to his lips and then chuckled. "It's Jake, isn't it?"

Hattie's stomach clenched. Simon knew about her and Jake? She did her best to hide her discomfort, but Simon read her like an open book. He snorted in derision and melodramatically put a hand over his heart.

"Oh, did he tell you that he loved you? That he'd take you away from all this?" he gestured to the room.

Hattie's chin lifted, "As a matter of fact, he did."

Simon's mocking laughter filled the room. "And you believed him?" He threw his hands in the air. "Oh, I would have loved to have been a fly on the wall for that conversation." He walked over to stand in front of Hattie who was trembling now. "Let me guess. You love him because he's trustworthy and honest?" He smiled but there was only malice in his eyes. "Tell me my dear. Did he tell you about me?"

Hattie's eyes widened. "Why on earth would we talk about you?" she said evenly, but her stomach was roiling now.

Simon opened his mouth to answer when Jake walked into the parlour from the kitchen. "Simon!" Jake barked. "That's enough."

Simon smiled and opened his arms wide. "Look who it is!" he said to the room at large. "My dear, big brother."

CHAPTER FIFTY

COALMONT, BRITISH COLUMBIA—MARCH 1920

"Simon is your brother?" Hattie was incredulous.

"Half-brother," Jake corrected, as if that made the admission any less astonishing.

After Simon's revelation, Hattie had raced upstairs to her room and Jake had followed. Hattie walked over to the window, the tears streaming down her face.

Jake said, "I wanted to tell you so many times. I was going to tell you the night of Rose and Emmett's party, but then you told me you loved me and how much you trusted me… and I just couldn't bring myself to do it. I was afraid I'd spoil everything." He touched her shoulder, but she jerked away. He let his hands drop, his fists balled at his sides. He ached to take her in his arms, but he knew it was too soon.

She whirled to face him, angry now. "Why couldn't you tell me?"

Jake ran his fingers through his dark hair and sighed. "I don't know. I guess when I found out he was in Coalmont, I just couldn't face it."

Hattie looked at Jake and then the realization dawned on her. "Your fiancée cheated on you with your brother."

Jake nodded. "She left me for Simon." Jake sat down on the bed, his elbows on his knees. "It took me so long to get over that betrayal. Then, when I met you and found out you were in business with Simon, I assumed you were cut from the same cloth." He looked up, smiling at her. "I tried not to like you, but it was futile. After we fell in love, I knew I had kept the secret for too long. I was afraid of what you'd think of me if you knew Simon was my brother." Jake stared at his clasped hands between his knees. "I should have told you right from the beginning, but I guess I hoped he'd just disappear and not come back."

Hattie sat on the edge of the bed beside Jake. "He does have a habit of doing that." She placed a hand on his knee and he took it, kissing her warm palm.

"I'm so sorry," he said. "I should have been honest with you from the first day."

She leaned her head against his shoulder and said, "It's all right. Now that I've gotten over the shock."

He turned to face her and said, "Let's be honest with each other from now on, okay?"

Hattie stiffened and he felt her reaction immediately. "What?" he said, alarmed.

Hattie stood, hugging herself protectively. "There is something I need to tell you." She turned to look at him. "I was going to wait another week or two, but you said we should be honest." She came back to the bed and sat down.

Jake searched her face. "You're scaring me."

Hattie smiled, her eyes brightening. "I'm sorry, I don't mean to. It's just that I don't know how you're going to react to what I have to tell you." She took in a deep breath and slowly exhaled. "Jake," she said, "I think we're going to have a baby."

"You're pregnant?" Jake stared at Hattie in disbelief.

She nodded, searching his face. "I'm sorry to shock you like that but there was no easy way to tell you."

Jake nodded, his mouth hanging agape. "Are you sure?" was all he managed.

She shook her head. "Minna seems sure, but I don't know." She shrugged. "I've never been pregnant before." She was quiet for a moment. "Maybe I'm just afraid to believe it."

Jake wrapped his arms around her, drawing her close into his warm embrace. He kissed the top of her head as she burrowed deep within the safety of his arms.

"You're not mad?" The words were muffled as she spoke them into his shirt.

He reared back to look at her face. "Why would I be mad?"

"I've had some time to think about this, Jake. And I wouldn't blame you. This will change both of our lives forever. I know you love me, but we're not married."

Jake let her go and then lifted her chin to look into her eyes. "Is that what you're worried about? That our child will be a bastard?"

She looked chagrined but answered truthfully, "This child will have enough to deal with when he finds out that his mother ran a brothel. Being born out of wedlock sure won't help."

Jake laughed and kissed her again. "And if our child is half as feisty as his mother, I'm sure he'll understand that his mother had a past." He kissed her nose. "I promise to make an honest woman of you as soon as possible."

CHAPTER FIFTY-ONE

COALMONT, BRITISH COLUMBIA—APRIL 1920

"Good morning," Minna singsonged as she let herself into Hattie's bedroom. She carried an empty tray, save for a small pot of tea and soda crackers.

Hattie propped herself up on one elbow, looking pale and weak. Her morning sickness had not improved, in fact, it seemed to be getting worse. Minna squelched a moment of fear but kept a smile on her face. "How are you feeling this morning love?" she asked, though she well knew the answer.

Hattie managed to sit up, propping a pillow against the headboard. Leaning back, she exhaled, exhausted with the small effort. Pressing her palms to her forehead she said, "I've been better." She managed a weak smile. "Honestly Minna, if I didn't want this baby so badly, I think I would have stepped in front of a train a long time ago."

Minna frowned. "That's not funny," she said, looking quite worried now.

"Sorry," Hattie said, "but I'm so tired of being sick and it's only been a month." She threw the quilt over her head and spoke from under the covers. "How did Rose do this six times?"

Minna straightened at the mention of Rose's name. "Does Rose know you're pregnant yet?" Minna asked.

Hattie shook her head under the blanket. "No. At first I didn't want to tell her until I was sure and now, well, I'm just not up to it."

Minna was closing Hattie's bedroom door, when Jake came bounding up the stairs.

"How is she?" he asked quietly.

Minna shook her head. "Not good, Jake." She motioned for Jake to follow her back down to the main floor. "She's so pale and she hasn't eaten in days. I'm afraid for her. And for the baby."

Jake was alarmed. "What can I do?" he asked, panicking now.

"Go to King Valley Ranch and get Rose," Minna said. "I've never birthed a baby, but Rose and Emmett have six healthy children. She'll know what to do."

By the time Jake reached the ranch he was beside himself with worry. Rose met him at the door as soon as she saw him pull up with the buggy.

"Jake, what's wrong?" she said, the moment she saw his face.

"It's Hattie."

Rose held the screen door open for Jake and then followed him inside. He paced the confines of the kitchen while Rose watched him anxiously. "Tell me," she demanded.

"Hattie's pregnant," he said without preamble.

"What?" Rose sat down with a thump, sloshing her coffee on the table. Her face broke into an enormous smile. "Oh Jake! That's wonderful."

He smiled a tight smile and said, "Yes, it is wonderful, but it's hit her hard." He sat down beside her. "Rose, she's so sick that she can't keep anything down. Minna's pretty worried and she's wondering if you'd come and see Hattie. Maybe you have some suggestions?

Rose stood without hesitation. "Just give me ten minutes to collect some things and talk to Emmett. Then we can be on our way."

When Rose walked into Hattie's bedroom, Hattie was bending over a basin and emptying the contents of her stomach for the third time that morning. There was nothing left to expel, but the spasms came anyway and her muscles ached with the effort.

Rose threw off her coat and was immediately beside her friend. She brushed Hattie's long hair away from her damp cheeks and said. "So, I hear congratulations are in order."

Hattie opened one eye and managed a weak smile. "I am so happy, Rose." She dabbed her mouth with a damp crumpled hanky, "But I had no idea I would feel this terrible. How did you do this six times?"

Rose answered honestly, "Well, I wasn't sick with all of them. Only the first two, actually. Not every woman gets morning sickness."

Hattie chuckled without humour. "So, I'm one of the lucky ones, eh?" She looked down at her stomach and said, "Thanks very much, little one."

Tears sprang to Rose's eyes. "Oh, Hattie. I'm so happy for you and Jake." She gave Hattie a gentle hug and then said, "Now, let's see what we can do to make you feel better."

Opening the small canvas bag she had brought along, she asked. "Tell me. Are you sick all day or just in the morning?"

"Just in the morning."

"Well, that's a good thing," said Rose. "If you were sick all day, I'd be more concerned." Rose brought out a small jar of dried green leaves and turned to Minna who was hovering at the end of the bed. "Minna, would you be a dear and boil up a new pot of tea using these leaves?" She handed Minna the small jar and Minna took them gratefully, eager to be doing something to help.

"Steep them for about five minutes," Rose called to Minna as she left the room. She then took out a small paper bag and extracted a tiny golden cube.

Hattie looked at it curiously. "What is that?"

"Dried ginger," Rose explained. "My mother buys it from a Chinatown shop in Vancouver. I always bring a supply back with me whenever I visit." She handed Hattie the tiny piece and said, "Take a small bite and then chew it very slowly. Does wonders for an upset stomach."

A few moments later, Minna and Jake came back into the room, Minna carrying the tray upstairs for the second time that morning. Rose poured the tea for Hattie and said, "This is raspberry leaf tea. It's the best tea for pregnant women. It'll help settle your stomach, too, and it apparently helps with the birthing later on."

Hattie closed her eyes and slowly chewed on the ginger. She took a small sip of the tea and settling back onto the pillows, closed her eyes. "I'm so glad you're here and I'm sorry you found out like this," Hattie said without opening her eyes. "I should have told you sooner."

Rose patted Hattie's leg. "Do not apologize. You've had enough on your plate to worry about. I'm just happy I'm here now."

Hattie placed her hand over Rose's. "Me, too."

Rose stood and said, "So here's what I suggest: stay in bed for at least half an hour after you wake up. Have some soda crackers on the bedside table and chew one slowly before you get up. Don't eat anything until the morning nausea has passed, except those crackers and tea." She smiled at Hattie and said, "My guess is that this will be over in a couple of months."

"Months?" Hattie and Jake both exclaimed together.

"Unfortunately, yes," said Rose. "It could be even longer, I'm sorry to say. And you should send for the doctor."

Hattie's eyes grew wide in alarm. "No!" she exclaimed. "I don't want anyone to know that I'm pregnant."

Rose came back to sit beside Hattie. "For heaven's sake," she said, searching Hattie's eyes. "Why ever not?"

Hattie gripped the quilt and tugged it tighter over her stomach. "Don't you know what people will say? They'll talk about that woman who ran a brothel. I can just hear them speculating on who the father is and dragging Jake's good name in the mud along with mine. And everyone knows that I don't have a husband. I won't have the entire town calling my child a bastard. It breaks my heart just to think of it."

Jake spoke up for the first time since entering the room. "Minna. Rose. Would you give Hattie and I a minute alone please?" Nodding, the two other women left quietly.

Hattie looked at Jake and shook her head. Before he could speak, she said, "I don't want anyone to know about the baby." She grimaced as a wave of nausea hit her, waiting until it passed. "But I don't know what to do," she continued. "I can't stay in this bedroom for two more months. Lena was hoping to open the boarding house soon and the last thing I need is our boarders to hear me sick every morning. The whole town would know before long."

"Then come and live with me on the mountain." Jake said.

"What?" Hattie asked wide-eyed.

"Why not?" Jake continued. "Listen," he said, "I've been doing a lot of thinking since you told me I'm going to be a father and I think it's the perfect solution." Hattie opened her mouth to speak but he put a finger on her lips to shush her. "Hear me out." He said. "I don't give a damn what people say about me, but I do agree that our child deserves all the love in this world and not condemnation before it's even born. So, I'm thinking, let's give our baby, and us, a brand-new start. You and Minna come to live with me at the cabin. If anyone asks, Lena and Henry can say that you and Minna went on a trip for a while." She was about to respond when he continued. “I was talking to Emmett the other day and he was telling me about some beautiful ranch land for sale just north of Princeton.”

Hattie interrupted him then. “Ranch land? Jake what are you saying?” He took both her hands in his and said. “Don’t you see? You can have the baby at the cabin and no one will know, just as you want. Then, after the baby is born, we’ll move to a new home.” He grinned. “I’ve always wanted to have a spread of my own and I’m done mining.” She looked dubious so he pressed on. “We’ll move where no one knows who we are and start fresh.” He stopped to search her face, quite excited with his solution, now that it was taking shape. “What do you think?”

“We’d be a real family?” Hattie asked, still not believing it.

“Yes.” He grinned. “We’ll get married and bring our child to its new home. You’ll be my wife, Hattie Pearson.”

She didn’t answer and Jake saw the uncertainty in her eyes. “What?’” he asked. “I thought you wanted to start over.”

She nodded. “I do,” Hattie said quietly. “But my name isn’t Hattie. It’s Sarah.”

“What?” Jake said again. He was confused. “What are you talking about?”

She took a small bite of ginger, and then, choosing her words carefully, continued. “After I realized that I had no choice but to run the brothel, I changed my name to Hattie.” She grimaced, remembering that day when Simon demolished her.” I was so mortified and humiliated. It was a rash decision, but I didn’t want anything left connecting me to my past.”

Thinking of Simon and the sordid role his brother had played, Jake felt his blood grow hot. But he was slightly piqued at her too. “I thought we weren’t going to keep secrets from each other anymore?” he said.

“I’m sorry,” she offered. “But I’ve been Hattie for so long that I never really thought about it until just now. I guess I never expected to be that woman again." Looking out the window, she smiled as if glimpsing her future. "How could I have known that I'd meet Minna and Rose and Henry and you." She turned back to look into his eyes and he saw the dream she carried. "I never dared to hope…" her voice caught, and she couldn't finish.

But it didn't matter. He felt the same. Jake smiled, taking her hand in his. "It's a future that I always dreamed of too. I fell in love with you and it doesn't matter to me what you did or what your name is." He kissed her. "As long as you become my wife, that's all that matters."

She was thoughtful for a moment and then said, "I think it would be perfect to start my new life with the name I was meant to have."

He nodded his head and smiled. "Sarah," he said, trying the name out for size. "Jake and Sarah. I like it."

CHAPTER FIFTY-TWO

COALMONT, BRITISH COLUMBIA—OCTOBER 1920

SIMON STEPPED OUT OF the hotel into the sunshine and immediately groaned. It was a cloudless autumn day and everyone was enjoying the beautiful weather, except for him. He made it as far as the second step when the world began to spin, forcing him to sit down to regain his equilibrium.

For the umpteenth time that week Simon cursed his brother for putting him in this situation. If it hadn't been for Jake meddling in his private life he'd still be living in luxury off the profits of the brothel. Now he was drawing seriously near to the end of his funds and he was in peril due to his gambling debts. He had managed to stave his debtors off with a payment after his last visit to Hattie's Place, but they would not be placated for long. He sported a split lip and black eye to prove it.

"Well, you look like the dog's breakfast."

Simon looked up to see Nellie standing in front of him. He sighed heavily. "What do you want Nellie?"

"Nothing," she shrugged. "I saw you sitting here and I thought I'd come over and say hello," she said.

"Well, now you did, so you can move along." He swept his fingers in front of her, like he was sweeping a dusty porch. He had no desire to talk to this skinny former prostitute.

She whistled, not bothering with his suggestion. "That's quite the shiner you got there!" she laughed. "What happened? Did you walk into a door?" Nellie had just been at McTavish's and Angus had regaled her with the latest regarding Simon and his travails. She knew full well why Simon's face looked like a bowl of diced beets, but Nellie fed on other people's misery and this was the perfect opportunity to heap abuse on the man's narrow shoulders.

Despite his decrepit state, Simon would allow only so many insults to be flung his way. "So, how's it going at the boarding house?" he asked. "How do you like being an upstairs maid?" The grin fell from her face, so he continued, knowing that he had found her soft underbelly. "How do you like emptying chamber pots and washing sheets? Is it everything you thought it would be?" He laughed, despite his pounding head.

Nellie crossed her arms over her chest and said, "It's dreary as hell, if you must know. I miss the days when I could sleep in. A few hours on my back every night and I was done." She looked at her hands, now rough and red from cleaning every day. "I don't plan on staying there much longer."

Simon couldn't have cared less. "Really?" he said. "I thought you all loved working for the perfect Hattie."

Nellie snorted. "Hattie left months ago with Minna. Lena and Henry are running the place now."

Simon straightened. "Hattie is gone? Where did she go?"

Nellie shrugged. "Beats me. One morning we went down to breakfast and Lena told us that Hattie and Minna had gone away for a while." She leaned forward, as if to share a deep, dark secret and said, "I do know this. I overheard Henry telling Lena that Hattie and Jake are planning to buy a ranch together."

Simon jerked as if he'd been shot. "A ranch? How can they afford to buy a ranch?"

Nellie looked at Simon, trying to gauge whether he was baiting her or if he was just plain stupid. When his expression didn't change, she said, "Did you honestly think that Hattie gave you everything that was owed you?" She shook her head in disbelief. "She hated you, Simon. We never heard the end of it." She rolled her eyes for effect.

"What are you telling me?" he said, feeling a weight growing in his stomach, like he had swallowed a lead ball.

"You know," she said, leaning forward so that she got his full attention. "Everyone thought I was this ridiculous girl from California, but I'm a lot smarter than they gave me credit for." She tapped the side of her head and Simon resisted the urge to make a snide comment, but he bit his tongue. "I know when to listen." She studied him for a second and then decided to throw him a bone. "For someone who loves money as much as you do, you didn't pay very close attention to where the money went."

"What are you talking about?" Simon sputtered. "I made Hattie show me the books and receipts at the end of every month."

Nellie shook her head and chuckled. "Please. Hattie showed you exactly what she wanted you to see."

Simon's face grew dark, the rage building like an approaching storm. Suddenly, Nellie lost her bravado. Fearing that she had said too much, she turned to leave but Simon grabbed her wrist so fiercely that she cried out in pain.

"Tell me what you know," he hissed.

"Let go of me." She tried prying his fingers from her arm in a futile effort to get free.

"Not until you tell me everything," he said through gritted teeth.

"All right. I overheard them one night."

"Who?" Simon growled impatiently.

"Hattie and Minna and Henry," she said, yanking her arm free. "They were in the kitchen talking and they didn't know I was listening." She rubbed her wrist and continued. "Hattie asked Henry where the receipts were for that week." She paused, thinking back to the evening that Henry had spurned her. "Henry said something about how his little sister had better penmanship. They talked about copying Angus's chicken scratch and they were all laughing about it."

"Angus who owns the mercantile?" Simon asked, the light beginning to dawn.

Nellie nodded. "Hattie said something about rewriting the receipts so that they looked the same as the month before."

Simon felt his blood grow cold as the reality of what Hattie had done to him became clear. "She stole from me. All this time." He said it so quietly that Nellie was sure he had forgotten she was there. She turned to make a hasty retreat, but he grabbed her before she could escape. "Not a word." He spat the words into her ear, so close that Nellie could smell his foul breath. He grabbed her face with his other hand so that she was forced to look into his eyes. "You hear me? You don't tell a soul what you just told me."

She tried to shake her head, but the pressure of his fingers was bruising her cheeks. "I won't tell anyone. Just let me go," she pleaded. Pushing her away in disgust, he watched her run back to the east end of town, a cloud of dust trailing behind her.

CHAPTER FIFTY-THREE

COALMONT, BRITISH COLUMBIA—OCTOBER 5, 1920

HATTIE WOKE SLOWLY AS the sun began to dawn through the bedroom window of the cabin. She opened one eye to see Jake smiling down at her. "Good morning," he said, touching her cheek. Leaning over, he planted a kiss on her stomach. "And good morning to you, too," he said to her enormous belly.

Hattie laughed and playfully shoved his face away. "Don't you let Minna see you doing that. She'll be certain that you've taken leave of your senses."

"I am saying good morning to my son," Jake said with mock hurt. "What is so wrong with that?"

Hattie smiled at him, placing a hand on his whiskered cheek. "Not a thing," she said, arching one eyebrow. "Except that you keep saying 'our son,' like you're certain it's going to be a boy."

Jake handed her a soda cracker, like he had every morning for the past six months and beamed. "I would love to have a little girl, especially if she's as beautiful as her mother." He kissed her fingertips. "But I have to admit that I would love to have a son." He squeezed her hand. "Just wishful thinking, I guess."

Hattie chewed slowly on the cracker and pushed herself upright. Although the morning sickness was not as bad as it had been during her first trimester, the mornings were still the worst. She pushed through a wave of nausea and grimaced slightly.

"Are you all right? Should I get Minna?" Jake asked.

She shook her head, "No. I'm fine. It's no worse than usual." The words were barely from her mouth when she felt her stomach muscles tighten. Clutching her abdomen, she made a small grunt of pain.

"What is it?" Jake's voice rose in fear.

She waited for the pain to subside; her eyes closed. "I think I just had a contraction," she said fearfully.

Jake felt his heart clench. *It's too soon*, he thought. *Dear God, it's too soon.*

Hattie reached for his hand. "Go tell Minna—and then you need to get Rose." She could see that he didn't want to leave so she did her best to reassure him. Placing a protective hand over their child she said, "We're going to be all right. Now go."

By the time Jake returned to the cabin with Rose, Hattie's contractions were fifteen minutes apart and Minna looked like she was in labour herself.

"What took you so long?" Minna exclaimed as soon as they entered the cabin.

Rose hurried to the bedroom where Hattie was bent over the bed and panting, beads of perspiration collecting on her forehead. Seeing the panic in her friend's eyes, Rose placed a comforting hand on her back.

"It's too soon," Hattie whispered to Rose. "And it's happening so fast."

Rose brushed the damp hair from Hattie's forehead and shushed her. "You're at least seven months along. This baby has got more than a fighting chance." She helped Hattie get back into bed, bolstering the pillows behind her. "I had Ida in four hours. Did I tell you that?" she forced a laugh. "That girl came on like a runaway horse and hasn't stopped since." Despite her pain, Hattie managed a weak smile.

"What can I do?" Minna was hovering at the foot of the bed, anxious to be useful.

"We'll need some warm water, soap, twine, scissors, and as many clean sheets that you can find," Rose said. "Boil the scissors," she added. "And ask Jake if he has an oil cloth and some leather straps would be helpful, too."

"Leather straps?" Hattie asked, her eyes wide.

"You'll need them for when it's time to push," Rose explained. "Helps to have something to hang on to." Rose watched Hattie's face go white. She tucked the blanket around her friend. "Women do this every day. You're going to do just fine." Rose wondered who she was trying to convince; herself or Hattie? She was putting on a brave face, but inside she was quaking to her bones. Lord, give me strength and the wisdom to bring this baby into the world. She breathed the prayer over and over as she and Minna assembled the room, preparing it for Hattie to deliver.

Jake and Henry sat on the front porch of the cabin. Henry did his best to make conversation; he told Jake about the boarding house, how all the rooms were full, and how well Lena was running the new venture. He talked about anything that would distract but Jake heard nothing but the agonizing sounds coming from behind the door.

Another moan of pain reached their ears, making Henry grimace.

"How long has it been?" Jake asked again.

Henry glanced at the pocket watch that he held in his hand. "About three hours since Rose got here," he said, shaking his head. How did women do this again and again? It was beyond his imagining.

The front door opened and Jake jumped to his feet. Minna came out, carrying a tray of sandwiches and hot tea. Jake ignored the food and asked, "How is she?"

Minna smiled. "She's doing good, all things considered." Setting the tray down, she said. "Rose doesn't think it will be much longer."

"Really?" Jake felt his heart jump in his throat. "And the baby?" He was terrified to ask but the words came out anyway.

Walking over to Jake, Minna placed a hand on his shoulder. "God only knows." She turned to go back into the cabin, giving him a little squeeze. "Try to eat something. There is nothing we can do but wait and pray. Hattie is doing the rest."

Hattie stared at the embroidered daisies on the small blanket by her face. She counted the yellow stitches, one by one, to take her mind off the pain. When the contraction was over, she exhaled a long breath.

"That's it," Rose encouraged. "You're doing just fine."

Hattie was bent over the bed, her forearms braced on the mattress. "They're coming quick now," she panted, reaching her hand out to Rose. "I'm so glad you're here. I don't think I could have done this without you." Her grip tightened as another contraction began. Rose rubbed Hattie's back, wishing again that they had sent for the doctor, but it was far too late now.

Another pain hit Hattie, this time accompanied by a great gush of fluid. "What's happening?" Hattie cried, staring at the puddle between her feet.

Rose smiled. "Nothing that isn't supposed to happen. Your water just broke. That means it's almost time." She turned to Minna. "Let's get the oil cloth on the bed." Together Minna and Rose spread the cloth over the bare mattress and then covered it with a soft flannel sheet. Then, they helped Hattie climb into bed.

"How will I know it's time to push?" Hattie asked when she was settled.

Rose chuckled, despite the situation. "Trust me. You'll know."

Rose wasn't lying. Just moments later Hattie felt an overwhelming need to bear down. "Rose," she cried. "I need to push."

Rose guided Hattie's hands to the bedrails and into the leather straps that were looped there. Then she helped lift her nightgown to her waist. "I can see the head!" she exclaimed. Rubbing Hattie's swollen belly, she said, "Okay, on the next pain, you push that baby out as hard as you can."

Hattie nodded, unable to speak. When the next contraction hit, Hattie pushed with all that was within her. A guttural moan escaped her as Rose watched the head emerge, pink fluid staining the sheet crimson. Rose ignored everything except for the baby. With the next push, the baby's head emerged fully.

"The head is out," Rose said. "Now don't push."

"What's wrong?" Hattie cried.

"Nothing at all," Rose reassured. "I just want to get his mouth clear." Rose inserted her pinky finger into the baby's mouth and removed as much mucus as she could. "There you go," she whispered. You're almost here." The shoulders emerged next and with a massive gush the infant slipped into the world and Rose's waiting hands.

"It's a boy!" Rose and Minna exclaimed together. He was tiny, not much bigger than a fledgling, but he was pink and perfect. Minna handed Rose two pieces of twine, which she tied about three inches apart on the umbilical cord. Cutting the cord with the scissors and then carefully turning him over, she expelled the last of any fluid in his lungs. *Come on*, she thought, imploring him to breathe. When he didn't make a sound, she gave his little bottom a tiny smack. His arms flailed wildly and then suddenly he let out a lusty cry. "He's breathing." The enormity of what she just witnessed overwhelmed her and her tears flowed freely.

"Is he all right?" Hattie tried to lift her head off the pillow, but she was exhausted.

Minna kissed Hattie's forehead and said, "He's small, but he seems to be breathing just fine."

Rose carefully placed the baby on Hattie's chest and Minna covered them both with a quilt that had been warming by the fire.

Hattie stared at her son, marvelling that this perfect little creature was hers. "Oh, my," she said, kissing the top of his damp head. The urge to kiss him was undeniable. "I can't believe you're here, little man."

Rose and Minna sat on either side of the new mother, revelling in the perfect moment. "You did good," Rose said, wiping her tears with the back of her hand. Hattie gazed down at her son and then at these two extraordinary women.

"How can I ever thank you?" she said to them both, her words transcending beyond this day.

"Well, now that the hard part is done, I can tell you I was terrified!" Rose laughed, her relief coming in waves.

"I would have never known." Hattie shook her head in amazement.

When the baby snuffled at their laughter, Rose said, "I think there's an anxious daddy out there waiting to meet his son. Let's get you cleaned up and give this boy his first bath."

Minna was beaming when she came out on the porch for the second time. "It's a boy." She said to a pacing Jake. "You have a son."

Jake sat hard, like someone had shifted the earth. "I have a son?"

Minna nodded, joy spilling from her heart. She held out her hands to them both. "Come inside and meet him."

When the men entered the room, they would never have guessed of the drama that had unfolded only an hour before. Minna had cleaned like a whirling dervish, removing the straps, rinsing bloody sheets, and disposing of the afterbirth while Rose bathed and diapered the baby. They changed Hattie into a clean gown and finally placed the swaddled infant into her arms.

For a long moment, Jake was speechless. He saw Hattie smiling, looking as lovely as the Madonna, with a dark-haired baby in her arms. Finally finding his voice, he asked. "He's all right? You're both all right?" He seemed unable to process this new reality.

"We're fine," Hattie said, lifting the baby to him.

Jake gingerly took the bundle from her, mesmerized by this tiny miracle that fit into his palms. "He's all right?" he repeated, looking at Rose.

Rose nodded. "He seems fine and I'm guessing about six pounds." Jake hefted the baby a little until Minna gave him a glare.

Rose said to Hattie, "You may have been further along than you thought, so that would account for him coming earlier than you expected.

Jake sat in the chair next to the bed, nestling his son into the crook of his arm, unable to take his eyes off the newborn.

Rose looked at the happy little family and asked, "So have you two decided on a name?"

Hattie started to laugh and then cringed, holding her stomach. "We haven't been able to agree on any name yet. His favourites were Nathaniel and," she rolled her eyes, "Gertrude."

Rose covered her mouth to smother a laugh. "Well, Nathaniel is not bad," Rose conceded, "but I'll just say I'm glad it's not a girl."

Jake laughed. "I still like my choices over hers." He nudged Hattie softly.

"What's wrong with Elliot or Bertha?" She asked.

He shuddered, "I had a schoolteacher named Bertha who tanned my hide on more than one occasion, so you can't blame me. And I knew a boy named Elliot who was always digging." He put one finger on his nose. "I always wondered how he could mine that far."

Hattie held her stomach to keep it from quaking. "Jake, please stop." She shook her head but still chuckled, "What are we going to name him? We can't call him 'the baby' for the rest of his life."

Watching the two of them, Henry suddenly had a thought. "What about Isaac?" he ventured. Before they could say anything, he continued. "In the Bible it means laughter. When Abraham and Sarah had a baby boy, they couldn't stop laughing so they named him Isaac."

Jake and Hattie exchanged looks and Hattie asked. "In the Bible… Isaac's mother was Sarah?"

Henry nodded. "It was always one of my favourite Bible stories," he said. "My *mutti* would tell it so as to make us laugh."

Jake stood, placing the baby in Hattie's arms. He walked over to Henry and shook his hand. "What do you think?" he asked, turning to Hattie.

"I think it's perfect." Nodding at Henry, she said, "Thank you Henry." Kissing their beautiful son, she said. "Welcome to our family, Isaac."

Jake could not stop staring at his son and marvelling at the newborn's perfection. Isaac was sound asleep on the bed, his soft cheek pressed against the mattress and his legs, still tight as clock springs, were tucked underneath him. His downy hair was dark and stuck up in tufts around his head like a halo. Jake touched the baby's fist with his pinky, and Isaac's impossibly tiny fingers opened, then closed, around his father's.

Gazing across his son, Jake looked at Hattie and took in the same dark hair strewn across the pillow. She too, was sound asleep, exhausted from giving birth just three days ago. The baby wriggled slightly and Hattie opened one eye.

Jake held a finger to his lips. "He's okay," he whispered.

Hattie winced and sat up very slowly. "Is it morning?"

Jake nodded. "Yes, but it's still early." He gestured to the other room. "Minna's not even up yet. I'm sorry; I didn't mean to wake you."

Hattie smiled at Jake and then at their son, her heart overflowing. She picked up the warm bundle and held him to her, taking in his newborn scent. She winced again, her breasts aching. "You didn't wake me. I'm expecting this little one to be hungry soon."

Jake slid into bed beside them and for a perfect moment they were silent, as if afraid to break the spell they were miraculously living. "Well, before my son has his breakfast, I want to give you something." He pulled a small box from his shirt pocket and handed it to her. Hattie's eyes grew wide, but she had no words. "I'm sorry it took so long," Jake apologized. "I had Rose buy it for me and it took longer than we expected."

Hattie took the box and opened it to reveal a beautiful gold locket laying in blue satin. "Oh, Jake," she whispered. "It's gorgeous."

Jake lifted the locket from the satin. "Rose had them engrave lilacs on the front. I know they're your favourite." Turning the locket over, he showed her the inscription: "Jake & Sarah, October 1920." Her eyes brimmed with tears when he opened the locket, revealing their photos that Rose had inserted inside. He kissed her cheek softly. "I can't imagine my life without you. Will you marry me, Sarah McBride?"

Hattie had known all along that this was coming, yet his official proposal hit her with the force of a tidal wave. She cried and nodded, kissing him until Isaac began to protest.

Jake slipped the locket around Hattie's neck and then watched as she nursed their son. They stayed there until the sun came up over the mountain and the smell of Minna's fresh coffee wafted in from the kitchen.

CHAPTER FIFTY-FOUR

COALMONT, BRITISH COLUMBIA—NOVEMBER 1920

HATTIE GENTLY LIFTED HER baby boy over her shoulder and began to stroke his back, attempting to coax a burp from his little body. Despite arriving too early to the world, Isaac Henry Pearson was thriving and, to reiterate that fact, emitted a resounding little belch.

Bouncing from foot to foot, Ida hovered near them both, waiting for the baby to be done his breakfast. Ida's mother had made it very clear that she was, in no uncertain terms, to ask to hold the baby. "Aunt Hattie may offer but you are not to ask. Is that clear?" Rose had reiterated this to Ida on the trip to Jake's cabin, but it took every ounce of her will power to be silent.

When the baby burped again, Ida giggled and Hattie smiled indulgently at the little girl. To say that Ida was taken with baby Isaac would be a gross understatement. From the moment she first met Hattie and Jake's baby boy, she had been smitten.

Winking at Rose, Hattie asked, "Would you like to hold him, Ida?" The girl nodded so hard that her braids bounced. Hattie stifled a laugh and stood to pass the baby to Ida who had settled herself on a nearby chair. The moment that Isaac was placed in her arms Ida was lost to the rest of the world.

With Isaac settled, Hattie walked across the room and sat next to Rose. Tucking her feet under her, she reached for the cup of tea that Minna had set out before. Rose watched her take a small sip and close her eyes.

"You getting any sleep?" Rose asked.

Hattie opened one eye to peer at Rose and managed a smile. "Some," she said, "but he's still not sleeping through the night."

Rose smiled in empathy. "Well, he's only a month old. Every baby is different." She patted Hattie's knee. "Try to enjoy this time. I know it's hard but, believe me…" she nodded towards Ida, "…sometimes I feel like Ida was born just a few months ago. They are grown before you know it."

The little girl looked up at the mention of her name. "Mama?"

"Yes, dear."

Ida sighed dramatically. "Do I hafta go with Papa and you and Uncle Jake to Princeton?" She kissed baby Isaac on the cheek. "Can't I stay here with Aunt Hattie? I could be a big help." She turned a thousand candle-watt smile on Hattie, just in case it would help.

Rose smiled. "I know you would be sweetheart, but Minna is here to help Hattie." She walked over to Ida and crouched down so that they were face to face. "And what about me?" She pointed to her chest. "I would be terrible lonely with no one to talk to except Papa and Uncle Jake. She winked at Hattie and said, "I'm sure that all those two will talk about is cattle and ranches. And then maybe they'll talk about cattle again."

Ida giggled and conceded. "Papa does talk about cows a lot."

At that moment, Jake and Emmett walked into the cabin. "Wagon's all loaded," Emmett said, after closing the door. Hattie stood and walked over to Jake. "You're sure you'll be all right while I'm gone?" Jake asked, giving her a quick hug.

"I have Minna and Henry's going to come every day to check on us," Hattie said, walking over to take the baby from Ida's reluctant arms. "What more could we need?" She smiled at the sleeping infant. "Besides, you and Emmett need to concentrate on finding the perfect ranch for us."

Emmett chuckled. "Hopefully we find you a place with a perfect price tag as well."

Jake took his son from Hattie and gently brushed the baby's forehead with a whiskery kiss. Hattie watched him, still awed that she was loved by this gentle man. After losing all faith, her heart had been healed; only one thing was still missing.

As if reading her mind, Jake said quietly. "Pray we find a place we can afford because I don't want to hide any more. I want everyone to know that we have a son and I can't wait to make an honest woman of you." She laughed, but he was serious. "Once I find us our own land, we'll be able to start a proper life together, starting with finding a preacher."

Hattie's heart swelled at his words. "Promise?"

He handed Isaac back to her and said, "If it's the last thing I do."

For two days, Hattie could not forget what Emmett said about the cost of buying their own land; and on the third morning she woke with her mind decided. Walking out the small bedroom, dressed for the day, she was glad to see that Minna was up and Henry was already in the yard, tending to the stock. She smiled when he saw her through the window and she waved for him to come inside.

A few minutes later, he was sitting at the kitchen table, a mug of steaming coffee cradled between his cold hands. "It's chilly out there," he said. "Sure feels like snow."

Hattie poured herself a cup as well, then sat down beside him. "Henry," she began with no explanation, "I need you to take me down to town today."

He looked perplexed. "You want to go to Coalmont? I thought you didn't want anyone to know you had a baby."

She shook her head. "I don't. That's why we'll leave Isaac here with Minna."

"Leave what with Minna?" Minna said as she came in the back door." She set a basket of eggs on the table by the door and then looked at the two of them. "What are you two planning?"

Hattie pulled a chair out and motioned for Minna to sit. "I want to go to town today. One last time."

Minna looked dubious. "Why now? Shouldn't you wait until Jake gets back?"

Hattie shook her head. "Once Jake gets back, I'm hoping we'll be moving right away. He'll be too busy packing us up. And the last thing he'll want to do is go to Coalmont. Everything has been going so well; I don't want to take the chance that he'll run into his brother."

"Did you hear?" Henry interjected. "Simon's working at the hotel."

Hattie looked shocked. Henry couldn't resist a grin. "Lena told me. Apparently, he's in debt to his eyeballs."

At the mention of Lena's name, Hattie added, "And I can't leave without saying goodbye to Lena."

She forced a smile, but Minna wasn't buying it. "What is it you're not telling us?" she asked.

Hattie pressed her fingers to her lips and then answered. "The money I stole from the brothel; it's still hidden in the barn."

Henry's eyes widened. "It is? I thought you used it to pay Simon for his half of the brothel?"

Hattie shook her head. "I scraped up everything that was left and hoped it was enough for Simon. To tell you the truth, I was shocked that he took it. He must have been more desperate for cash than we realized." She took a sip of coffee. "I had full intentions of taking the money out of the barn after we paid him off," she explained, "but Simon was always lurking around; there never seemed to be a good time. I knew no one would find it so I left it there." She smiled ruefully. "Then I found out I was pregnant."

Minna whistled. "It's got to be a nice sum after all these years," she said. "Does Jake know about it?"

Hattie looked chagrinned. "No," she admitted. "But not because I didn't want to tell him. I decided to save it for a wedding present. To surprise him. When Emmett suggested that we may have trouble finding a ranch we could afford, I knew I needed to get it soon. She was quiet for a long moment, "You know, there is a small part of me that wants to leave it there; it represents a time I'd sooner forget.

Minna shook her head. "You took that money for us and you know it. So that we could leave and start anew." She pressed her wrinkled hand over Hattie's. "You were trying to make it right and you did the best in a situation that was beyond your control." She looked at Hattie with love. "Now you can use that money for your new family. And no one deserves it more."

Hattie's eyes grew bright listening to her words. She asked Minna, "Are you ever sorry you said 'yes' to my job offer?"

Minna chuckled. "When I married Nathan, I knew I was bound for an adventure. Then, when he died, I thought the adventure was over." She squeezed Hattie's hand with affection. "But one day I sold a pie to this beautiful young woman." She closed her eyes remembering that day so long ago in Princeton and smiled. "You, Jake, and Isaac are the family I never thought I'd have." She turned to Henry and covered his hand with her other. "And you too, dear boy." She let go their hands and wiped her eyes with the corner of her apron. "I've not regretted it for a single moment."

CHAPTER FIFTY-FIVE

COALMONT, BRITISH COLUMBIA—NOVEMBER 21, 1920

SIMON STRUGGLED TO PUT on his overcoat as he made his way down the hotel steps. He had worked behind the bar, serving 'near beer' until two o'clock in the morning and then, before he knew, had gambled away his tip money in an all-night poker game. This morning all he had to show for his work was a fuzzy head and a tongue that felt like it was covered in fur. He contemplated staying in bed all afternoon but the confines of the small room he rented was driving him mad. Besides, all he did was lie there, dwelling on Hattie and Jake and the life he felt was his due. Every day he experienced afresh the humiliation of his brother taking everything that should have been his. He needed some fresh air to clear his head.

As he began to exit the hotel, Simon saw a familiar buggy entering the town limits. He stopped. It was that blasted Henry Thiessen. Simon took a step back into the shadows, watching the man drive by. It was then that Simon saw that Henry wasn't alone. There was a hooded passenger sitting in back, bundled against the cold. Simon watched the retreating four-seater, focusing on the mysterious rider. He didn't recognize the heavy woolen cape, but long strands of black hair had escaped the hood. Simon straightened and he couldn't believe his luck. Hattie McBride had come back to town.

Simon was stupefied. After months of believing she was gone with his money, here she was, in Coalmont right in front of him. His conversation with Nellie came back to mind and his rage, so near the surface, erupted. Slamming his hat on his head and abandoning all reason, he ran to follow Henry's buggy.

Moments later, Simon peered around the corner of the old barn beside Hattie's Place and saw Henry and Hattie talking in the wagon. Straining to listen, he heard Hattie say, "I won't be long, Henry. Go tell Lena I'll be there in a minute. We shouldn't stay long. Jake said he'd be back today." Henry hesitated but she said, "Go on. I'm fine."

Watching them from the shadows, Simon bided his time. Henry helped Hattie from the buggy and then, much to Simon's relief, Henry left Hattie alone and entered the house. As Hattie walked past the corral, she took a moment to say hello to the Appaloosa mare, running her fingers under the horse's mane. The horse nudged at her for more affection and Hattie laughed. The sound of her laugh reminded Simon of their first days in Greenwood when she still loved him. *You should be mine*, he thought as a wave a desire swept over him. He moaned softly and she turned, glancing around, but he was in the shadows and didn't see him. Seeing nothing, Hattie turned and walked into the barn. When she was out of sight, he moved like a cat, slipping in behind her.

"Hello, Hattie," he said quietly.

She whirled at the unexpected sound of his voice, her hand pressed to her throat. "What are you doing here?" She said.

"I believe you owe me something," he said, running his gaze up and down her body, her gorgeous black hair tumbled loose around her face.

She knew he was after more than just money. Hattie opened her mouth to scream, but Simon was too fast. In a heartbeat he was behind her, with one hand on her throat and the other over her mouth. "Where is it?" he hissed. His voice was deadly quiet. Her eyes widened and she nodded. Thinking she was going to confess, he removed his hand but then, to his utter amazement, she bit him.

His retaliation was instantaneous. Turning her, he slapped her face and her heart constricted with fear. Before she could react, he covered her mouth again and dragged her to the old cabin beside the brothel. She fought like a feral cat, but he was so much stronger. When they were in the cabin, he slammed the door and shoved her to a chair.

"Where is it?" he demanded again.

"I don't know what you're talking about," she said, defiance in her voice.

"I know you stole from me," he said, his face inches from hers. He grabbed her shoulders and shook her, as if the answer would fall from her, but instead he caught sight of something gold. "What's this?" he said, hooking a finger around the chain.

"None of your business," she said, slapping his hand away. His finger was still hooked on the chain and when she hit him the delicate strand snapped. Hattie's locket bounced on the floor. Simon reached down to pick up the locket and without a glance, slipped it into his pocket. "Collateral," he said, patting his pocket with his hand. Simon took a deep breath to calm himself and then took a cigar from his inside vest pocket. He lit it and took a long pull before he spoke again. "I know you were skimming from the brothel profits. That money is rightfully mine and you're not leaving here until you tell me what you did with it." He turned to lock the door to ensure they would not be disturbed.

Jumping at the opportunity while his back was turned, Hattie lunged for the poker beside the wood stove. She swung it wildly, hitting Simon on the small of his back, felling him to his knees.

As he shrieked in pain, she raced for the door, groping for the key, but she wasn't fast enough. His hand caught the edge of her skirt and he pulled in desperation, yanking her back into the room. Her arms wind-milled wildly as she tried to regain her footing, but it was too late. There was a sickening sound as her head hit the edge of the cast iron stove. Her body landed on the cabin floor with a thud and was still.

The cabin was remarkably silent after their struggle and Simon could hear his own laboured breathing.

"Hattie?" Simon stared at her inert body. "Hattie?" he said again, his voice rising with fear. He pulled himself up, rubbing his bruised back. "Hattie?" he said once more, nudging her with the toe of his boot, but still she did not move. With his heart racing, Simon crouched down and shook her. With the movement, her head lolled to one side. That's when Simon saw the blood. It was everywhere, pooling under her black hair, dark red rivulets filling the cracks in the pine floor, like a spider's web.

Staring in horror, Simon fell back. "Dammit," he said under his breath. "Dammit. Dammit." He managed to stand and ran a shaking hand through his hair. Trembling, he drew the flask from his vest pocket and gulped the fiery liquid. *Think*, he commanded himself, *think*. It wouldn't be long before Henry came to look for Hattie and Simon knew that no one would believe that what happened here had been an accident. He stared for a long moment at the silver flask in his hand and then, without thinking, he poured the remainder of the contents over the table. Picking up a discarded newspaper and, taking one last puff of his cigar, he held the paper to the red hot embers. It caught instantly, and he tossed it into the centre of amber liquid that was now dripping on the floor. The whisky caught fire and he watched it for a moment as it burned, the flames licking the table like a rabid dog. Sparing one last look at the woman lying on the floor, he turned and ran for his life.

CHAPTER FIFTY-SIX

COALMONT, BRITISH COLUMBIA—NOVEMBER 21, 1920

HENRY AND LENA WERE chatting in the parlour when the front door burst open. "Simon's old cabin is on fire!" Nellie exclaimed as she burst through the door.

Henry jumped to his feet. "What?" He wasted no time and was out the door in moments, Lena and Nellie racing close behind.

They ran up to see the entire structure already engulfed in flames. There were a few men from the town with buckets in hand, but it was already too late. All they could do was make sure that the nearby barn and boarding house didn't catch fire, too.

Henry stood for a moment, watching the blaze, and then his heart clenched. Where was Hattie? He whirled around, scanning the surrounding yard but didn't see her. She must still be in the barn, he reasoned and ran there.

"Who are you looking for?" Lena panted as she chased after him into the barn.

"Hattie. She said she'd only be a minute and then she was going to come in to say her goodbyes." He turned again, hoping he had missed her. He scanned the crowd that had gathered, but she was nowhere to be seen.

"What was she doing in the barn?" Lena asked. Henry had an uneasy premonition as he walked to the corner of the milking stall. His fingers ran along the logs to a point where the chinking was loose and then pried it free. Lena watched, amazed, as he drew out a small tin box. "She came for this," Henry said. "And she wouldn't have left without it." Henry's unease grew tenfold as they walked out the barn. The smoke from the cabin fire had now filled the air, settling around them like a heavy, rank blanket.

"Henry," Lena tugged on his arm. "What is wrong?" She could see the fear in his face.

"I'm not sure," he said. "But Hattie came for this. Why would she leave without it?" He tucked the tin into his coat pocket.

Lena looked in the corral. "Dolly is gone," she remarked.

"She is?" Henry felt his heart lift for a moment. Maybe Hattie decided to go back without him, and she took Dolly. Everyone knew that the mare was her favourite. Henry turned to Lena and gave her a quick kiss on the cheek. "I'm going back to Jake's," he told her. "I need to find Hattie."

Simon was panicking. Images of Hattie's lifeless body were flashing in his mind and he fought to keep the bile from rising in his throat. The horse underneath him caught a hoof on a fallen branch and Simon clutched the reins and mane in a death grip. He was, by no means, a proficient rider, but when he saw the horse in the corral by the barn, he grasped at the only opportunity he felt he had. He took the nearest bridle hooked on the barn wall and prayed that he'd be able to stay on long enough to get out of this desperate situation.

Once he had reached a safe enough distance from town, he reined in the horse to catch his breath and regroup. He saw the dark smoke billowing from the east end of town and grimaced.

Damn you Hattie, he thought. *I had it all planned for us. This was supposed to be our destiny.*

Thinking of Hattie, he remembered the necklace that he had taken from her and pulled it from his pocket. He held the gold heart up to examine it and, turning it over in his palm, read the inscription: Jake and Sarah, October 1920. Seeing his brother's name renewed his panic. There was no doubt that Jake would see him in hell when he discovered what he had done. He couldn't let that happen.

The horse pawed the ground, anxious to get back to her warm barn. It was turning colder and already Simon could feel the frigid air seeping into his bones through his suit jacket and his feet were going numb. He was in such a panic to get away from the fire that he had left with nothing but the clothes on his back and not a cent in his pocket. He pressed his fists to his mouth, suppressing a scream of frustration. The horse pawed again, unaccustomed to this strange behaviour and she pulled on the reins.

"Just a minute," he said to her, yanking her back. "Let me think." Thrusting his icy hands deep into his pockets, he felt the warm locket. His gaze travelled north and then, seeing the mountain looming in front of him, he smiled a thin smile and knew what to do.

The cabin seemed quiet and deserted when Simon rode to the edge of the clearing. He had heard Hattie say to Henry that she wanted to get back before Jake did and Simon was counting on that. It would be much easier to search the place without having to deal with his brother as well.

He should have reined the horse east and headed for Princeton, but Simon was a sweet talker; he could talk anyone into doing anything, including himself. By the time he reached Jake's cabin he had convinced himself that he would take whatever he could find from it. Jake had taken everything from him; it was the least his brother owed him, he reasoned. He'd go down south, he decided, maybe to Nevada where there was lots of gambling and plenty of women. He'd change his name and start all over again. It was the perfect plan.

Simon silently slid off the horse and looped the reins over the nearest rail. He crouched low, making way to a small cabin and carefully peered inside. He saw no one, so he crept onto the porch and, turning the knob, let himself in. The inside of the cabin was warm and it smelled like bread; instantly he knew that he was not alone. He was about to turn around when a snuffling sound caught his attention. He turned to see a small cradle in the corner of the room. He walked over in disbelief and peered down at a tiny dark-haired baby. A thousand thoughts ran through his mind and then the baby cried.

Simon turned, ready to bolt through the door, when he came face to face with Minna.

"What are you doing in here?" She tried not to yell, but her voice was shaking.

Simon pointed at the baby, saying the first thing that came to mind. "Whose baby is that?" he demanded.

Minna snorted but said nothing.

He stared at the baby, refusing to believe it, but he knew. "It's Hattie's, isn't it?"

Minna ignored him and instead bent to pick up Isaac and rocked him, cuddling him close to her soft body.

"Hattie's been living here with Jake? All this time?" He was incredulous. How could he have been so stupid? Suddenly his eyes widened. "Where's the money?" he said to Minna. Minna's rocking stopped for only a moment, but it was long enough for Simon to notice. "You know where it is, don't you?" He took a threatening step towards her and the baby.

"Don't come any closer," Minna warned.

"Or you'll what?" he sneered. "Can't do much with that baby in your arms, now can you?" He held out his hands and said, "Why don't you just give him to me? I'll hold him while you go fetch me my money."

"Step away from my son." Jake's words were low and ominous. He was standing in the doorway, fury clouding his face like a thunderhead.

Simon took a step back and raised both hands in mock surrender. "Your son?" Simon cocked one eyebrow. "That's a pretty bold statement, considering that his mother was a whore."

Jake was across the room in a moment, his fury released like lit dynamite. "How dare you come to my home and insult my family!" Jake's fist caught Simon on the jaw and sent him flying across the room.

"Your family," Simon shouted, as he righted himself, "should have been mine." He lunged and shouldered Jake in the stomach, sending him backwards, knocking over chairs and skittering them across the floor.

Jake pushed a chair out of the way as he stood, his fists balled at his sides, resisting the urge to hit his brother again. "What's the matter Simon? Didn't get your way this time?" he taunted. "Our whole lives, you were the chosen one. You could do no wrong. You only stole Deborah from me because you couldn't stand the thought that I might be happy." Jake spit blood from his mouth. "You don't want a family. You're far too selfish for that. You just want *my* family." He took Isaac from Minna and his voice was low, "Get out. Now. I don't ever want to see you near me or anyone I love again."

Simon's mind raced. He assumed that Jake's anger was because of Hattie, but obviously Jake hadn't heard about the fire. "You're right." Simon hung his head in contrition, hoping to placate his brother for just a few more moments. "I had decided to leave but," he cleared his throat, "I'm a little short on cash." He said the words meekly, hoping he sounded remorseful since he was never very good at it.

Jake stared at his brother and marvelled at his duplicity. He could not fathom that this man carried the same blood in his veins. "Fine," Jake said. "Anything to get you away from us."

Simon was elated and truly believed he had gotten away with murder when Henry ran into the cabin. He stopped instantly when he saw Simon. Fearing the worst, he asked Minna, "Is Hattie here?"

Minna shook her head. "No. I thought she was coming back with you."

Henry felt his stomach begin to churn.

"Henry?" Jake said, with growing unease. "Where is Hattie?"

Henry said, "We went down to Coalmont today." His voice started to shake. "She said she was only going to be a minute…"

"What happened?" Jake demanded.

"There was a fire. Simon's old cabin," Henry exclaimed. "I looked everywhere for her, Jake, but I couldn't find her." His voice cracked. Henry had never been so afraid. He whirled on Simon. "Where is Hattie?" he shouted, reaching to grab Simon by his shirtfront.

Simon took a step back. "I don't know," he whispered, but Henry heard the fear in his voice.

"You're lying!" Jake screamed at his brother. "What happened to Hattie?"

"It was an accident," Simon blurted out the words before he could stop himself. "We were in the cabin and she fell." He took another step backwards towards the door.

Jake felt his blood run cold. "She fell and you just left her there?" Prickles of shock crept over him and he had to force himself to say the words, "You burned down the cabin?" The bile rose in his throat. "With her inside?"

Henry's cry of rage filled the room and he charged towards Simon but, before he could reach him, Simon pulled a small revolver from his boot. He pointed it straight at Jake's chest and the baby he held there.

"One more step," he warned Henry, "and they both die." Henry stopped instantly and dropped his hands. "All I want," Simon said shakily, "is my money."

Henry nodded and slowly placed his hand inside his coat pocket. "I've got your money," he said. "Just don't shoot."

The shot rang out so loudly that for moments, it reverberated within the cabin walls. Isaac wailed and Jake waited for the pain to begin, but it didn't. Instead, it was Simon who had a look of astonishment on his face. He took one step forward and then, without another word, crumpled to the floor.

Jake and Henry looked behind the fallen man and saw Minna standing there. She held Jake's hunting rifle in her trembling hands, tears of sorrow streaming down her cheeks.

CHAPTER FIFTY-SEVEN

PRINCETON, BRITISH COLUMBIA—PRESENT DAY

THE ROOM WAS SILENT when Isaac finished. "My father and Henry moved Simon's body to the mine that night and covered the entrance," he said.

Hannah shook her head, overwhelmed. "But why hide the evidence?" she asked. "Simon was going to kill you and your father. Minna was protecting you. It would have been self-defence."

Isaac smiled. "It was because of me and Minna, that my father decided to hide the body. My mother was the love of his life; if the police had been involved, there would have been an investigation. The thought of my mother's past and my parentage being dissected and publicized was more than he could bear." Isaac dabbed at his eyes with his hanky. "I was born out of wedlock and my mother ran a whorehouse. "That secret has stayed in our family until today.

Ed and Hannah exchanged looks but said nothing. Jim continued, "After the murder, my grandfather transferred the mining rights and the land to your great uncle. I think they thought it was best to sever any connection of that land to the Pearson name. Henry agreed—with one stipulation."

Ed asked, "What stipulation?" But he felt he already knew the answer.

Jim said, "That, upon his death, our family would transfer a piece of land to his mother's family."

Ed leaned back in his chair. He let out a long breath and said, "When I was about eight, our family was together at my oma's for dinner. I overheard my parents and great aunts talking about their wayward brother and my oma crying." He smiled ruefully, "I had never heard her cry like that before."

Hannah reached over and held Ed's hand. "That must have been the night they learned of his bequest."

Ed nodded, "A few months later my parents told us that the family had bought some land for a family cabin." He shook his head. "I never imagined that it was a lie."

The room was silent for a moment and then Isaac spoke again. "Your uncle talked about his family a lot. He missed his mother and his sisters every day."

Hannah was confused, "But then why didn't he come home? Why distance himself from people he loved?"

Isaac said, "Partly to protect your family, I suppose. If Simon's body had been found, Henry would have been a material witness to a murder."

Ed agreed, "My family comes from Mennonite heritage. A large portion of our faith is based on peace and pacifism." He steepled his fingers in front of him. "Having a family member involved in murder would have ruined them. Uncle Henry would have realized that."

Isaac said, "There may have been another reason he didn't go home." He grinned a little. "It might have had something to do with his wife."

"His wife!" Ed and Hannah exclaimed together. "He was married?"

"Yes," Isaac said, "to a beautiful woman named Lena."

Both Ed and Hannah were astonished.

Ed finally spoke. "We had no idea."

Isaac said, "Well, hearing you talk of your faith and family, I can't say I'm surprised."

Hannah was mystified. "Why do you say that?"

Isaac said, "When Henry first met Lena, she worked for Hattie."

It took a moment for Hannah to realize what Isaac was saying. "She was a prostitute?" Hannah asked.

"She was." Isaac nodded and continued his story, "When Henry died in '67, the land was transferred back to our family. Minna lived with us, taking care of me and my father until her passing in 1937. No one ever said a thing about Simon Lamont. It seems that no one ever missed him."

Ed said, "I can't believe no one ever discovered him. All this time."

Jim said, "I think, for the first few years, they were probably holding their breath, waiting for his disappearance to be reported. Neither Jake nor Henry went back for a long time, while the body was..." He didn't finish his sentence as they could all imagine. Hannah shuddered involuntarily.

Jim walked over to a small fridge and.pulled out four bottles of beer. He handed one each to Sam, Ed, and Hannah and said, "We should have moved the bones but, understandably, no one was eager to do it. I'd go up there after ever spring thaw and make sure that everything was covered. Put a few more logs and stones over the opening. When Sam told me that you had been asking questions I went there and saw that someone had been in the mine." He looked at Hannah. "I can't believe you found the mine entrance. Or got him out of there." He clinked his bottle to hers. "You must be pretty strong."

Hannah remembered how driven she had been that day and said, "It's amazing what adrenalin will do to your body when you're motivated. All I could think about was getting my husband out of there."

Jim said, "You should know that I moved the bones."

Ed was surprised. "You did?"

"Yes," Jim said. "I buried him here on the ranch."

Hannah looked at Isaac and he smiled back. His fragility hit Hannah hard and she mourned the time he never had with his mother. "There's one thing we haven't shown you yet," said Hannah. Reaching up to the nape of her neck, she undid the clasp of the chain and pulled out the locket that was hidden beneath her blouse. "After I got Ed out of the mine, I went back in."

Jim's head reared back. "You did?" It was his turned to be surprised.

She nodded. "Yes. We weren't sure if we planned on going to the police, so I took some photographs for our own reference." She held out the locket for them all to see. "That's when I found this." She shivered a bit, remembering. "It was in his pocket." Isaac held out a shaky hand to take the necklace but, before he could, Hannah inserted her thumbnail into the edge and popped it open. "It's a locket," she said, placing it in Isaac's waiting palm. "And I believe those are your parents inside."

Isaac began to weep quietly. Jim came and, kneeling beside him, stroked his father's hair as they looked at the photographs together. "My father told me that he had given a locket to my mother when he proposed," Isaac whispered. "He assumed that it had been destroyed in the fire."

"There's one thing I don't understand." Hannah said. "You said Hattie McBride was your mother. So why does the engraving say, 'Jake & Sarah' on the back? Was that her middle name?"

Isaac shook his head. "No. Sarah was her real name; the name she had before she came to Coalmont." He rubbed his thumb over the faces of his parents as he spoke. "Apparently, she planned to change it back to Sarah when they married." His voice broke then, but he continued. "But, as you know, that never happened."

Jim took the warm locket from his father, resentment lining his face. "Simon obviously took it when he killed her." Jim's words were bitter. "You are right, Dad, he was a bastard." He stood, obviously angry now, but Isaac stopped him with a weathered hand.

He placated his son. "It's time that we let go of the past, don't you think? All our secrets have been unearthed." He winked at Ed and Hannah. "Quite literally in fact. Now our family's secret has become yours as well." He looked around the small cabin. "The only people who know what happened to my mother and Simon are in this room. "I think we'll let you two decide what you want to do with it."

CHAPTER FIFTY-EIGHT

PRINCETON, BRITISH COLUMBIA—PRESENT DAY

Isaac Pearson passed away peacefully in his sleep two weeks later. It was a beautiful summer day when they laid him to rest in the Princeton cemetery beside his beloved wife, Ida.

Sam stood with Ed and Hannah beside their graves. "Aunt Ida said she loved him from the moment he was born." Sam said, "She was six years older than him, but that didn't seem to matter to either one of them. When she got cancer, she told me about the family secret. She knew I'd look out for them. I'm sorry I couldn't come clean with you sooner."

Ed put a hand on his friend's shoulder. "No worries. But I was wondering later, why you told me so much about Hattie when we met at the hotel? Why admit you knew anything about her?"

Sam shrugged. "At the time I didn't know that you had fallen into the mine. It wasn't until Jim told me that the mine entrance had been disturbed that we started to wonder if you were involved."

"I'm sorry, too," Ed said. "I should have trusted you."

"Guess we were both looking out for our families," Sam surmised. "And that's what's most important."

Jim came over to where they were standing. "Thank you both for coming," he said to Ed and Hannah. "Dad was so grateful that he met you both."

Sam said, "I think he knew his time was up soon." He smiled at the couple. "He's the one who asked me to bring you to the cabin."

"We're so glad you did," Hannah said. "It was good to hear the truth about Uncle Henry."

Ed added, "It's nice to know that his family was important to him. And in his way, he was trying to protect us, too." Ed glanced around the cemetery to make sure they were alone before he continued. "We want you to know," he said quietly, "that Hannah and I have decided to keep your secret."

Jim smiled, but Ed saw the relief on his face.

"There's no one alive that it would matter to," Ed reasoned.

"The only part that bothers me," said Hannah "is that no one will know Hattie's real story. People will always think that she was just some prostitute and that no one cared that she was murdered." She looked around the cemetery and then was reminded of Hattie's grave in Granite Creek. "You know," she said, "when we found her grave, there was a dried bouquet of flowers laying by her tombstone."

Jim smiled a knowing smile, "My father told me that my grandfather went there every year to place flowers on her grave. She was the love of his life and we have continued to remember her for him. Don't worry about the memory of my grandmother." He looked around them, taking in the family that had gathered to celebrate the life of their patriarch. "Her memory will live on, in all these people."

CHAPTER FIFTY-NINE

ABBOTSFORD, BRITISH COLUMBIA—PRESENT DAY

HANNAH AND ED WALKED down the hallway and stopped when they reached Aunt Elsie's room. Ed knocked softly on the door before they entered and saw Aunt Elsie, laying in her bed, her eyes closed.

"Looks like she's having a nap," Ed whispered. "Maybe we should come back later today."

"I'm not asleep," Elsie said, without opening her eyes. "Just resting a bit." She smiled at them both and motioned for them to come in. "Don't even think about leaving without a proper visit," she chided.

Walking to the side of the bed, Hannah placed a kiss on Elsie's wrinkled cheek. "How are you doing today?"

Elsie smiled. "I'm still here, so I can't complain." She laughed, patting the bed so that Hannah would sit next to her. "How are you two doing?" she asked, always eager to hear their news.

Hannah apologized. "I'm sorry we haven't been to see you for a while. We had a lot going on, but things are back to normal," Hannah explained without elaborating further.

Kissing Elsie as well, Ed said, "But we brought you something."

Hannah drew the old Bible from her purse and placed it on Elsie's lap. "We thought you might like to have this," Hannah said. "It was your brother's."

Elsie's eyes grew bright, but she shook her head. "No." she said. "This wasn't Henry's. It was Papa's."

Hannah and Ed exchanged looks. "But we found it in Uncle Henry's suitcase," Ed explained.

Elsie's smile was sad. "Papa put it there." She wiped away the tears that threatened. "They were so angry at each other and both too proud to forgive." She picked up the old leather book and hugged it to her chest. Papa loved this Bible, but he wanted Henry to have something from home. Something to remind him of where he came from." She laughed a small laugh. "I saw him put it in the suitcase." She turned the pages, seeing the many verses that Henry had underlined. "I'm so glad to know that he kept it." She closed the book and rubbed her hand over the worn leather. "You keep it," she said, passing the book to Ed. "I want you to have it."

Ed took the Bible and then her hand. "We've learned a lot about Henry's life and we wanted you to know that he loved his family very much. It may have not seemed like he did, but we know that he cared about all of you. More than you know."

Elsie looked at Ed then, and he was surprised to see a small grin cross her face. She pointed to a tiny storage closet in the corner of the room. "Be a dear," she said to Ed, motioning to the closet. "There's a box in there, on the floor, underneath some old quilts. Could you bring it to me?"

Ed did as she asked and unearthed the box. He brought it over and set it carefully on her lap. Lifting the lid, Elsie removed a plethora of birthday cards and random photos. Underneath the pile was a bundle of letters wrapped with an old elastic band. She stared at them for a moment before handing the stack to Ed.

"When Papa died," she began, "Henry came home for a while." She closed her eyes, reliving the past. "Helen and I were so happy to see our brother again and I think Mama was, too." She sighed. "But Frieda." She shook her head remembering her oldest sister. "Frieda was so angry at him for leaving us. Nettie too. And then when they found out where Henry had been working, neither could find it in their hearts to forgive him."

"Where he had been?" Hannah asked, wondering how much Aunt Elsie knew about her brother's past.

Elsie looked at her and nodded. "Yes, he told us where he had been working. He tried to explain how desperate he was and why he needed to go back, but Frieda would hear nothing of it. She believed our family would be excommunicated if word got out." She sighed heavily. "When he left, he promised to write, and he did, but his letters were addressed only to me." She pointed at the letters that Ed still held. "He wrote as often as he could."

Ed asked, "What did he tell you?"

Elsie nodded her head from side to side. "Oh, nothing of importance. Funny stories of things that happened in the town. Friends he had made. That sort of thing. But something must have happened because then his letters stopped."

Hannah asked, "Did you ever hear from him again?"

Elsie nodded. "It was some years later and he had moved up north." She smiled again and added, "With his wife."

Ed and Hannah were both amazed. "You knew he was married?" Ed was incredulous.

Elsie nodded. "I told you he wrote me. Of all the people he wrote about, Lena was the one he mentioned most." She chuckled, "I think it was inevitable." Digging through the photos, Elsie plucked out a small black-and-white photo and handed it to Ed. "She was beautiful." Elsie's smile was one of regret. "I think I would have liked her."

EPILOGUE

GRANITE CREEK—PRESENT DAY

THE GRANITE CREEK CEMETERY was peaceful and quiet when Ed and Hannah went back to visit Hattie. They walked through the dappled sunlight to her grave. Ed sat on the bench by the gate and watched as his wife tidied the grave, removing twigs and branches that obscured the inscription. When she was done, she sat next to the headstone, taking Uncle Henry's old Bible from her purse.

"Hi, Hattie," she said, touching the head stone. "My name is Hannah. I know you don't know me, but I wanted to tell you that we met your family." She took a brand-new photo from the Bible and leaned it against the headstone. "See? This is all of them." The photo showed Isaac's and Ida's four children and their progeny. "They are an amazing family and they love each other very much."

She started scratching the dirt in front of the tombstone with her fingernails, creating a small depression in the earth. When she was finished, she lay the photo in the tiny grave, covered it with the fresh dirt and said, "I wanted you to know that you should be very proud of the legacy you left behind."

The Janzens drove away, their truck rumbling down the dirt road until the forest was silent again. Somewhere in the distance, a mourning dove called, and a gentle breeze blew through the jack pines, filling the air with the scent of lilacs.

CPSIA information can be obtained
at www.ICGtesting.com
Printed in the USA
LVHW110011030422
714933LV00020B/147